# PRAISE F

"In such explosive times ___ captures fanaticism in all its extremes and tells a story as thrilling and vibrant as *America Libre*. Future and history collide in a cautionary tale of a new civil war on American soil. A must read for all, no matter where you draw your line in the sand."
—James Rollins, *New York Times* bestselling author of *The Last Oracle*

"An engaging, fast-moving story of love, intrigue, and personal and ethnic conflict, wrapped in rich, thought-provoking political and cultural commentary."
—Richard W. Slatta, PhD, professor of Latin American history, North Carolina State University

"A fast-moving and intriguing novel about the dangers of racism and extremism in a future America."
—*Catalina* magazine

"Thematically similar to T. C. Boyle's enormously popular *The Tortilla Curtain*, Ramos's *America Libre* is a story of what we all struggle with when we decide where we stand on the issue of immigration."
—Professor Edward J. Mulens, University of Missouri-Columbia

"A window into the despair, brought about by racism, faced by many of our Hispanic neighbors."
—Miguel Del La Torre, PhD, director of the Justice and Peace Institute, Iliff School of Theology

"Realistic storytelling…a frighteningly plausible future…This book is begging to be a screenplay."
—Dunia-Buku.com

"Exciting."
—*Valley Culture*

"An intense novel of action, reaction, and consequence…unforgettable characters."
—MyShelf.com

"A powerful premise…intriguing…a scary and fascinating scenario of what could happen in the future."
—RedRoom.com

Also by Raul Ramos y Sanchez

America Libre

# HOUSE
## DIVIDED

### Raul Ramos y Sanchez

**GRAND CENTRAL**
**PUBLISHING**

NEW YORK    BOSTON

Grand Central Publishing
Hachette Book Group
237 Park Avenue
New York, NY 10017

www.HachetteBookGroup.com

Printed in the United States of America

First Edition: January 2011
10 9 8 7 6 5 4 3 2

Grand Central Publishing is a division of Hachette Book Group, Inc.
The Grand Central Publishing name and logo is a trademark of
Hachette Book Group, Inc.

Library of Congress Cataloging-in-Publication Data

Ramos y Sanchez, Raul.
  House divided / by Raul Ramos y Sanchez.—1st ed.
    p. cm.
  ISBN 978-0-446-50776-9
  1. Hispanic Americans—Fiction.   2. Latin Americans—United States—Social
conditions—Fiction.   3. Illegal aliens—United States—Social conditions—Fiction.
4. Insurgency—United States—Fiction.   5. Ethnic conflict—United
States—Fiction.   6. Imaginary wars and battles—Fiction.   7. Radicalism—
Fiction.   8. Fathers and sons—Fiction.   9. Los Angeles (Calif.)—Fiction.
10. Political fiction. I. Title.
  PS3618.A4765H68   2011
  813'.6—dc22.

                                                                2010011267

*To those who understand our only enemy is extremism*
*in any form*

# ACKNOWLEDGMENTS

March 8, 2010

Most people leave the movie theater once the credits start rolling. Industry insiders, however, know the names scrolling by on the screen are perhaps the most important people of all: those who brought the project to life and helped create the storytelling magic. The same holds true for books.

While a novel has no producer or director, much less a key grip or best boy, the book you're holding is the collaboration of a number of exceptional people. The list of credits begins with my agent, Sally van Haitsma. Her persistence, patience, and tact were instrumental in turning a raw manuscript into a marketable novel. Grand Central Publishing editor Selina McLemore believed in the story—and helped refine its narrative. Production editor Siri Silleck and editor Laura Jorstad were responsible for copy editing. Linda Duggins led the GCP publicity team, and assistant editor Latoya Smith supported the book at every stage.

The sociological and historical underpinnings for *House Divided* came from the work of an international team of scholars I had the good fortune to recruit for a public television project. These included Dr. Oscar Alvarez Gila, Dr. Miguel De La Torre, Dr. Henry Louis Gates Jr., Dr. Franklin W. Knight, Dr. Edward Mullen, and Dr. Richard W. Slatta.

Another key name on the list of credits is Rueben Martinez,

a MacArthur genius grant recipient and advocate for Latino literacy whose guidance and support I will always treasure. I want to credit Dr. Jess Nieto, Veronica Jacuinde, Scott Willis, and Michael Steven Gregory for their efforts in spreading the word about *America Libre*, the predecessor to *House Divided*. I also want to recognize the support of my many friends on Facebook, Twitter, Red Room, National Society of Hispanic Professionals, OC Gente, Nunca Sola, Latinos in Social Media, and the BronzeWord Authors group. Credits listings for research go to James Adams, Barbara Estes, Jason Johnson, and Colonel John M. Volpe, USAF (ret.).

The credits for *House Divided* end with the most important people of all: my wife, my siblings, and my mother. Their love and support are the foundation of everything I've accomplished.

# THE MARCHA OFFENSIVE

*The day we strike together across the United States, we'll send an unmistakable message: We are united. We are a nation.*

*Josefina Herrera*

# THE MARCHA OFFENSIVE:
## *DAY 2*

**S**ome things had not changed. The dawning sun in East Los Angeles was still a feeble glow in the gray haze. But the city's infamous smog was no longer a residue of its endless traffic. These days, the smoke of cooking fires clouded the sky. The vehicles that had once clogged Los Angeles were now charred shells littering a war-scarred city divided into two walled-in Quarantine Zones.

A rooster crowed outside a white stucco cottage on the north side of Quarantine Zone B. Inside the small house, Manolo Suarez got out of bed and began to dress.

Lying naked on the bed, his wife, Rosa, yawned, stretching languidly. "What time is it, mi amor?" she murmured.

"Time for me to go, querida," Mano answered, fastening his weathered jeans, his left forearm bandaged to the elbow.

Rosa sat up suddenly, her eyes flashing. "Where are you going?"

Lacing a scuffed brown boot, Mano looked up. "The less you know, the better it is for all of us, Rosa. I wouldn't leave you if it wasn't important."

"We've been apart over a year, Mano," she said, her long

black hair still sleep-tangled. "Can't someone else take your place—at least for today?"

Mano stopped dressing and stared at her somberly. "There's no one else left."

"I'm sorry, Mano. I understand," Rosa said, the edge in her voice gone. Rising from the bed, she slipped on a tattered robe. "Will you have time to eat?"

"No, it's nearly daylight," Mano said walking toward the bedroom door. "I should have left an hour ago."

Rosa stopped him in the doorway, putting her palm on his broad, muscled chest. "When will you be back?"

"When I can," he said, looking into her dark brown eyes.

"Is this how our life is going to be, Mano?"

"This is a war now, querida. I wish it could be different."

She sighed and embraced her husband. "At least we're together again."

Mano gave her a reassuring squeeze, then stepped away. "I have to go."

"Wait. Come with me," she said, taking her husband's hand. "This won't take long."

Mano followed Rosa as she led him through the narrow hallway into the living room. On the couch, covered in a thin patched blanket, slept their son, Pedro. Rosa leaned toward the thirteen-year-old, reaching out to wake him.

Mano gently pulled her back. "Let him sleep," he whispered.

"Doesn't a son deserve to see his father?"

"Not now, querida," he said softly. "I don't have time."

"Pedro was asleep when you got in last night," she said, looking up at Mano, nearly a foot taller. "It's been over a year since your son has seen you," she added, her voice rising. "And when you leave, it may be the last time we—"

Rosa stopped as Pedro rolled over and opened his eyes. The boy stared glassy-eyed around the room for a moment before his gaze fixed on Mano. "Papi, is that you?"

Mano knelt by the couch and touched the boy's cheek. "Yes, m'hijo."

"Papi, Papi!" he called out, wrapping his arms around Mano's thick neck. "I saw your name in the newspaper at the camp!" he said, his hoarse adolescent's voice cracking with emotion. "The paper said you were a traitor but everybody in the camp thinks you're a hero—except for the vendidos. But I told them—"

"Listen, Pedro," Mano interrupted as he tenderly unwound the boy's arms clinging to him. "I have to go now. It's very important. We'll have to talk later, okay?"

The boy's smile faded. "It's just like before," he said, blinking back tears. "You never want to be with us."

"No, m'hijo. That's not it at all," Mano answered, cupping the boy's face in his large hands. "There are things I have to do...right away. I'll be back as soon as I can. I promise."

Pedro said nothing and turned away from his father.

Rosa wrapped her arms around the boy. "Go, Mano. We'll be fine," she said unconvincingly.

Mano rose and peered cautiously through the windows. "Stay inside today—both of you. I think the Baldies will be coming into the zones in strength," he said, opening the front door.

"May God keep you, mi amor," Rosa whispered, unheard by Mano as he closed the door behind him.

Once outside, Mano moved along the deserted street with a resolve born of necessity. He had nothing left to lose. If captured by the government, he would be sentenced to death under the Terrorist Arraignment Act. Passed five months earlier, the draconian bill most people called the "needle law" charged anyone supporting the insurgency with high treason. The punishment was death by lethal injection. Even Mano's wife and son faced a similar fate for abetting an insurgent. Although he was happy to have Rosa and Pedro back after a year at the relocation camp, they were now in greater danger than ever. Mano shook his head, trying to clear his mind of the guilt. He had a more immediate crisis.

Yesterday's nationwide offensive had been a disaster, derailed by a mole who'd alerted the government to the rebel attacks. A terrible question now plagued Mano: How much damage had the informer caused? Since leading a failed assault against an Army outpost yesterday morning, Mano had been cut off from news of the outside world. What little he knew was bad enough.

Guided by the mole, the Army had discovered the rebel command center in Los Angeles directing their widespread offensive. Mano had returned from his raid to find their communications equipment seized or destroyed and his comrades killed.

The sight of spent bullet casings on the street brought him back to the present. Most of the insurgency's leaders across the continent were now out of touch or dead—and he did not have time for the luxury of grief. He was now the sole survivor of the rebel's inner command in the area. The next few hours might decide the future of their cause. Turning onto Whittier Boulevard, Mano quickened his steps.

A quarter hour later, Mano approached a run-down duplex on Fraser Avenue. The man who lived inside was his last resort for help—Angel Sanchez, the leader of Los Verdugos, a street gang that had become the palace guards of the rebel leadership in Los Angeles.

Mano needed to see Angel right away—if he was still alive.

———

The armored vehicles raced through downtown Los Angeles stirring eddies of dust in the empty streets. As the convoy crossed the viaduct over the vacant Union Pacific rail yards, the voice of the column's commander came on the radio.

"Tango Five to all units," Captain Michael Fuller said. "Convoy halt."

Moving in unison, the five vehicles rolled to a stop and Fuller emerged from the Humvee leading the column. Studying the road ahead through his binoculars, a tight smile formed on Fuller's face. The rusting steel doors of the North Gate into the Quarantine Zone B were open, creating a glowing portal in the long, early-morning shadows cast by the ten-foot concrete wall topped with razor wire. *So far, so good,* Fuller thought with relief.

The North Gate was one of only two passages into the twenty-two square miles of Quarantine Zone B. Although a likely place for an ambush, Fuller was betting the rebels would not be lying in wait at the gate this morning.

Fuller climbed back into the Humvee and picked up the radio's handset. "Tango Five to all units. Deploy in combat formation and proceed into the Quarantine Zone."

The four tank-like Bradley Fighting Vehicles behind Fuller's Humvee began moving into position at the head of the column. As the Bradleys lumbered past the Humvee, Fuller's driver nervously stroked the blue figurine taped to the dashboard. "All right, Hefty," he whispered to the grinning Smurf. "Pancho's waiting for us inside. Get us through that gate, dude."

"Don't worry, Springs," Fuller said to his driver. "Getting inside won't be a problem." *Save up Hefty's luck for later,* Fuller kept to himself. *We're going to need it.*

---

Angel Sanchez entered the living room of his duplex apartment cranking the dynamo on a shortwave radio. Shirtless, with crude tattoos covering his face and muscled torso, the gang leader was an imposing figure despite his short stature.

He handed the radio to Mano, who tuned it to the familiar

setting for the BBC and placed it on one of the steel milk crates serving as chairs and coffee table in the sparsely furnished living room. Most wooden furniture in the Quarantine Zones had been burned for fuel, along with almost anything combustible.

Following a report on the London Stock Exchange, the dulcet-toned BBC announcer reached the news they'd been waiting to hear.

> ... and now our top news story: the widespread Hispanic insurgent attacks across the United States being called the Marcha Offensive ... Mary Ann Kirby reports.

The scratchy quality of the female voice now on the air indicated her report had been recorded over a telephone line.

> Yesterday, at precisely noon U.S. Eastern Time, Hispanic insurgents from California to Connecticut emerged from their walled-in barrios and stormed the military outposts guarding the forty-six Hispanic Quarantine Zones throughout the United States. Timed to match the rebel assaults, explosions rocked hundreds of communications and power facilities across the continent, destroying electrical relay stations, power lines, transformers, and vu-phone towers. Not since the American Civil War, over a century and a half earlier, has a conflict of this scale taken place on U.S. soil.
>
> A body count released by the U.S. Army claims two hundred fifty-four insurgents were killed and seven captured during the attacks. U.S. Army losses were reported at eleven dead and wounded. Preliminary reports indicate fewer than thirty non-Hispanic civilians lost their lives, most as a result of auto accidents in the panic following the attacks. Despite the heavy rebel losses, the carefully coordinated attacks were a shocking psychological blow to the U.S. public.

At four thirty p.m. on the East Coast, President Carleton Brenner addressed a shaken nation. *"The attacks are over. You are not in danger. Stay home and remain calm. While today's terror attacks were unprecedented in scale, civilian casualties were minimal. The assaults on our military installations were courageously repelled. Our nation remains strong and secure."*

President Brenner's speech stemmed the tide of panic. But the Marcha Offensive—launched on the birth date of the rebels' patron saint, José Antonio Marcha—marks the start of a dark new era in U.S. history. According to Oxford expert on American studies Sir Bernard Spaulding, *"The Balkanization of the United States now seems inevitable."*

This is Mary Ann Kirby reporting from New York.

Angel turned off the radio and faced Mano. The gang leader had understood much of the news despite his limited grasp of English. "Muchos muertos, eh?"

"Yes, a lot of dead," Mano answered grim-faced. If the news report was accurate, they'd lost nearly half their fighters, many not much more than children.

"They die in fight or die like this," Angel said, raising his tattooed arm and jabbing his finger into the crook of his elbow, mimicking an injection.

Mano closed his eyes and rubbed his temples, swamped by a wave of guilt. He was the architect of the Marcha Offensive; he had insisted their fighters attack military installations and not civilian targets. The price for avoiding the tactics of terrorists had been very high. *At least only a few civilians died,* he reminded himself. Still, like any guerrilla, his primary weapon against the military had been the element of surprise. The informer had robbed them of that advantage—and the Army would be quick to exploit their heavy losses.

"The Baldies will be coming, entiendes?" Mano said, rising to his feet. "We need to be ready."

"Sí, Mano," Angel replied, already striding toward the door. "I talk con mis vatos. They tell me when Baldies come."

———

Captain Fuller leaned forward in the Humvee's seat, scanning the rooftops visible over the Quarantine Zone wall for snipers. He was relieved—but not surprised—to find their entrance into the zone unopposed.

Most Army patrols entering the nation's Quarantine Zones over the last year had suffered heavy losses. Michael Fuller, however, was determined to avoid that fate for the five vehicles and forty-three soldiers under his command. That's why he'd chosen this time and place to enter. Still, the thirty-one-year-old captain had qualms about his decision. He was breaking an unwritten truce with the Panchos by launching an armored patrol into the zone during the Army's weekly delivery of food.

Once inside the solid-steel doors, Fuller's convoy skirted past a line of open-bed Army trucks loaded with sacks of cornmeal parked along the boulevard. Civilians in blue armbands were hastily transferring the sacks from the trucks into an odd assortment of vehicles, while a platoon of National Guardsmen stood warily nearby. The civilians stopped their work, staring hard at Fuller's trespassing column.

From the rear bench of the Humvee, Lieutenant Gerald Case gazed expectantly out the window. "You think we're going to see some action, Captain?"

"Not if I can help it."

"C'mon, Cap. What's wrong with stirring up a little firefight? I missed out on the action at the outpost yesterday. A combat commendation would be a fast way out of this shithole."

Case's words stung Michael Fuller—mostly because they were true. A domestic assignment in today's Army was for bottom-feeders. Overseas duty was the fast lane to promotion. "Stow it, Case. I'm not going to risk getting anybody hurt to help your career...or mine."

"We ain't likely to get anybody hurt with a platoon of Brads around, Cap," Case said, nodding toward the four treaded vehicles trundling ahead of them. Each Bradley was armed with a turret-mounted 25mm chain gun and carried seven heavily armed troopers.

"What about civilians, Case? Don't you think...Watch the kid, Springs!" Fuller yelled to his driver as a naked toddler wandered into the path of their vehicle. The screeching of the brakes brought the boy's mother running into the street.

"Sorry, Captain," Springs said, his face pale. "I didn't see the kid. I guess I was looking out for the Panchos."

Lieutenant Case sneered. "Wouldn't have made much difference if you'd taken him out. They breed like rats," he said as the boy's mother swooped up the child and retreated into the doorway of a dingy apartment building. "Why we fight these people on one street and feed them on another one is beyond me, Cap."

"If we starved the QZs, every person inside would be fighting against us, Case. Beans are a lot cheaper than bullets. And besides, it's the right thing to do."

"They teach you that kind of bleeding-heart crap at West Point, Captain?"

"Yeah, right after the mandatory class on the virtues of appeasement."

Case stared at Fuller blankly. "Appeasement?"

"Never mind, Lieutenant. We don't have the time right now."

"Well, explain this for me, will you, Captain...How the hell did an Academy ring knocker like you wind up with this dead-end posting anyway?"

Fuller turned slowly toward Case. "Lieutenant, your mouth is going to get you in deep shit one of these days...possibly very soon."

As their convoy drove deeper into the zone, Fuller silently cursed the politicians who'd hatched the Quarantine and Relocation Act—and then left the military to clean up their mess. At the core of the law was a new type of citizen: Class H—those who were Hispanic, married to a Hispanic, or had at least one grandparent of Hispanic origin. The Q&R Act called for the relocation of all Class H citizens to quell the ethnic violence sweeping the country.

Two years after the bill was enacted, most Americans now saw the attempt at the largest ethnic internment in the nation's history as an epic failure.

The construction of new Relocation Communities for Class H citizens in North Dakota had been halted after the deaths of more than two thousand internees during the first winter. Meanwhile, the once-temporary Quarantine Zones—built around Hispanic urban enclaves to end the bloody street battles between vigilantes and Hispanics—had become rebel strongholds from which the Panchos launched strikes and then melted back into the civilian population.

Yesterday's offensive by the Panchos had changed the game. Thanks to a government mole, they'd uncovered the operation's command center—an abandoned Holiday Inn near the center of Los Angeles Quarantine Zone B. A Delta Force team arriving in two helicopters had wiped out the enemy personnel and hauled away all the rebel communications equipment the helos could hold before pulling out. Now the brass wanted a more thorough intelligence sweep of the Pancho command center and had created Fuller's ad hoc task force to ferry an intel team to the rebel command center and let the G2 wonks snoop around. The mission was considered so important, Fuller had even been assigned an air surveillance drone—a first for a state-side unit.

From the touch screen on the Humvee's dashboard, Fuller studied the drone's-eye view of the road ahead. What he saw made the captain shiver under his flak vest despite the eighty-degree heat: A barricade of rubble and abandoned cars blocked all four lanes of Whittier Boulevard.

After nearly a year of duty in Southern California, Fuller had come to know the insurgents' tactics well. He was sure the Panchos were watching every move his convoy made. No matter which detour he chose, the Panchos would likely have an ambush waiting.

From the second floor of a vacant office building, Angel peered through a gap in the boarded-up window. Three blocks ahead, the armored column was moving slowly toward the rebel barricade on Whittier. "Mira, Mano," he said. "Baldies come."

Pressing his six-foot-three frame against the window, Mano watched the Army convoy approach their roadblock. He'd heard about the patrol soon after it entered the zone—the volunteers from La Defensa Del Pueblo unloading the food trucks had alerted Angel. Mano had always believed the Army would exploit its food distribution for military advantage someday. The move could not have come at a worse time.

"See the little plane?" Mano said, pointing to the drone circling over the column.

Angel squinted into the gap between the boards. "Sí."

"That's the commander's eyes. Keep your people out of sight when you move around them." Mano held out his palm like a roof and made finger-walking gestures below it. "Use the storm sewers. Move inside buildings. Entiendes?"

"Sí. Entiendo. Baldies see from sky."

A third-generation Mexican-American, Mano spoke only a handful of words in Spanish. Angel, who had slipped across the border four years earlier, spoke little English. Until her death yesterday, their translator had been Josefina Herrera. Now, facing the first tangible measure of her loss, the enormity of Jo's death came flooding back to Mano.

When Jo had entered his life three years earlier, he'd been an out-of-work mechanic, one unemployment check away from eviction, desperate to provide for his family. Jo hired Mano, first as a mechanic for her recycling business, and later as security director for La Defensa Del Pueblo, a community organization she'd created in response to the outbreak of vigilante killings in East Los Angeles.

Jo had been more than a boss. She'd opened Mano's eyes to the plight of their people. For a long time, he'd resisted two disturbing impulses: the pull of the Hispanic liberation movement and his attraction to Jo. Ultimately, the former U.S. Army Ranger's loyalty to the United States had withered. His devotion to his wife had not. Shortly before her death defending their command center, Jo had used most of her remaining wealth to reunite Mano with his wife and son, interned in a Relocation Community in the Dakotas. That gesture had erased all of Mano's lingering questions about Jo and their cause—and renewed his will to fight.

"How we fight Baldies?" Angel asked, breaking Mano's reverie.

Mano rubbed his face and looked again at the line of vehicles now turning north around their barricade. "That's a strong force," he observed drily. "Muy fuerte."

Angel curled his hands together as if strangling a neck. "I send vatos with RPG to Guirado Street," he said.

"Yes, I know Guirado is a choke point. But we have very few people or weapons left, Angel. Muy poco hombres. Entiendes?

We need more time to plan an attack. Mas tiempo," Mano said, tapping the watch on his brawny forearm bandaged from the bullet that had grazed him yesterday.

Angel looked unblinkingly into the taller man's eyes. "We no fight, more Baldies come."

Mano nodded. "You're right, but we can't risk losing more men—or our RPGs. We need a better plan." After yesterday's disastrous raids, Angel's eight men armed with four rocket-propelled grenade launchers was their only fighting team left intact.

Angel shrugged in disgust. "What we do?"

Mano rubbed his wispy beard. From his days as a Ranger, he knew the five-vehicle column was a formidable force—but still clearly a sortie into the zone. "Let's wait and see where they're going. Sooner or later, they'll be leaving—and there are only two ways out."

Angel nodded and smiled.

————

Half an hour after entering the zone, Fuller was surprised when his column reached the Holiday Inn unopposed. His respite was short-lived.

Shortly after setting up their defensive perimeter, civilians began gathering around the abandoned hotel, pressing against the crime scene tape left behind by the Delta Force team the day before. In less than an hour, several hundred men, women, and children surrounded Fuller's position, staring in unnerving silence.

Fuller gazed into the crowd less than fifty paces away. He was sure there were Panchos staring back. How long this standoff would last was anybody's guess.

"I don't like this, Captain," Lieutenant Case said nervously. "If one of these beaners has a bomb, all he has to do is walk through the tape and we're chipped beef."

"The Panchos haven't used suicide bombers before, Case. I doubt they're going to start now."

"What if they charge us, sir? We're outnumbered ten-to-one. I say we fire over their heads and scare them off, Captain."

"Chill out, Case. The last thing we want to do right now is start shooting."

Fuller had no fear of being overrun. He'd deployed his Bradleys in the hotel's front and rear parking lots, forming two bases of fire that could easily mow down a charge from the crowd. His concern was for the innocent onlookers. *If the spooks don't finish up fast, this could turn into a bloodbath.*

Standing among the crowd around the Holiday Inn, Mano studied the captain's face, trying to read the man's thoughts. The officer looked concerned but unafraid, coolly scanning the onlookers. It had been months since he'd been this close to a Baldie.

*Could this be one of the men who killed my son?*

Although it had been more than two years since Julio had been run down by a military convoy, the memory brought back a surge of anger. The incident had killed more than Mano's nine-year-old son. It had destroyed Mano's respect for the uniform he'd once worn. The armored vehicle that crushed Julio had not even bothered to slow down. Unknown to Mano, the green sergeant driving the vehicle had never seen his son.

Mano stifled his anger, trying to think clearly. He should have guessed the Baldies would come back for a closer look at their command center. In any case, the soldiers would be leaving soon—empty-handed. Jo had equipped the temporary location with outdated communications equipment that would be difficult to trace. The soldiers would find nothing of value.

The convoy had been at the abandoned Holiday Inn more than an hour when Angel emerged from a vacant building and approached Mano.

"When Baldies go?" Angel asked.

"Pronto."

"Where we put vatos?"

Mano nodded toward the ground below him. "Right here."

"Baldies come from there," Angel said, pointing toward the street north of the soldiers.

"Yes, but they won't leave that way. They'll head for the South Gate this time."

"Esta bien, Mano," Angel agreed. Despite his insolent manner, the gang leader had grudgingly come to respect Mano's judgment in battle, proven many times over the last two years.

Mano gestured toward the people along the street. "We need to move everyone away before we attack, Angel. Entiendes?"

"Sí."

Mano then began a half pantomime of his plan for Angel's men.

---

"Find any bodies?" Fuller asked the intel officer.

"No, Captain. The Delta Force team said they wasted three Panchos. But the stiffs are gone," the reedy lieutenant answered.

"I'm not surprised. The Panchos weren't likely to leave any of their leaders around for us. Anything else?"

"Our electronic sweeps came up empty. We just started the caveman stuff...dusting for prints, gathering DNA material."

"Well, pick up the pace, Lieutenant. The longer we hang out around here, the harder it's going to be to get out."

While the intel geeks worked, Fuller huddled with his Bradley commanders to plan their exit route. When the intelligence team wrapped up their investigation forty minutes later, Fuller wasted no time getting his convoy on the move.

"Everyone's ready to roll, Captain," Private Springs said

as Fuller hopped into the Humvee's passenger seat.

Fuller grabbed the radio's handset. "Tango Five to all units...
move out."

The Bradleys lumbered forward, their diesels snorting.
"Okay if I give Hefty a rub, Springs?" the captain asked his
driver.

Springs swallowed hard. "Sure, sir."

"This is when we're going to need some luck," Fuller said,
stroking the blue figurine.

From the second floor of an empty office building nearby,
Mano and Angel watched the column begin to move.

Angel's eyes widened in alarm. "Mira, Mano!" he said as
the convoy headed north, away from them.

Mano was stunned. The officer commanding the column
was backtracking, an obvious blunder.

Angel bolted toward the door. "I move vatos to Whittier."

"Yes, pronto," Mano agreed, falling into stride behind the
smaller man, silently cursing his own poor judgment. They
had a slim chance of damaging the convoy now—and his
men would be more vulnerable as they scrambled into improvised attack positions. Clearly, he'd overestimated the Baldie
captain. Facing the same situation, Mano would have...

"Wait, Angel," Mano called out.

The gang leader turned, his expression puzzled. "Que?"

"Keep your vatos where they are."

Fuller's convoy had moved three blocks north when the
captain picked up the radio handset. "Tango Five to all
units...execute Code Green," he said into the unit.

The Bradley leading the column made a hard left. The convoy was doubling back. *I hope this throws off the Pancho recep-
tion committee*, Fuller said to himself. The insurgents were
probably abandoning their ambush right now, scrambling to
intercept him as he headed north. He hoped to catch them in
the open by reversing his direction.

The street was deserted as the convoy rolled past the Holiday Inn, this time heading south. *This is not a good sign,* Fuller thought as the convoy entered the corridor of taller buildings south of the hotel. "Tango Five to all units...Stay sharp," he said over the radio. Fuller didn't like moving through confined areas like this, but there was no other way out. He knew the Panchos liked to attack up close, neutralizing their firepower.

As if on cue, the metallic barking of an automatic rifle rang out.

"This is Tango One, Captain," said the commander of the lead Bradley over the radio. "We're taking fire up here. Looks like Pancho's coming out to play."

"Halt and engage, Tango One," Fuller replied. Turning to the drone operator in the backseat, Fuller said, "Ash, give us a look at what's happening up there." As the camera panned toward the skirmish, the Humvee's radio blared with the excited chatter of the Bradleys' commanders.

*"Anybody see them?"*

*"Behind the burned-out car at two o'clock. I've got somebody with a weapon."*

*"I see him."*

*"Smoke him, Jackson. Smoke him."*

From the drone's-eye view, Fuller saw a figure huddled behind a charred car. A puff of smoke appeared from the turret of the lead Brad followed by the jackhammer burst of a chain gun. The thumb-size bullets tore through the vehicle as if it were paper.

*"Got him!"*

*"Good shot, Jackson! He's down."*

*"Anybody else taking fire?"*

*"Negative."*

*"Watch the rooftops! There's gotta be more of them."*

*"Roger that."*

Fuller stared into the drone's display, waiting for Pancho's next move.

"Holy shit, Captain!" the Humvee's driver shouted suddenly. In the street ahead, a manhole cover opened from below.

"Pull up between the Brads. Hurry!" Fuller said, pointing to the armored vehicles.

The Humvee lurched forward, racing past the manhole, narrowly missing the rear of the Bradley ahead as it swung around the armored vehicle, seeking shelter. "Tango Five to Tango Three and Four," Fuller said into the radio. "We've got Panchos coming out of the manhole between you. Take them out!"

The turrets of the Bradleys spun toward the target—but not quickly enough. The insurgent in the manhole fired a rocket-propelled grenade, hitting the third Brad in its lightly armored rear panel. The vehicle began to smoke as the chain guns sprayed the manhole, obliterating the man inside.

"This is Tango Three. We're hit," the commander of the crippled Bradley shouted, his voice cracking with tension. "Our engine's dead and we've got..." Three rocket-propelled grenades fired from the buildings along the street ended the commander's transmission. The vehicle exploded, disappearing into a billowing orange ball of flame.

"Tango One and Two—take the two targets on the west walls!" Fuller yelled into the mike. "Tango Four, take out the RPG on the east side!"

The armored vehicles raked the buildings with their guns, sending up clouds of dust from the pulverized masonry. Passing easily through the walls, the projectiles would shred anyone inside. "Cease fire," Fuller ordered after a few seconds. He knew the Panchos would not hang around to fight.

A bitter taste rose in his throat as he looked back at the charred, motionless Brad. Thick black smoke billowed from its dislocated turret. There was no chance anyone inside had survived. He'd just lost ten men. His efforts to protect his command had been useless.

They had nearly five miles of hostile territory left to cross and a quarter of his command was already dead.

Peering around the corner of a building behind the convoy, Mano watched joylessly as the bloodied column drove away. Yes, they'd managed to destroy one of the Bradleys, but the swift return fire from the convoy had cost him five more men and two RPGs. It was not an even trade. In a war of attrition, the U.S. Army would win.

He'd sent a detachment to the South Gate, giving them one more chance to attack the convoy. But what would they do to stop the next patrol inside the zone? Or the one after that? Without more weapons and supplies, it was only a matter of time before the Baldies would end the rebel resistance.

Fuller's column made a wide turn on Whittier, staying clear of the taller buildings. Inside the command Humvee, Private Springs broke into a wide grin. "That's a sweet sight, Captain," he said as the South Gate of the Quarantine Zone came into view.

Fuller's own smile faded when he looked into the drone's display. "Pull over, Springs!" he ordered. "We've got people on a roof up there." He pointed to a shuttered, one-story body shop just ahead.

As the vehicle skidded to a halt, a volley of bottles sailed though the air, each trailing a comet-like flame. The Molotov cocktails crashed onto the pavement, bursting into flames just ahead of the Humvee.

"They missed us, Cap!" Springs shouted. "Good call!"

"They're lighting up another round," Fuller said, watching the drone's display. "Back up, Springs! Now!"

The second salvo of firebombs fell short of the retreating Humvee. But the street was now a wall of fire, cutting them off from the Bradleys ahead.

"Tango Five to all units," Fuller yelled into the radio.

"Suppressive fire on the body shop to the east! We've got Panchos on the roof."

The turrets of the Bradleys homed in on the body shop and fired in a deafening roar. Through the dashboard display, Fuller watched the figures on the rooftop retreat to the back of the building. Several were cut down as they ran.

"What are we going to do, Captain?" Springs said, staring in terror at the barrier of flames ahead.

Fuller knew the Panchos might have an even nastier surprise if he tried to detour around the fire. The safest way out of an ambush was to fight through it. "Tango Five to all units," Fuller said into the radio. "Keep the guys on that body shop pinned down."

Fuller grabbed the Humvee's fire extinguisher and stepped outside. "Get out of throwing range, Springs. I'll signal you when we're ready to roll."

As the Humvee backed away, Fuller began dousing the flames, expecting another firebomb at any second. Each time he managed to extinguish the flames from a section of pavement, the gasoline would reignite. With the $CO_2$ nearly depleted, Fuller finally managed to open a corridor. "C'mon!" he yelled, waving to his driver. "Let's get the hell out of here!"

Fuller jumped inside and the Humvee sped away, swerving wildly past the slower Bradleys toward the safety of the gate. Once outside the zone, the shaken driver turned to Fuller in awe. "Damn, Captain! That took some kind of balls, man."

"I don't want any mention of this in your debriefing, Springs. Understand?"

"Whatever you say, sir."

A combat commendation might get him shipped overseas, and Michael Fuller did not want that right now.

He had a score to settle with the Pancho commander.

# THE MARCHA OFFENSIVE:
## *DAY 3*

**O**ctavio Perez shed his overcoat and dropped heavily into the chalet's couch, his rain-soaked shoes staining the sofa's white leather. "I need a drink," he said, eyes glazed with fatigue.

"How about some wine?" Ramon Garcia asked, pulling a bottle from the large chrome rack by the fireplace. "I picked up an excellent cab from the French delegation."

Octavio grimaced in disgust. "What I'd like is some real cerveza. These Swiss beers taste like piss."

"Sorry, hermano, I'm all out of beer. How about a nice single-malt?"

"Whatever. Just get me a drink," Octavio said wearily. "I'll tell you, Ramon, all this fucking talk is driving me crazy."

Since arriving in Geneva five weeks earlier, Perez and Garcia had kept up a hectic schedule of meetings with other U.N. delegates. The reason for the widespread interest in the non-voting delegation from the Hispanic Republic of North America was no secret: Many countries saw the presence of the HRNA in the United Nations as a way to settle old scores with the U.S.A.

In fact, the U.N.'s recognition of the HRNA as a stateless people had been a landmark event. The United States had withdrawn from the world organization in protest, prompting the U.N.'s move from the banks of the East River to the shores of Lake Leman.

Ramon poured three fingers of Glenlivet into a glass and handed it to Octavio. "Have you heard the latest news from the States?"

"No, I was meeting with the pinche Chinese all afternoon. What's up?"

"There's a lot of concern about another wave of attacks," Ramon said, uncorking the wine bottle.

"Are you kidding me? We got our ass kicked."

"Sure, we took some losses, Tavio, but look at the public reaction. The Marcha Offensive turned out just as Jo said it would. It may have been a military setback, but it was a psychological victory—like the Tet Offensive in Vietnam. The American people are in shock. They know we're united across the continent now. Eventually, they'll negotiate with us." Ramon's eyes turned toward the floor. "I have to admit, though, I'm worried that we haven't heard from Jo."

Octavio's face puckered in disgust. "Mano's plan was soft-headed," he said, downing the eighteen-year-old scotch in a single gulp. "We lost a lot of good people attacking military targets. And the explosives were a waste, too. We should have really hurt them, Ramon, not just dicked around blowing up unmanned power stations like Mano insisted."

"No, Tavio. Killing civilians isn't just immoral—it's bad politics. World opinion would turn against us," Ramon said, refilling Octavio's glass. "Our cause needs public support. Look how little terrorism's gotten the Islamic militants."

"The gabachos won't take us seriously if we don't put some fear into them," Octavio said, thrusting his chin defiantly.

Although both men shared a gold complexion and high

cheekbones, the similarities ended there. While Ramon was wiry and average in height, Octavio was tall and heavily built. But the differences went deeper. Octavio displayed a bull-like belligerence that matched his frame. Ramon's mind and body reflected the cunning of a fox.

Ramon had argued with Octavio before—and knew it was pointless to continue. He poured himself a glass of wine and sat down. "So what did the Chinese have to say?"

"The chinos dropped hints about giving us money, but they won't support us publicly. I think they're afraid of pissing off the gabachos."

Ramon sipped his wine. "You can't really blame them. It'll be a long time before the Hispanic Republic buys as many Chinese jogging suits as the U.S.A."

"Yeah? Well, I told them they were a bunch of gutless worms."

"What did you hope to gain by insulting them?"

Octavio scowled. "You think too damn much, Ramon. Fuck the chinos." He drained his glass again. "How did your meeting with the French go?"

"Our Gallic friends promised to back us for U.N. voting seats...if we can get the rest of the E.U. to go along. It's a big step," Ramon said with a slight smile.

"A big step?" Octavio laughed bitterly. "A big step would be for them to give us some of their Famas, Minimis, and maybe a few mortars."

"Be realistic, Octavio. The French can't be seen giving us weapons. Washington, D.C., is today's Rome. The U.S. is too powerful for any single country to resist."

"Here's what you need to do, Ramon," Octavio said, wagging his finger like a whip at Garcia. "You tell the French that if they give us weapons, it will force the U.S. to bring its war machine home. Then the Frenchies—along with the rest of these puto Euros—can quit worrying about an Islamic uprising at home each time the U.S. invades another Muslim country. Tell them supporting us will make the U.S. stop whacking the Islamic hornet nest."

"The French are walking a tightrope, Tavio. Of course they're worried about their Islamic immigrants. My God, in another generation there'll be more Muslims in France than Christians. And it's the same for most of Western Europe. But we can't expect the French to take on the U.S. alone."

"Sounds to me like the gabachos are right about the French. They don't have any cojones."

Ramon sighed. "Well, amigo, you certainly have a knack for simplifying things."

*The man is a blunt instrument*, Ramon reminded himself. *Octavio is useful for smashing stubborn obstacles but worthless for prying open delicate ones.* In the barrios, Perez's fiery passion had been valuable in rallying people to their cause. But here in Geneva, his coarse simplemindedness was threatening their negotiations to win allies.

Ramon sipped his wine, studying Octavio over the rim of the glass. *I have to find a way to get rid of this man.*

———

"It looks infected, Mano," Rosa said, unwinding the bandages around her husband's forearm. "But I don't know much about bullet wounds."

"The bullet went all the way through. Just put a fresh bandage on it. I've got to go," he said glancing toward the living room door.

"I'll look for some medicine when I go shopping," Rosa said, wrapping Mano's beefy forearm in strips of an old sheet. When she was done, Mano kissed her quickly and hurried outside.

Rosa had long ago stopped asking Mano what he was doing for the cause—or expecting an explanation. He'd convinced her it was safer for their entire family to have nothing to reveal if captured. Still, something was troubling her husband. Although a quiet man, Mano had always been affectionate. Now he seemed distant and distracted. The tender words and caresses that had once been part of their daily life were missing. *Could Mano be sorry Pedro and I are back with him?* It was a thought she didn't want to dwell on.

Gathering her purse and sun hat from the bedroom, she headed outside, determined to stock the kitchen. The meager stores her husband had kept as a bachelor would not do for a family. Following the directions of a neighbor, she discovered the store closest to her new home; the apartment her family had called home before she'd left with the children for the relocation camp was in a barrio farther south in Zone B.

Like most barrio bodegas, the door to Alejandro's Market was lined with iron bars. After Rosa stepped inside the small grocery store, she realized the bars were a relic from better times. There seemed little left inside worth stealing.

Besides Alejandro, who sat forlornly behind the counter near the door, a lone female shopper hovered in the narrow aisles. The woman frowned in disgust as Rosa approached.

"Por lo menos en Oaxaca las bodegas tenían comida," she said under her breath.

"I'm sorry. I don't speak Spanish very well," Rosa answered.

The stranger gestured to the near-empty shelves. "In Oaxaca, store has food, no?" she said in broken English. "Here, nothing."

Rosa shrugged and moved down the aisle. What was the point of complaining? She needed to feed her family, and bellyaching certainly was not going to help. However, the high prices and shortages of goods in the Quarantine Zone were a shock after the relocation camp where food and other necessities were meager but doled out free. Thankfully, Rosa still had some of the cash Josefina's courier had given her for their escape.

After scouring the shelves, she managed to find a paltry haul of beans, rice, and other staples. Looking at the hand-written prices on the torn packages and dented cans, it was clear they would take a large bite out of her money. *At least we won't starve*, she reminded herself. Mano had explained how the Army delivered cornmeal and other grains in bulk each week, and La Defensa Del Pueblo distributed a pound to each person free.

Alejandro brightened noticeably as she approached the counter with her purchases. "Welcome, señora," the merchant said, smiling broadly. "It's been a long time since a woman of your beauty has graced these walls."

Rosa blushed, paid for the groceries, and asked the merchant about medicine. With elaborate gestures, Alejandro gave her directions to the only source of medical supplies left in the barrio: a botanica several blocks away.

Reluctantly, she began walking toward the folk medicine shop. Following her mother's views, Rosa had always disdained the women who ran most botanicas, faith healers known in the barrios as curanderas. Her mother had called them brujas—witches. Even as her mother's health worsened from the MS that eventually took her life, she'd resisted them. Still, Rosa knew she had no other choice. She needed to treat Mano's wound—quickly.

The botanica was hidden from the street at the end of a narrow alley between two buildings, adding to its sordidness in Rosa's mind. Walking through the unmarked door, she covered her nose, assailed by the spicy-sweet scent of incense mixed with acrid medicines and moldy paper. The sight of the shop was no less overwhelming.

In a barrio where store shelves were mostly bare, a dizzying array of brightly colored goods covered the walls and counters of this tiny room. Displayed without any apparent order were medals and amulets, books and pamphlets, boxes of shiny stones, porcelain and plastic statuettes of saints, prayer cards, holy cards, Tarot cards, numerology charts, crucifixes, candles, framed portraits of Jesus and the Virgin, feathers and beads, and endless bottles of vitamins and medicines.

"Buenos dias," a voice said softly, making Rosa start.

In a corner of the room, peering just above the glass counter and blending with a display of brown feathers behind her, was the close-cropped head of an elderly woman seated in a low chair. Her face, tawny and wrinkled, wore a broad smile.

"Do you have any antibiotic ointment?" Rosa asked, trying to regain her composure.

"No, but I may have something better," the woman said, rising to her feet. "Is this for a cut, a scrape, or a burn?" she asked in the singsong English of the barrios.

Rosa hesitated, unsure if she should tell a stranger her husband had been shot. "Well...it's not really..."

"So it's a bullet wound then."

"I didn't say that."

"You didn't have to, m'hija, I've seen too many like you. Is this for your man?"

Rosa nodded slowly. "Yes, for my husband."

"Don't worry. We'll fix him up," the curandera said, patting Rosa's arm. "Does he have a fever?"

"No fever. But the skin is very red and hot to the touch."

"It's infected. That's for sure. Where is the wound?"

"Here," Rosa said, touching her left forearm. "Gracias a Dios, the bullet went all the way through."

"Ah, that's two good things then."

"What do you mean?"

"Your husband is lucky the bullet went through...and that his wife has faith in God."

From the shelf behind her, the curandera brought down a glass jar filled with a gray paste.

"What is it?" Rosa asked, examining the unmarked container.

The old woman laughed softly. "Magic, m'hija. Magic."

Rosa bristled and put down the jar. "I don't believe in magic."

"The magic isn't in this jar. The magic is in the healing power of the human body...and in the goodness of God," she said, handing the jar back to Rosa. "All that's in that jar is some mashed garlic and a few herbs."

Rosa studied the curandera's eyes. "How much is it?"

"Nothing. If it works, you come back and pay me."

"Can I set my own price, then?" Rosa asked, sensing a trick.

"Oh, no," she said, laughing again. "I set the price."

"How much?"

"From the moment you walked in, I could see you had doubts, m'hija. If this cure works, my price is that you come back and tell me."

Rosa nodded and left, grateful to have avoided another dip into their dwindling supply of money, but not really convinced the cure would work. Unfortunately, she had no other choice but to try it.

# THE MARCHA OFFENSIVE: DAY 7

The oily scent of pastries hung in the air of the windowless office in Outpost Bravo. Seated behind a gray metal desk, Southwest Regional Director of the CIA Henry Evans finished another cheese Danish, wiped the crumbs from his mouth with his fingers, and waved for his deputy to start their weekly media briefing. "Go ahead, Bill," he said, still chewing.

Bill Perkins tapped the keys on his laptop and a slide with a long list of bullets appeared on the wall-mounted plasma. "You want to go through the official briefing sequence this week or just skim through it like you usually do?" the young deputy asked.

"I see you're learning how to suck up to the boss, Bill," Evans said, smiling. "That's an honorable Agency tradition." Now nearing fifty, Henry Evans had managed to survive more than twenty-seven years in the CIA by deftly navigating its formidable bureaucracy. But the stress and long hours had left their mark. Overweight and balding, with an LDL count that would make a great bowling score, Evans's career had cost him his health—and his marriage.

Still, Hank was more buoyant than he'd been in some time following his regional office's recent coup: placing the informer inside the rebel ranks that had led to their Marcha Offensive victory.

"Yeah, I get it," Perkins said, adjusting his heavy glasses and forcing himself to smile. "So where do you want to start?"

"Let's start with the important stuff. How's the Marcha Offensive playing in D.C. this week?"

Perkins brought up a new slide on the plasma. "Calls and e-mails from constituents are up seventy-eight percent in all congressional districts."

"Forget the numbers, Bill. What's your gut telling you."

Perkins raised his head from the keyboard, eyes tiny behind his thick glasses. "Well, for the first few days after the Panchos hit us, it seems people were in shock. Now they're angry. A lot of demands for military retribution against the zones are coming in."

"What's the reaction been in Congress?"

"We've got an inside source that says Bates is going to call for punitive air strikes against the zones."

"Yeah, that should get him some headlines. Old Mel's never seen a camera he didn't love," Evans said with a dry laugh. Congressman Melvin Bates of the Nationalist Party was the author of the Quarantine and Relocation Act and the Terrorist Arraignment Act. Evans knew both of the draconian bills had started out as hard-line political posturing that, unfortunately, had gained popularity and become law as the Pancho insurgency worsened. "Is Gates going to get support from any other House members?"

"Not likely. A bipartisan committee in the House is drafting a resolution to cut off food and water to the zones." Perkins pushed a lock of stringy blond hair away from his forehead. "As a carrot, there's going to be a bounty for information that leads to the arrest of any insurgent. They're hoping that starving the civilians will get them to turn in the Panchos."

"And the White House?"

"They're in a holding pattern, waiting to see how the House bill plays with the public."

Evans was suddenly reflective. "You know, Bill, sometimes it's hard for me to get used to these domestic issues. Before the merger, anything inside U.S. borders was off-limits." Throughout most of Evans's career, domestic surveillance by the CIA had been forbidden. But the Brenner administration's consolidation of all intelligence divisions under the CIA three years ago had brought homeland security under Agency control.

Perkins saw Hank's observation as an opportunity to impress his boss. "On this next slide, I've got data from this really cool program that queries national editorials and blogs and—"

"Good, good, Bill," Evans interrupted. "Maybe we'll have time for that next week. Right now, I want to move on. Have we got any media leads on our local Panchos this week?"

Perkins sighed softly. "Hang on, I'll jump ahead in the deck," he said, tapping at the keyboard. Seconds later, a new slide appeared on the plasma. "Nothing much has changed. The only local Pancho leader that appeared in the media last week was Ramon Garcia. He's still in Geneva and issued a statement saying the Marcha Offensive was a moral victory for the rebels."

"I see it's not just our side that tries to spin the news," Evans said with a faint smile. "Okay, at least we know Garcia hasn't changed address. Any word about our mole? What's his name? Fernandez?"

"Alvarez—Ernesto Alvarez," Perkins corrected. "No word about him in the media or from any of our field contacts."

"Well, he served his purpose. There's nothing he knows that can hurt us, is there?"

"No. We kept him in the dark about our side of the deal."

"What about the other two in La Defensa Del Pueblo? The blonde and the big guy."

Perkins tapped the keys, and bios for Josefina Herrera and Manolo Suarez appeared on the screen. The photos that accompanied each were grainy, evidently taken from a distance. "Nothing's surfaced on Herrera or Suarez in the media. But we do have a photo from the Delta team that might be a clue. I've got to warn you, though, it's pretty gross."

"Can you tell me about it instead? I just ate."

"The Deltas who took out the Pancho command center snapped photos of the bad guys they snuffed before cutting out in the helos. One of them was a blonde about the right build. She'd been shot in the head, though. Not enough left of her face for a positive ID. You want to see the picture?"

"No," Evans answered, suddenly queasy.

"In any case, we can't confirm it was Herrera. The intel unit the Army sent in to follow up on the Delta raid didn't find any bodies at the Pancho command center. We just got their report yesterday."

"Did they come up with anything useful?"

"Not really. They found a laptop, but couldn't crack the security encryption on it."

Evans laughed bitterly. "Who was the CO on the intel sortie?"

Perkins scanned his laptop screen. "Captain Michael Fuller. He's stationed here in Bravo."

"Set up a briefing with him, will you? I know his mission didn't come up with any hard evidence, but Carol Phelps said the White House wants to get a read on the morale inside the zones from someone on the ground. The losses the Panchos took last week had to hurt them. They'd like to find out how bad."

Perkins blanched at the sound of Carol Phelps's name. A

political appointee at CIA headquarters in Langley, Virginia, Phelps was the assistant director of the CIA—and no friend of their regional office. "You sure Fuller's a good choice, Hank? The dude just led a patrol that came up with a goose egg—and got ten soldiers killed. Wouldn't you rather talk to one of the intel officers on the mission?"

"Naw, I want a regular Army guy. The Army intel nerds like to use big words and talk in circles. Most of them don't know shit but they never want to admit it."

Perkins shrugged. "Whatever you say, boss," he said, then turned back to his keyboard. "What else you want to see?"

"That's all for this week."

"But, Hank. I've got a lot more data to review."

Evans rose to his feet, indicating the briefing was over. "Thanks, Bill. I think we've covered everything important. I've got a lot on my plate. We'll see if there's time for your data next week."

Crestfallen, Perkins silently closed his laptop and left.

Alone, Evans felt a pang of guilt. Perkins was a good kid—and his computer skills were a godsend. But he could also waste your entire day with trivial details.

Evans leaned back and noticed the chair creaking under his corpulent frame. *I've got to start dieting soon,* he promised himself once again. Then his eyes drifted to the last Danish on the paper plate atop his desk. *Tomorrow. I'm going to start tomorrow.*

---

After four days of treatments with the garlic balm, to Rosa's surprise, Mano's infection had cleared up. That afternoon, Rosa returned to the botanica as she'd agreed.

Entering the shop, Rosa found the curandera carefully dusting the cluttered shelves.

"Buenos dias," the old woman called out before putting down the duster and approaching Rosa.

"Why didn't you charge me for the balm?" Rosa asked without preface.

The curandera smiled. "How much would I have made if you paid me? A few dollars?" She flicked her gnarled hand dismissively. "I wanted something much more valuable. I wanted to make a friend."

Rosa studied the older woman. Maybe the curandera believed a lot of nonsense—but she also had medicine that could help her family. "Perhaps you have," Rosa said warily.

"Good. Do you have time for some tea?"

Over a cup of herbal tea, Rosa learned that the curandera was named Celia Alonzo, a widow who had bought the shop with her husband's insurance settlement nearly thirty years earlier. Celia's unassuming manner and gentle humor put Rosa at ease. Their talk soon turned to faith and Rosa was surprised to learn Celia's views were not so different from her own. Before long, an hour had passed.

"I have to go," Rosa said reluctantly. "It's nearly time to start supper."

"Come back again...even if it's just to talk."

"I will," Rosa said, then reached into her purse and pressed a ten-dollar bill into the curandera's hand. "This is for the medicine."

Celia smiled, her eyes twinkling. "God bless you, m'hija."

Returning home to begin the evening meal, Rosa entered the kitchen and smiled as she looked out the window.

Seated on the ground under the shade of a eucalyptus in the backyard, Mano and Pedro were sharing a book. The thirteen-year-old leaned against his father as Mano read aloud, his finger tracing the lines of the text.

The sight warmed Rosa's heart. She had feared Pedro would balk at returning to school. Her son had hated the mandatory classes in the relocation camp. Staffed by frightened and uninspired detainee teachers, the camp's school had been little more than babysitting—with armed guards at the doors. That's why she'd asked Mano to persuade their son to attend the classes in the zones taught by La Defensa Del Pueblo volunteers.

Suddenly Pedro was on his feet. By her son's agitated gestures, Rosa could see the boy was upset. He turned and walked away from his father, heading toward the house.

"Finished reading with your father?" Rosa asked as Pedro entered the kitchen.

"I don't understand why I have to go to school," Pedro protested. "It's not like I'm going to get a job or anything."

Rosa stroked her son's shoulder. "It won't always be like this, Pedro. Someday our lives will get back to normal."

"If that ever happens, I can go back to school. But we need soldiers now, Mami. There's nothing in a book I need to know."

"You're wrong, m'hijo," Mano said, walking into the kitchen. "Even soldiers need an education. You think the Baldie officers are ignorant?"

"Why can't I just learn from you, Papi?"

Mano tapped his broad chest. "I'll be glad to help you, Pedro. But I don't know enough. You need real teachers."

"Teach me how to fight. That's all I want to know."

"If our people don't learn anything but fighting, we'll always be at war."

Rosa drew Pedro closer, putting her arm around his shoulder. "Listen to your father, m'hijo. This fighting will end someday and you'll need to make a life for yourself— and your family, if you're lucky enough to have one."

"These barrio schools are for cholos, anyway," Pedro said, stepping away from his mother. "I'm going to be somebody."

"Do you trust me, Pedro?" Mano asked, moving close to his son.

"Yeah." Pedro shrugged, staring at his feet.

"Then trust me when I say you will not regret attending school."

Pedro gazed toward the door. "Can I go now?"

Rosa patted Pedro on the backside, relieved the confrontation was over for now. "Be back before sundown for supper."

Exhaling heavily, Mano sat down at the kitchen table. "I don't think he's convinced," he said after Pedro had left the house.

"He's just disappointed. He'll get over it," Rosa said, getting an iron pot down from the cupboard and placing it on the stove. "I'm sure you didn't like to see the end of summer vacation when you were his age."

Mano laughed softly. "I hated going back to school."

"It's good to hear you laugh, mi amor," Rosa said as she scooped cornmeal from a burlap sack into the pot. "You haven't done that very much lately. I know things aren't going well for our people, but I thought being together with your family again would make you happier."

"I'm happy you're here…," Mano said, his voice trailing off.

"Then what is it?"

"It's nothing, querida. Let me help you with supper." Mano rose from his chair and began piling wood into the stove as Rosa added water to the cornmeal from a plastic jug. From a box in the corner, Mano grabbed a handful of mattress padding and placed it under the wood in the stove. He then took flint and steel from a drawer and began striking sparks. Moments later, the mattress padding was smoldering. After Mano blew on the cotton padding to nurture a flame, the wood began to ignite.

"The fire's going," he said, rising to his feet. "I'm going to wash up."

Rosa stopped stirring the pot and reached for his arm. "Mano, I don't think you're telling me everything you know.

People are saying most of our fighters are dead and the Baldies will be back in control soon."

Mano stared at the floor, reluctant to answer. He'd always kept silent about the grim business of war, wanting to shield his family from even secondhand knowledge of the brutal carnage he faced daily. More importantly, his training as a Ranger had taught him that his wife and children were civilians. Anything they knew about military matters endangered them and others. But the self-imposed silence was wearing on him.

Without Jo and Ramon, he was now alone in deciding matters that were no longer just military. He had little experience with logistics and supplies, precisely the areas where their situation looked most hopeless.

They had no way of getting more provisions to survive, much less weapons and ammunition. Even if they continued to fight, the war would likely turn into a bloody stalemate. Worse yet, if the resistance collapsed, they'd be captured. That meant a death sentence for all of them. Gnawing hardest at Mano was the realization that bringing Rosa and Pedro back from the camp had been a terrible mistake. They were in greater danger than ever.

Telling Rosa any of this, however, would do nothing to change it.

"We'll be all right," he said finally.

# THE MARCHA OFFENSIVE:
## *DAY 10*

Hank Evans studied the young officer on the other side of his cluttered desk. Michael Fuller sat erect but relaxed, his dark brown eyes probing. Around thirty, Fuller seemed a bit old for a captain. Perhaps that explained why he lacked the hollow swagger so many junior officers affected these days. During his three decades with the CIA, Evans had developed an instinct for reading people, and Fuller seemed like an officer whose judgment he could trust. Although Fuller had lost ten men on his sortie, sadly, that wasn't a bad record for a patrol into the zones.

"The report on your mission into Zone B last week reached some pretty high places, Captain," Evans said.

Fuller's eyebrows arched slightly in surprise. "It's rare when news of the Baldies in QZB gets all the way to Washington."

"Baldies?"

"I'm sorry, sir," Fuller said, nodding his head deferentially. "Baldies is what people in the zones call the Army—because of our helmets. *Balde* is Spanish for 'bucket.' It's also a pun in English because of our haircuts."

"I see." Evans rubbed his own smooth pink head. "Well,

my boss, Carol Phelps, wants to ask you some questions about your mission," he went on, dialing an antiquated desk phone. A moment later, the voice of the assistant director of the CIA came over the speaker.

"I read your report, Captain," Phelps said cordially. "It seems the Panchos aren't ready to roll over and die just yet."

"We met some strong resistance, ma'am," Fuller answered evenly.

"How did the civilians in the zone respond to your presence? Have they become more hostile?"

"I don't think it's fair to generalize, ma'am. Some people were hostile. Others seemed tolerant of us."

"I appreciate your effort to be precise, Captain. But I've been asked by the president to evaluate enemy morale. The administration is considering some new options. I'm sure you've heard about the calls for punitive raids against the Quarantine Zones."

"Yes, I have. I think that would be a mistake, ma'am."

"What?" Phelps said, her voice rising in surprise.

"Ma'am, I've been stationed in California for the last year and I've gotten to know the people in the zones. In my opinion, indiscriminate attacks would be counterproductive."

"Why?"

"Hispanics sitting on the fence will turn against us," Fuller said calmly. "Lashing out at everyone in the zones might be politically expedient, but in the long run, we'll make more enemies than we eliminate."

"Surely we could use surgical strikes to limit civilian casualties."

"As I'm sure you're aware, ma'am, we don't know who the rebels are or where they're hiding. And even if we did, the population density in the zones would still create a bloodbath."

"Suppose the U.S. public was willing to stomach high civilian casualties?"

"Urban combat is the last resort of any army. The risk of fratricide cancels out our superiority in firepower and technology. If we have to fight house-to-house, our losses would make the Marcha Offensive look like a Maypole dance."

"Spare me the lecture on MOUT, Captain. It's the same song and dance we've been getting from the Pentagon. I thought you military types liked to fight."

"Believe me, ma'am, every soldier since Sun Tzu has tried to avoid urban combat."

"What about more moderate measures? How do you think people in the zones will respond if we cut off the food supplies?"

"Same result, ma'am. The rebels want to paint us as the bad guys. Cutting off food to innocent people plays right into their hands."

"Look, Captain. It's time to turn up the heat on the terrorists. We need to get tough."

Fuller leaned forward in his chair, but his voice remained steady. "If the administration wants to get tough, then we should bite the bullet and convince the public that aggression against the zones is the wrong approach."

"I see, *Captain*," Phelps said, stressing his modest rank. "And what approach would *you* suggest the administration take instead?"

"I realize the public doesn't understand this, ma'am, but the Marcha Offensive was the biggest win we've had so far against the Panchos. We need to lure the insurgents out of the zones again. If they go toe-to-toe against us without civilians around, we'll win every time. And if we brought more of our better-equipped units stateside, we'd win sooner rather than later."

"What about the Pancho bombings? Do you suppose we can let them destroy strategic facilities and get away with it?"

"The sabotage was the Panchos' smartest play. They

**HOUSE DIVIDED**    43

managed to spread panic and demoralize us without spilling much blood. If the Panchos *had* indiscriminately killed civilians, they would have lost public support around the world. Right now, we still look like Goliath bullying David. Attacking the QZs is only going to make us look worse."

"We can't let enemy attacks go unpunished, Fuller," Phelps said, her voice suddenly sharp. "It only makes us look weak—and that's going to invite more attacks. If we could get some informers in the zones to come forward and finger the ringleaders, we could be more selective with our response. But since they won't, it's clear to me they're all supporting the terrorists."

Fuller sat calmly, unfazed by Phelps's ire. "Ma'am, the main reason no one comes forward is the Terrorist Arraignment Act. The way the act is written, informers could be tried and executed if they're involved in the insurgency in any way. And that's not even the worst of it. With a death penalty for taking up arms, why should an insurgent ever surrender?"

"That's strange talk coming from an Army officer."

"My duty is to serve my country, ma'am. I don't think punishing innocent people serves our national interest," Fuller said evenly.

The line was silent for a moment. Evans knew his boss was stunned. Junior officers did not openly question government policy. Fuller was committing career suicide.

After several long seconds, Phelps finally answered. "Well, it's apparent we have different opinions on the national interest. Thank you, Captain. Your views have been duly noted," she said icily before hanging up.

After an awkward silence, Evans rose and smiled at the young captain. "I admire your candor, son. It's not a very popular opinion right now. Thanks for stopping by." He extended his hand.

With a pang of guilt, Evans watched the young officer leave. He agreed with the captain's assessment, but had once again stifled his dissent. The administration's heavy-handed attitude was only the latest arrogant blunder.

Evans dropped back into his chair and stared sullenly at the haphazard stacks of documents on his desk. For the last few months, Brenner appointees had been routinely ordering CIA staffers to doctor their reports about the full extent of overseas military deployments. Done under the pretext of misleading our enemies, Evans had no doubt the real motive for obscuring troop commitments was political. It was nothing less than a systematic deception of the American people. Although he found it hard to stomach, Evans had kept quiet. The Brenner people were zealots. His dissent would only get him fired.

He'd contemplated going public, but who'd listen to a mid-level spook from the West Coast? In the end, he'd lose his job—and his GS15 salary. In this lousy economy, he couldn't take that risk.

Still, Fuller's courage in standing up to Phelps shamed him. *The kid doesn't have alimony payments and a daughter to put through college*, he told himself. *He can afford to take it on the chin.*

Michael Fuller closed the door to Evans's office and made his way down the corridor, mulling his future. *Well, I've crossed the Rubicon. There's no turning back now*, he realized. His open dissent with the CIA bosses was sure to get him blackballed. Their punishment would be to keep him stateside—and that would give him exactly what he wanted: another crack at the Pancho commander.

Fuller hoped he'd made the right choice. Because there was little doubt he'd just kissed off his chances for a successful military career.

Ramon checked his laptop again. There was still no word from Jo.

He shut down the computer's encrypted connection and returned to the Web, searching for news from the States. The articles were more of the same: a blame storm over the Marcha Offensive.

A sudden blast of static from the security radio startled him. "Mr. Perez is here to see you, sir," the bodyguard stationed outside his apartment reported.

Ramon pressed the reply button on the handheld device. "Thanks, Retief. Send him up."

By the time Ramon had powered down his laptop, the doorbell buzzed. Opening the door, he motioned Octavio inside. "I'll save you the trouble of asking," Ramon said wearily. "I still haven't heard from Jo."

Handing Ramon his rumpled jacket, Octavio said, "I was never in favor of controlling the attacks from a single place... and I was right. Face it, Ramon. Jo's command center's been taken out."

"Absence of evidence doesn't necessarily mean evidence of absence," Ramon answered, leading Perez into the chalet's living room.

"You're playing fucking word games with me, Ramon. Jo's dead—or she's been captured. Otherwise we would have heard from her by now."

Ramon lowered his eyes. "Perhaps you're right," he said softly, hanging the dated jacket on a stylish chrome rack.

"Not much doubt of that," Octavio said before walking to the fireplace, where he held out his palms to warm them.

Ramon filled two glasses with scotch from the small bar along the wall. "Maybe it's time to call another meeting of the Quarantine Zone leaders and decide what we do next. Getting together in Mexico should work again. But we can't use Santiago this time."

"Forget it. We don't need another big fucking meeting," Octavio said over his shoulder.

Garcia set the glasses on the coffee table and sat down. "That's ridiculous. We need to rebuild our national front. Otherwise, our resistance is going to fall apart."

"It won't fall apart if we organize it right... *this time*," Octavio said, settling into one of the leather chairs and picking up his scotch. "You and Jo set things up so we couldn't take a piss without getting everyone else involved. Well, that's over, Ramon. We need to be like that monster bitch with a bunch of heads. You cut off one head and two more take its place."

"Your reference to Hydra is not without merit..."

"Goddamn right," Octavio interrupted, stabbing his finger toward his host. "We work in small cells this time. Nobody can rat out more than a few others if they're caught."

"Think this through, Tavio. We need to outline our objectives."

"There's only one objective... Hurt the gabachos every way we can."

Ramon shook his head. "All that's going to accomplish is a bloody, pointless rebellion. We'll have no coherent strategy, no way to shape the media message. We can win this thing if we play it smart. What you're suggesting will only lead to endless killing and retribution. Do you want to end up like the Palestinians... pariahs who get no sympathy because of their senseless terrorism?"

"Yeah? Well, what has your 'smart' way gotten us so far? Most of our fighters are dead and we're totally out of touch with our people back home. If these pendejos in their embassies ever figure that out, you think they're going to hook us up with any weapons? Shit, they won't give us the fucking time of day."

Ramon stared coldly at Octavio. "Well, we at least agree on one thing: We need to keep our mouths shut about how bad things really are."

# THE MARCHA OFFENSIVE: *DAY 14*

**A**fter finishing another crab cake, Hank Evans searched the hors d'oeuvres table for a napkin and, failing to find one, wiped his fingers on his pants before refilling his wineglass. Evans had planted himself near the impressive array of finger foods and beverages while eavesdropping on the conversations around him at the beachfront cocktail party.

Hank had no illusions about why he'd been invited. Hosted by California congressman George Whitehead Nixon, the affair had presidential aspirations written all over it. Most of the guests were from the local intelligence community or the diplomatic corps, with a strong sprinkling of military officers. Although everyone wore name badges, they did not include titles of office. All the same, Hank's surveillance skills were still sharp enough for him to discern the profession of most guests he didn't already know.

The great-nephew of the former commander in chief desperately needed foreign policy experience on his presidential résumé, and being on a first-name basis with some spooks, diplomats, and generals would certainly pad Nixon's credentials. On the other hand, the party was a two-way street.

Catching the eye of an up-and-coming politician never hurt a career in government service.

As the liquor flowed, the conversations around Evans grew louder and more animated. Two weeks after the Marcha Offensive, the repercussions of the rebel attacks seemed to be the main topic of every discussion. A few feet away from Evans, a trio he'd pegged for senior military officers in civvies were deep into their cups and proving to be very informative.

"The Joint Chiefs told the Brenner people air strikes against the zones would be a bad move," said a tall, gray-haired man in his fifties holding a whiskey. By his commanding manner, Evans figured him for an Army one-star. "Thank God they had the sense to listen to the Pentagon for once."

"Bates lobbied pretty hard for air strikes," a shorter and younger man observed. His Air Force Academy ring left no doubt about his branch of service. Evans guessed he was a bird colonel at least.

The one-star tapped the fly boy's arm. "Yeah," he said with a cynical grin. "I bet your B1 wing commanders would have been lining up outside your office to volunteer for a bomb run on U.S. soil."

The officers laughed, downing another swallow from their glasses.

The third member of the group had been the easiest to spot as a military officer out of uniform. She was the only woman in the place with sensible shoes—and they were white oxfords, a good clue she was Navy. "So what's the White House going to do?" she asked the one-star.

"Brenner's people talked him into putting a blockade around the zones. They think that's a safe play politically," he said, taking another pull from the glass. "We've just got the orders. The food and medicine shipments stop tomorrow."

The news sobered the group.

Evans already knew about the siege. His office had received a memo from Langley that morning. He was not surprised to see the officers shared his own apprehensions about the move. Most U.S. military people did not like waging war on civilians.

The naval officer seemed especially concerned. "What about water and electricity?"

"Well, most of the zones have been without electricity for some time. Not many utility workers willing to go inside to fix anything. But we've got orders to kill the electrical service anyway," the one-star explained. "We're going to keep the water flowing, though. If people start dropping like flies right away, that wouldn't play well in the press—and that's the last thing the White House wants. Brenner's people are hoping after a week or two with empty bellies, the civilians will start turning in the Panchos."

"Who's going to keep these people inside the zones once they start getting hungry?" she asked. "Nobody's going to sit around and watch their families starve to death. I figure they'll start foraging outside the walls pretty quick. You think they'll bring some overseas units back stateside for security?"

The one-star took another sip of whiskey and shook his head. "Nope. The White House is using the War Powers Act to draft off-duty local cops as border guards around the zones."

"Are you kidding?"

"Hey, you can't blame the president," the one-star argued. "Our foreign deployments are already stretching us pretty thin. If we bring many units stateside, it's going to be a disaster for our overseas missions."

The naval officer seemed unconvinced. "Sounds like trouble to me, Chuck. Those local cops will be stretched a lot farther than our troops overseas if this blockade lasts more than a week. I don't think they've thought this thing through very well."

"It's a done deed, my friend," the one-star said drily. "Beginning tomorrow, our choppers will be flying over the zones, dropping leaflets with a five-thousand-dollar bounty for anybody who turns in a Pancho. We'll have speaker trucks driving around the walls telling them the same thing."

Evans felt his pulse rise as he listened to this last bit. A five-grand bounty for fingering a Pancho meant the CIA would be following up on thousands of useless leads—many of them simply personal vendettas. Most good intelligence tips came from insiders. But the needle law would silence anyone with real knowledge of the Panchos. Who would give information that could lead to your own prosecution? Evans agreed with the naval officer. The Brenner people were bungling this insurgency. The worst part was feeling helpless to do anything about it.

He finished the rest of his wine and turned back to the table for a refill. As Evans poured another glass, he spotted the party's host. Congressman Nixon was working his way through the guests, methodically greeting everyone on the terrace, occasionally stopping to pose for a photo. An aide trailed the congressman providing a quick bio for anyone Nixon did not recognize.

Hank was on his third helping of crab cakes when the congressman finally approached, his palm extended. Over Nixon's shoulder, the aide said, "Mr. Evans is regional director for the CIA in our district."

"Thank you for coming. Glad you could join us," Nixon said heartily.

"Thanks for the invitation, Congressman. The crab cakes are excellent," Evans said, washing down the last bite with some white wine.

Nixon glanced at Evans's name badge. "That's the pride of California you're tasting there, Henry. Dungeness crab, caught right in our waters. I've been working on legislation to keep our coastal fisheries free from pollution so people all over the world can keep enjoying California seafood. And that zinfandel is Napa Valley, too."

"I've always believed protecting the environment is good for business."

"Well now," Nixon said in mock amazement. "Don't let your bosses hear you. They'll think you're one of those wild-eyed greenies they're always bashing."

"I'm not an appointee, Congressman. I'm career CIA."

"I didn't think there were many of you guys left around."

"They haven't managed to scrape off all the barnacles yet."

Nixon laughed loudly and slapped his back. "A spook with a sense of humor. This is a man I'd like to remember. Mind if we have a picture taken?" he said, gesturing to the photographer hovering nearby.

"I'd be honored, Congressman."

Evans smiled as Nixon nestled closer and the camera flashed. It would not be wise to keep a copy of the photo at the office—but a man on the way up was always good to know.

Nixon handed him a business card. "Here's my number, Henry," he said, already walking toward the next guest. "Give me a call if there's ever anything I can do."

# THE MARCHA OFFENSIVE:
## *DAY 19*

Rosa approached her shrine to the Virgin of Guadalupe and, just as Celia had shown her, softly brushed the porcelain statuette with an eagle feather to clear away any evil spirits that might weaken the power of her invocation. She then lit a garlic candle and replaced the almost spent one burning on a small plate above one of the bounty leaflets dropped by the Baldies. "Señora, please protect us from this evil," she said solemnly.

The invocation against the bounty leaflets was simply a precaution. Rosa and everyone else in the zones who personally knew a rebel fighter understood the needle law made the bounty toothless. Most of the leaflets dropped into the zones had quickly become highly prized kindling.

The feather and garlic candles, purchased from Celia's botanica, were new additions to Rosa's daily rites. Recalling her first visit to the folk medicine shop, Rosa was still astonished by how many misgivings about the curandera she'd overcome.

Hanging the eagle feather back on the wall, she finished the morning ceremony with a more familiar ritual, placing a small saucer of cornmeal before the Virgin's battered statuette. She'd broken the figurine in despair after her daughter's death at the relocation camp, but repaired it shortly afterward as her faith was restored. "Lupita, please provide for your servants," she whispered before making the sign of the cross and returning to the kitchen.

When Rosa entered the room, she found Mano and Pedro already seated at the kitchen table waiting for breakfast. She walked to the stove and spooned two portions of thick gruel from a cast-iron pot into bowls. "This is the last of the government cornmeal," she said softly to Mano, bringing the bowls to the table.

Mano nodded glumly. The start of the government siege against the Quarantine Zones four days ago had presented him with an agonizing choice—a decision he could no longer postpone. Would he let innocent civilians in the Los Angeles zones starve or would he share the caches of food and supplies Josefina Herrera had stockpiled for the fighters?

Mano pushed his bowl back slowly. "Thanks, querida. I'm not hungry right now. Save this for later."

"Mano, you can't keep doing this," Rosa said gently. "You have to eat, mi amor."

"We need to conserve food. Our people are going to need it."

"One bowl of mush won't make much difference, mi amor," she said, sliding the bowl toward him again. "I know what's really bothering you ... and I can tell you that giving away the food Josefina stored for the fighters will only keep everyone alive a few extra days before it's gone."

"I can't let people go hungry while I still have food."

"Josefina was a complicated woman, Mano. I didn't understand her for a long time. In the end, though, I realized she wanted what was best for all our people. So don't forget this: She gathered those supplies for those fighting for justicia, not to feed all of Los Angeles."

"Even if we only feed those fighting, we don't have a way

to break the blockade yet, querida. We need to train new fighters and find weapons for them."

"Then why keep fighting?" Rosa asked, scraping out the last remnants of cornmeal in the pot.

Pedro raised his eyes from his bowl. "We have to keep fighting... isn't that right, Papi?"

"Your mother was speaking to me, m'hijo," Mano gently corrected him. The thirteen-year-old had recently begun asserting his opinion without being asked, a sure sign of adolescence.

Pedro scowled. "Don't I get to say anything around here?"

"You can speak anytime," Mano answered calmly. "But you can't interrupt an adult conversation. That's disrespectful."

The boy rolled his eyes. "I'm finished eating. May I be excused?"

Mano nodded and Pedro huffed away.

"Be home right after school," Rosa called out after him without looking up from the pot she was cleaning.

Once Pedro was out of the kitchen, Mano rose from the table and faced his wife. "Rosa, there's something I have to tell you," he said tenderly. "It's something very difficult for me to say."

Rosa put down the pot, wiped her hands, and met his gaze. "What is it, mi amor?" she asked calmly.

"Rosa, you and Pedro are everything I care about," he said, taking her hand. "You know that, don't you?"

Rosa nodded. "Of course, mi amor."

"Then please understand... I want all this talk in our house about food, about the Baldies, about the war... I want this talk to stop."

"I don't understand," Rosa said evenly. "What's wrong with talking about these things?"

Mano rubbed his mouth, trying to find the words. "Rosa, my time with you and the children... I've always wanted it to be different from the rest of the world. I never wanted all the craziness out there to touch us. I've tried to keep what I do for the cause separate from our family." Mano lowered his eyes. "To talk about these things in front of you and Pedro . . . it makes me feel like I've failed you."

"No, Mano. You haven't failed us," she said, touching his cheek. "I know you've always tried to keep that part of your life from us. You say it's to protect us, and I believe you, Mano. You're a good husband and good father. But times have changed, mi amor. Don't you see? There's nothing that will save me or Pedro if we're caught now." She paused, dabbing at the tears welling in her eyes. "I don't want to know anything that could hurt you or anyone else fighting for our people. But at least let me help you think things through, to be someone you can talk to. Jo and Ramon are gone now and you don't have anyone else. You don't have to carry all this by yourself, mi amor."

Rosa spread her arms and Mano embraced her. With her head resting gently on his broad chest, they held each other silently for a time, the warmth of their bodies saying all they needed.

"Will you let me help you, Mano?" Rosa finally asked, looking into his eyes.

Mano exhaled slowly, trying to decide how to answer his wife. The camp had changed Rosa; there was no doubt of that. The woman who had left a year ago had lived only for her family and her faith. The woman who'd returned was more savvy, an ally who seemed ready to help their cause. Would he put aside his pride and accept her help? He knew it was the right thing to do . . . for his family and his people. "I'm going to need time to get used to this," he said.

"We don't have time, mi amor. People are already hungry. They'll be going outside the walls looking for food soon."

Tilting his head slightly, Mano said, "Have you changed

your mind? You want me to share the food we have stored for the fighters?"

"No, Mano. We can't give away that food. But we can give people hope."

"What kind of hope can I give them? Most of our fighters and weapons are gone…more Baldie patrols are coming into the zones every day…it's going to be nearly impossible to give them a win right now."

"Now you sound like Pedro," Rosa said gently, a faint smile warming her face.

Mano stepped away from her. "The boy is right, Rosa. With the needle law, we don't have a choice about fighting anymore."

"No, Mano. You don't have to keep fighting." Rosa moved closer to him, reaching for his hand. "I know that hiding is not in your nature, mi amor. You'd rather stand and fight. But if our people are too weak to keep the Baldies out right now, getting yourself killed won't change that."

"Maybe not. But I'd rather die fighting than by lethal injection."

"And what happens to the families of the fighters after you've thrown away your lives for pride?" She leaned against him, stroking his hard, muscled arm. "There are other ways to be brave besides fighting, Mano. You've always put your family first."

Mano slowly shook his head. "It's not that simple, Rosa. If we give up now, we might lose our last chance to reclaim this land."

"We don't have to give up, mi amor. We just have to stop fighting for a while," she said. "Maybe the government will stop the blockade if things are quiet for a while."

"We're not a regular army, Rosa. What keeps us together is hate for the Baldies. Take away that focus and our resistance could fall apart."

"Then give them something else to focus on. Put them to work. Convince them that the best way to fight back now is to figure out how to feed ourselves. My grandfather fed a family of six from a little field of beans and corn in Sonora."

"Your grandfather grew up in the country, Rosa. Most of the people here don't know much about farming."

"Celia told me some families near her shop have planted vegetable gardens. Can't more of our people do that?"

"What does a curandera know about farming? Does she think prayers grow food?"

"This has nothing to do with prayer, Mano. Celia just told me what she saw with her own eyes—and it's true. We've still got water, and there's good soil under all this cement. It may take some time, but our people have lived off the land before."

Mano rubbed his bearded chin. Rosa's words were very similar to something he'd heard before. "A while back, Jo started some self-sufficiency programs. We put them aside when we started planning for the offensive, but Jo always said we'd have to feed ourselves eventually."

"That could have been Josefina's plan all along, Mano. In any case, she paid for those supplies with her own money. Doing what she asked is the right thing to do."

"I don't think Jo ever imagined the situation we're in now," Mano said soberly. "Even if we stopped fighting for a while and started growing food, we'll still eventually need more weapons. That's going to take money."

"Can't Ramon Garcia help us? He has a rich movie-star wife."

"Margaret Zane is a producer, querida, not a movie star. Maggie and Ramon got divorced so she could avoid Class H and keep their money. She's still loyal to our cause and might have the money we need for weapons. But I don't have a way to contact Maggie—or Ramon. The Baldies destroyed our communications equipment the day we launched the attacks."

"So why hasn't Ramon tried to reach *us*?"

Mano stared at the floor. "I wish I knew," he said softly.

———

Octavio spotted Ramon in a corner of the ballroom holding a glass of wine and a beluga canapé, laughing with a bald Anglo. *Pendejo*, Octavio thought bitterly. *Boozing it up and eating caviar while our people back home starve.*

Walking uncomfortably in his rented tuxedo through the white-tie gathering, Octavio reached Ramon and brusquely pulled him aside. "Oye, I just heard that the Baldies started patrolling inside the Quarantine Zones again. We need to do something, Ramon. We're losing control."

Ramon turned his head and murmured, "Keep your voice down. This is hardly the place to discuss it."

"Well, we've got to do something, goddammit!" Octavio said. "We just can't keep on talking."

"Look, Octavio," Ramon said softly, but with an edge in his voice. "I found out through the showbiz blogs that my ex-wife is in Vancouver for a couple of months on a film project. The conversation you just interrupted was with a Canadian I was working on to smuggle a message to her."

"What good is that going to do?"

Ramon leaned closer. "She can use our money to help Mano...and your group in San Antonio, too."

"So we had to come to this fancy party just to do that? I can't believe you're here, having a good time, while our people are starving."

"Don't act so righteous, Octavio. It clouds your think-ing," Ramon sneered. "You should be smart enough to know I have to be careful about getting word to Maggie. The government gumshoes monitor all the embassies. If you or I were seen walking into the Canadian embassy, it would raise red flags. If they suspect Maggie's helping us, they might pick her up for questioning once she reenters the States."

"That sounds like a pretty lame excuse for coming here to me."

"I see. Then why did *you* show up?"

"To keep an eye on you."

Ramon glared at Octavio for a moment. "Well, enjoy the party," he said coldly and walked away.

Octavio stared at his back, fuming. Ramon liked this life too much. He was too easy and comfortable in the world of rich gabachos. The man was mayonnaise wrapped in a tortilla. On the inside, he was one of *them*.

# THE MARCHA OFFENSIVE:
## MONTH 1, DAY 4

The Army patrol moved slowly down Whittier Boulevard, hugging the center of the street. A pair of Bradleys led the column, shadowed by a platoon of infantry. Circling overhead, a camera drone kept a watchful eye over the heavily armed procession.

The civilians lined the street like a parade route—but no one was cheering. Instead, they stared in silence, wary of the soldiers but unwilling to hide in fear. A few blocks ahead of the patrol, Mano and Angel mingled in the crowd, studying the approaching formation for weaknesses.

"Where did they enter the zone this time?" Mano asked.

"South Gate," Angel answered. "Two times yesterday, same thing."

Now three weeks into the siege, Mano had yet to discover a pattern to the patrols. The Army was varying the routes and times of their sorties, making it impossible to prepare a kill zone. Mano's attempt to detour the patrols into a trap was also facing difficulties. "Have your vatos been able to build the new roadblocks yet?"

"No," Angel said, shaking his head dejectedly. "Too many soldiers come too many times."

Mano stared into the distance, trying to hide his disappointment. "Tell your vatos to follow this patrol and track their route. We need to keep watching if we're ever going to figure out their pattern."

"We fight Baldies soon?"

"Our attacks have cost us too much, Angel. We're almost out of weapons and ammunition. Each time we fight them, the soldiers kill more of our fighters. It's better for us to wait."

Angel's eyes narrowed in disgust. "We do nothing?"

"We'll fight later. Right now, we need to keep our people alive. Food is more important than fighting."

"Ramon Garcia...why he no help?"

Though Mano had asked himself that question more than once in the last few days, he couldn't afford to let Angel see his doubt. "Ramon hasn't forgotten us. He'll send help when he can."

The patrol had almost reached them when a knot of teenagers on the fringe of the crowd hurled a volley of rocks. The soldiers swung their weapons toward the fleeing teens but held their fire.

"Try that again and I'll waste you," one of the soldiers yelled. The other troopers laughed, but the incident darkened their mood. "Get back! Make some room!" they shouted angrily at the people nearest them along the street.

Mano moved away from the soldiers, but Angel held his ground.

Using his rifle like a staff, one of the soldiers shoved Angel backward, throwing him to the ground. "Are you deaf, beaner?" the soldier screamed.

Angel's eyes gleamed with fury as he scrambled to his feet, ready to pounce. Mano grabbed Angel's arm, holding him back.

"Sueltame, Mano!" Angel whispered angrily, demanding Mano release him.

But Mano only tightened his powerful grip, keeping the smaller man in place until the soldiers had passed. "The worst time to fight is when you're angry."

Angel locked his eyes on Mano's. "A dónde fueron tus cojones?" he said before walking away.

Even with his meager Spanish, Mano understood his question: *Where have your balls gone?*

# THE MARCHA OFFENSIVE:
## MONTH 1, DAY 18

**Z**ooming just over the treetops at a hundred seventy-five miles per hour, Simon Potts looked down from the helicopter's open cockpit and shuddered. The branches seemed close enough to reach out and touch with his feet. Although he'd filmed from a helicopter at least a dozen times in his career, he'd never lost his fear of aerial shoots—and it was easy to understand why. Perched on the edge of the doorless cockpit, his feet dangling freely and both hands on his VariCam, the only thing keeping Simon from hurtling to his death was a two-inch-wide harness.

"We're approaching the border of the no-fly zone, Simon," the voice of the pilot said in his earphones. "You want me to gain some altitude and see what kind of telephoto shot you can get from this distance?"

Doing his best to calm himself, Simon considered his options. The government had placed a no-fly zone around each of the nation's Quarantine Zones since the siege had begun some five weeks ago. The White House claimed this was to prevent any attempts to supply the insurgents. But Simon, like every other journalist, knew better. The real intent of the no-fly zone was to keep out the media. Cut off from food and electricity, innocents as well as insurgents inside the zones would suffer horrible privations, something the White House did not want the world to see—and the reason Simon Potts was determined to document it. The thought steadied his nerves.

As a filmmaker, he know the chance for another prizewinning documentary trumped the hazards of recording the conditions inside the wall. As an African-American, his connection with the plight of the people inside was an additional incentive.

"Take us in, Judy," Simon said, looking east toward central Los Angeles. "There's too much haze for a long shot."

"It's your party, Simon. This one could be a Pulitzer...or prison."

"Maybe both," Potts said with a dry laugh.

They had approached from the west, trying to keep their flight over water as long as possible to avoid detection. Their plan was to fly top speed at treetop level through the five-mile no-fly zone until they were over Los Angeles Quarantine Zone A.

Simon had gone into debt to charter the fastest chopper available. They would need every bit of the Agusta's hundred-seventy-five-mile-per-hour speed to avoid being caught by the Army's slower Comanche choppers patrolling the zones. If all went well, Simon estimated they would have about three minutes inside the Quarantine Zone and still make a clean getaway. Thanks to his old friend Ramon Garcia, he had directions to a park beside a community center just inside the walls. Once there, they could hover briefly, get the best images possible of the conditions inside, and be off before the Army could respond. The identification numbers on the side of the chopper had even been doctored as an extra precaution.

"I can see the wall, Simon," the pilot announced.

"Don't slow down until we're inside," Potts replied. Seconds later the helicopter was hovering inside the walls. Potts trained his camera on the abandoned landscape below and began to shoot.

His pulse pounding, Potts barely noticed what he was recording. He simply panned the camera, taking in as much as he could with a wide-angle lens. He'd have time to analyze what he was taping later.

Suddenly the helicopter lurched hard to the right. "We're out of here, Simon," the pilot's voice said over the radio. "We've got company coming in from the north."

Simon glanced in that direction and saw the hornet-like shapes of two Army choppers near the horizon. *This is going to be close*, he realized.

The Army helicopters, equipped with radar and armed with air-to-air missiles, could have shot them down outside of visual range minutes ago. Simon was betting their lives the government would not risk killing members of the media. So far, the bet was paying off. He knew the Army choppers would try to force them to land and arrest them or simply follow them until they ran out of fuel. Losing them was their only chance of avoiding prison.

"Sit tight. This is going to get hairy," the pilot announced as the Agusta dove lower to evade the Army choppers' air-to-air radar. Simon instinctively pulled his feet inside the craft as they raced along a deserted freeway less than twenty feet above the pavement, light poles zooming by at eye level like stakes in a picket fence.

Simon's stomach turned each time the Agusta shot up, then dove back down, to clear a highway overpass. "How much longer are we on this roller coaster, Judy?"

"Not long. Our freeway exit's coming up in a few miles," she answered.

Potts looked back toward the north. The sky above the

Quarantine Zone was obscured by buildings. *Good. If we can't see them, they can't see us.* The landing site they'd set up was outside the no-fly zone. Once their helicopter was on the ground and out of sight, they could wait until the sky was clear of the Army choppers for Judy's return flight.

"Please prepare for landing," Judy said calmly over the radio. "The captain asks you to put your seats and tray tables in their upright positions."

After flying the chopper at high speeds between buildings and power lines, Judy deftly guided the chopper into a small, tarp-covered landing area between two empty warehouses.

As soon as they'd touched down, Simon unbuckled his harness, jumped out of the craft, and helped Judy lower the tarp over the opening they'd just flown through. In the abandoned L.A. exurb, there was little chance anyone would report their landing.

Jumping into the rental car parked at the site, Potts was in a Las Vegas television studio four hours later. In the editing suite, Simon finally saw the details of the images he'd recorded: a trio of gaunt-faced children with protruding ribs and bloated bellies huddled in an apartment doorway; an emaciated old man staring vacantly, nearing the end of hope; a mother holding a scrawny toddler in her thin, bony arms.

These haunting scenes of hunger on U.S. soil, reminiscent of a third-world famine, would dominate the news cycle across the globe in the next twenty-four hours.

Reaction in the United States was muted. Most Americans, still outraged over the Marcha Offensive, had little compassion left for those they believed were supporting the rebels.

The rest of the world had a different response. They believed the suffering within the Quarantine Zone walls was proof of America's cruelty and prejudice. Almost invariably, film clips of the walled-in Jewish ghettos built by the Nazis in World War II accompanied Potts's footage. For the second time in six months, charges of genocide were leveled against the U.S. at the United Nations. This time, the accusations barely raised an eyebrow inside the United States.

The majority of Americans were more interested in another result of the siege: Rebel resistance was visibly diminishing. Although the five-thousand-dollar bounty had netted few insurgents, the rebels now seemed reluctant to engage government forces. As had happened before, the Southern California zones had led the trend—this time, toward pacifism.

For the first time in nearly two years, the Army was once again routinely patrolling inside the Quarantine Zones. This promising development raised hopes within the White House that the end might finally be in sight for the stubborn rebellion in the barrios.

---

The girl stared up at Mano steadily, her chestnut eyes unblinking. Barely fourteen, Isabel Sanchez already carried herself with a dignity possessed by few adults. "What is it you want me to tell my brother, Don Manolo?" she asked Mano.

Isabel sat between Mano and her brother Angel at the kitchen table of the two-bedroom duplex the orphaned siblings shared. Since crossing the border with Angel four years earlier, Isabel had absorbed English effortlessly, unlike her brother who was seven years older—a trait common among prepubescent immigrants.

Mano handed her a sheet of paper. "I need Angel and his vatos to help our people support themselves. I've made out a list of projects," he said. "Can you translate this?"

Isabel studied the list carefully. "I don't know this word," she said, pointing to *cistern*.

"It's a tank to capture rainwater."

She nodded and began translating the long list into Spanish for her brother.

Mano and Angel had considered using Isabel to translate their battle plans, but neither had wanted to risk putting the girl in harm's way. This topic, however, would require a vocabulary beyond the rough pidgin they'd developed to discuss tactics.

Based primarily on articles published by Jo in their sporadic underground newspaper, *La Voz del Pueblo*, the self-sufficiency projects on Mano's list included plans for planting, harvesting, crop storage, irrigation, water storage and purification, chicken breeding and egg production, domestic catfish ponds, and even folk medicine using herbs. Mano knew it was far from complete, but it was a start. He hoped that Angel and his vatos would help him spread the word and take part in these labor-intensive projects. The Verdugos had become respected role models for many of the young people in the zones.

Mano watched Angel as Isabel read from the list. The gang leader's expression grew increasingly sour as she continued. When the girl was finished, Angel answered in a long stream of Spanish.

Isabel faced Mano and translated. "My brother says he'll help you, but he's not happy about it. He said if he'd wanted to be a peon working in the dirt, he would have stayed in Coahuila."

# THE MARCHA OFFENSIVE:
## *MONTH 1, DAY 20*

**C**aptain Fuller stood outside his Humvee, inspecting the armored patrol about to enter Quarantine Zone B. "Close that hatch, soldier!" he yelled to the driver of a Bradley lumbering past. *You can't really blame the kid,* Fuller thought. The driver's compartment on the heavily armored Brad was notoriously hot. Still, six weeks ago none of his men would have dared enter a QZ with an open hatch. *Things have certainly calmed down,* he noted, climbing into the Humvee.

"Ol' Hefty's been doing a good job for us lately, Captain," his driver said, patting the blue figurine on the dash. "Pancho hasn't said *boo* for quite a while."

"Let's hope it stays that way."

As he uttered the words, Fuller realized he was not being completely honest. He was glad the fighting had died down, but part of him was disappointed, too. He'd probably thrown away his career to confront the Pancho commander again, and now it might never happen.

In a white stucco cottage less than three kilometers away, the Pancho commander was engaged in a decidedly unmilitary duty: the celebration of his son's fourteenth birthday.

The gathering had been Rosa's idea, an effort to keep family life normal despite the siege. Mano had agreed and they'd invited Angel and Isabel, along with Celia Alonzo. Having finished a meager meal of cornbread and beans, the group now sat around the dining room table, with Pedro in the seat of honor on the end nearest the kitchen.

Isabel rose from her chair and approached Pedro, her eyes cast demurely toward the floor. "Happy birthday," she said, handing him a shoe box with a bow made from an old skirt hem. "It's from my brother and me."

Pedro eagerly opened the box and found a hand-tooled leather belt. "Way large," he said, admiring the intricate pattern hammered into the dusky leather. He lifted the belt, proudly showing it to the others.

Isabel smiled shyly. "Angel made the buckle and I decorated the leather."

"Feliz cumpleaño, ese," Angel said, giving Pedro the thumb-and-pinkie *primo* sign.

Pedro returned the gang sign. "Gracias, hermano," he replied admiringly and placed the belt on a side table with the other gifts he'd received.

Noticing his son's response, Mano wondered if inviting Angel and his sister to his home over the last few weeks had been a good idea. Instead of exposing the orphaned gang leader to the calming influence of a family, Pedro had started mimicking Angel's haughty street 'tude.

Smiling with pride, Rosa emerged from the kitchen. "I have a special surprise for our guests," she said, carrying a small cake.

"Cake! Dios santisimo, where did you get such a thing?" Celia Alonzo said in astonishment. "Sugar is like gold these days."

"I've been saving every bit of sugar I could find," Rosa explained as she cut the small cake into six pieces for her guests.

Mano handed a fork and plate to Celia, concerned by how

quickly the curandera's friendship with Rosa had deepened. Her mumbo-jumbo reminded him too much of Santa Muerte—Sacred Death—a cult popular with drug traffickers and criminals. Adding to his misgivings, Rosa had invited Celia to the party but not his sister Teresa. Rosa's reasons were hard to deny. Inviting Teresa would mean feeding his sister, her husband, and their two children. Still, he was finding it hard to feel warm toward the old woman.

Celia kissed Rosa's cheek as she served the curandera a slice of cake. "I'm honored to be invited, Rosa. Very few of us are fortunate enough to have cake."

"I only wish all our people could be as lucky," Rosa replied. "I know Mano has—"

A rumbling from the street shook the house and stopped Rosa in midsentence. Everyone in the room fell into a tense silence.

"Tanks," Mano said, rising to his feet. "Angel, you're with me. The rest of you, stay here," he said quickly making his way to the living room, the gang leader trailing him.

Parting the curtains, Mano saw a column of Bradleys approaching the house. He exhaled in relief as he noticed the vehicles were in patrol formation. "The Baldies are just showing the flag. Nada malo," he said to Angel, who was watching the convoy through the other window.

"Mira, Mano!" the gang leader said excitedly, pointing to the second Bradley in the column. "Baldies have door open."

Mano looked again and saw that the driver's hatch on the armored vehicle had not been closed—a violation of combat rules. "The driver must be hot," he said, making fanning gestures. "Caliente."

Angel smiled. "We make him more caliente with Molotov, yes?"

Mano realized the gang leader was right. A Molotov cocktail hurled into the open hatch might take out the Brad completely. This security lapse by the Baldies was the best chance they'd had since their battle at the Holiday Inn to damage an Army patrol. But destroying a single Bradley would not end the siege. In fact, it would bring more patrols into the zones, making it harder for them to bring in supplies.

"No, Angel. Not now."

Angel's eyes widened in surprise. "Porque no?"

"We have to wait, entiendes? Too many more Baldies will come if we take out this Brad. No es bueno now," Mano said, frustrated by the language barrier that kept them from discussing complex ideas.

Angel shook his head in disgust, watching the convoy drive away.

The sound of footsteps behind him drew Mano's attention. He turned and found Pedro standing in the doorway into the living room. "Pedro, I told you to stay put," Mano said through gritted teeth.

"I just wanted to see what was happening, Papi…like, maybe I could help or something."

"Pedro, you know better than to—"

Angel stepped between father and son. "Pedro have cojones, no?" the gang leader said to Mano. "Have proud of him."

"Angel, this is a family matter and I don't…" Mano stopped, reconsidering what he was about to say. Dragging Angel into a family quarrel was a bad idea—especially during a social occasion. He would deal with Pedro later. "This is not the time," he said, gesturing toward the dining room. "Let's go back and join the others."

"What's happening, Mano?" Rosa asked as the men entered the room.

"Just a patrol," Mano answered. "Nothing serious."

Rosa made the sign of the cross. "Gracias, Señor," she said, noticeably relieved.

The old woman patted Rosa's hand. "Don't worry, m'hija.

El Señor will bring us peace soon and all this hunger and suffering will end. I pray for it every day."

"Well, we can't let a Baldie patrol spoil our party," Rosa said smiling, trying to lighten the mood. "Sit down and have some cake, Angel." She held out a plate to the gang leader.

Angel pushed the plate back toward Rosa. "No tengo hambre, señora."

"What's the matter, Angel?" Mano asked pleasantly. "Don't you like cake?"

"Many people die from hungry soon," Angel replied, his eyes narrowing. "Why we not fight?"

"Angel's right, Papi," Pedro added. "Our people need to fight back again."

Mano glared at his son, then turned his gaze back to the gang leader. "You're thinking with your heart, Angel, not your head. The Baldies will kill more people than hunger if we keep fighting."

Angel pointed to the cake and sneered. "You not hungry."

"Rosa made that cake to share, Angel. We live no better than anyone else."

"Maybe you more hungry, you want fight."

Mano smiled, unwilling to be affronted. "Trust me, Angel. We'll fight again, but we have to wait. The Baldies will leave once they think we're beaten," he said, hoping Angel understood him. "It's the only way to get our strength back."

"You and old woman talk the same," Angel said, jutting his chin toward Celia. "Sin cojones."

Mano's smile faded. "You have no need to insult one of our guests, Angel."

Angel answered Mano with an unblinking stare. "I go now. Gracias por el cake," he said coldly and then called out to his sister. "Vamonos, Isabel."

With a last look at Pedro, Isabel followed Angel out the door.

Breaking the tense silence following the gang leader's exit, Celia said, "Thank you for standing up for an old woman, Don Manolo. I know you're not a believer."

"What I believe doesn't matter. Angel had no right to insult you."

"Pardon me, señora," Pedro interjected. "But what Angel said is true. We need to fight."

Mano's forehead furrowed as he turned to face his son. "Pedro, you've been told before. Do *not* interrupt when adults are speaking."

"But Papi..."

"Enough, Pedro," Mano said, his voice growing tight. "Go to your room."

After a brooding sigh, Pedro retreated from the dining room.

"I should go, too," Celia said, standing up. "Please excuse me."

Rosa held out her palms. "Stay, Celia. Please."

Celia began walking stiffly toward the door. "It's getting late and I'm not feeling all that well. Thank you both for inviting me."

"Wait, señora," Mano said. "I'll walk you home."

When Mano returned half an hour later, he found Rosa still at the dining room table, her head propped in her hands. In front of her, all six pieces of cake remained untouched.

"These are hard times, mi amor," Rosa said wearily. "We can't even celebrate a birthday without a quarrel."

Mano sat down beside her. "Bringing up a child is hard enough in normal times, Rosita," he said, stroking her hair. "We'll get through this."

"I've got news that isn't going to make things any easier. I wanted to announce it during the party, but things went so badly." Placing a hand over her belly, Rosa's eyes filled with tears. "I'm expecting another baby."

# THE MARCHA OFFENSIVE:
## *MONTH 4, DAY 14*

**F**uller carried his coffee cup to the only open seat left in the officers' mess hall. A televised speech by President Brenner was scheduled at 1700 hours, and the choice seats nearest the plasma screen had been taken for some time. Ironically, it was the officers not assigned to combat duty who had arrived early to claim the best viewing spots.

As Fuller sat down, the president's image appeared on the screen and the crowded room exploded into applause. Brenner stood on a brightly painted stage with the words PEACE THROUGH STRENGTH emblazoned across the backdrop.

"My fellow citizens, four months ago we were forced to take decisive action to stop the violence erupting from the Quarantine Zones," Brenner said confidently into the cameras. "Today I am proud to report that our swift and resolute response has brought peace to our nation once again. We have successfully choked off the strategic resources that were fueling the insurgency within the Quarantine Zones and we have brought the terrorists to their knees.

"I want to thank the brave men and women of our armed

forces who have once again stepped forward and served their nation with distinction." A wave of applause washed over the mess hall following the president's praise.

"I also want to extend the thanks of a grateful nation to the law enforcement officers who have taken on the additional burden of security around the Quarantine Zones."

Fuller covered a wry smile with his coffee cup as he heard these words. The relative handful of troops flown stateside to quell the insurgency would be sent back overseas soon. But the cops guarding the borders of the zones would remain on duty—indefinitely.

For the next few minutes, Fuller listened to the president proclaim the siege of the Quarantine Zones as an unqualified success. And it was hard to argue the point. Rebel attacks across the nation had all but ceased. Despite the world reaction to the siege triggered by Simon Potts's infamous footage, the American people had held firm. They were too angry and afraid to be swayed by sentimentality.

The camera zoomed in on the president—a sign the speech was ending. "With this crisis at home under control, America must once again turn its focus on the terrorist threats we face abroad. The road ahead will be hard and long. But with God's grace and the spirit of freedom and justice to guide us, we will prevail."

The end of the president's speech brought a chorus of cheers and applause in the mess hall.

"Let's get back to kicking ass in Hajji land!" one of the officers shouted, drawing more cheers.

Fuller rose and carried his empty cup to the dish return, deep in thought. With the threat of the Hispanic insurgency apparently fading, Carleton Brenner was resuming the quest he believed would be his true legacy...the world stage.

Fuller hoped the president was right. But the young officer's instincts told him the president's proclamation of victory in the Quarantine Zones was much too premature.

---

"I don't understand why it's going to ruin your film if we include a box of Blemish Bomb on the kid's dresser," Margaret Zane said.

The twenty-something director rolled his eyes, appalled his producer could be so clueless. "Duh! It destroys the whole focus of the scene. The dresser is the first thing that explodes when the Gelmoid comes crashing through the door."

"Work with me, Chad. The Blemish Bomb people are major investors in this project. They're going to insist their product appears in the film. It's in the contract."

"But look at that box, Maggie. Oh, my God, it's blue! It totally clashes with the palette of the set."

"C'mon, Chad. You're shooting a teen horror flick for chrissake, not *Citizen Kane*."

"Citizen what?"

"Never mind. Just put the fucking box in the shot, okay?"

Chad sniffed in disgust. "All right then. Since you insist on this creative interference, I'm going to have to change the color scheme of the set. It's going to take at least another day to find new props. We're probably going to have to look all over Vancouver. That blue is hideous."

"You have half an hour to change the set. You're already way over budget, Chad," Margaret said and left the sound-stage before the young director could protest again. She'd check back later to make sure he was on schedule.

Stepping outside, she zipped up her jacket against the brisk breeze and lit a cigarette. Early fall in Vancouver felt far colder than winter in Los Angeles. As she exhaled a blue cloud of smoke, a man who had been standing across the alley began walking toward her.

"You're Margaret Zane, right?" he asked, drawing closer.

"Uh...yes," she said, nervously gazing around and finding they were alone. Her alarm diminished somewhat when she noticed the man's elegant clothes.

"A gentleman in Geneva asked me to give you this," the man said, holding out a folded piece of paper.

"Thank you," she said, opening the sheet eagerly. It had to be a message from Ramon. Her expression changed to bewilderment when she saw it was a promotion for some type of online dating service.

"The gentleman said you'd want to register at the Web site under your birth name."

Still puzzled, Maggie thanked the man, who quickly left. Returning to her temporary office on the soundstage, she logged on to the dating site from her laptop using her birth name: Zembrowski. A window popped up with a question she knew could have come only from Ramon. *What is position number two?*

Long ago, she and Ramon had given numbers to the positions they slept in. After she typed in *spoons*, a new window appeared...

ACCESS GRANTED

Leave a message, my love. This is a secure connection. I'll respond as soon as I can. Tu marido.

Maggie stared at Ramon's words, wavering between delight and dread.

Although she'd not seen Ramon for over a year, he was never far from her thoughts. Maggie had jokingly called their separation "a divorce of convenience." As an Anglo, the divorce had nullified her Class H status, allowing Maggie to keep most of their wealth and avoid internment. But separating from Ramon had been agonizing.

All the same, Margaret Zane was terrified. On a number of occasions, she'd considered contacting Ramon. Each time, she'd lost her nerve. She wasn't like Ramon and Jo, willing to face danger for their beliefs.

Only last month, more than a dozen captured rebels had been sentenced to death. Several wives and teenage children had been among those convicted. Although civil liberties groups had appealed the verdicts handed down under the Terrorist Arraignment Act, the mood of the courts was not sympathetic. The executions were upheld.

Maggie's hands trembled as she began typing her reply.

---

Bill Perkins entered his boss's office grinning widely.

"The Panchos just made their first mistake," the deputy operations officer said excitedly.

Hank Evans looked up from his third budget report of the day and slowly tilted his portly frame forward in his chair. "What are you talking about, Bill?"

"The HRNA delegates in Geneva," Perkins said excitedly. "I intercepted a transmission to Ramon Garcia's laptop that we can finally decrypt. Here, take a look." Perkins handed his boss a manila folder.

Evans placed the folder atop a pile of similar documents on his cluttered desk. "Good work, Bill," he said wearily. "Now, how about you just give me the Cliffs Notes?"

"Well, their network security was tighter than a baby's balls in a cold bath, but I finally cracked it. They tried to jury-rig something through an online dating service. Can you believe that?"

"Who sent the message?"

"Garcia's ex-wife, Margaret Zane. She's in Canada shooting a movie. Garcia hasn't responded yet. Should we get some field people ready to question her once she's stateside?"

Evans tapped his stubby fingertips together, mulling their next step. "No, let's find out what they're up to first. If we arrest Zane right away, Garcia will know we're on to them."

"You sure, Hank? This lead could score us some major points with the wicked witch of the east."

"I want to give Carol something juicier. Let's give this wound a chance to bleed a bit. Keep me posted on this, will you?"

Perkins nodded, clearly disappointed. "Okay, boss."

Evans watched his deputy leave and sighed. He wished the CIA had the resources to keep tails on secondary threats like Garcia and Perez, but human intelligence was just too costly. The bulk of CIA intelligence muscle these days was focused on the overseas conflicts. Spying outside the war zones these days was mostly online monitoring. Perkins's persistence with the HRNA had gone above and beyond—by the standards of today's CIA tech warriors anyway.

*Who knows? Maybe the kid will come up with something useful.*

---

"What an honor! The illustrious Señor Garcia has paid a visit to my humble abode," Octavio said as Ramon entered his apartment.

"Your sarcasm isn't any better than your decorator," Ramon said, looking around the high-rise flat where piles of clothes and empty food containers littered the rented Danish modern furniture. "I came because I've got some good news."

"It must be important to bring you slumming with us nacos."

"It *is* important...I finally got in touch with my ex-wife."

Octavio shrugged. "So?"

"Maggie will help us get some money into the zones."

"Let me guess...California is first in line for this generosity."

"That's where my contacts are deepest, Tavio. It makes sense."

"Sense to *you*, maybe. Not to me. I have contacts, too."

"Octavio, if I didn't intend to help the zones in Texas and the rest of the country, I wouldn't be here telling you, would I?"

"All right. What do you want from me?"

"You need to privately spread the word among the delegates that Brenner's going to eat his words. Let them know our rebellion is far from over."

Octavio smiled slyly. "*That*, I will be happy to do."

# THE MARCHA OFFENSIVE:
## *MONTH 5, DAY 25*

**A** cowboy ballad spilled into the night as Jennifer Hoying opened the door into the double-wide trailer. Seated in the makeshift nightclub, more than a dozen men locked their eyes on the shapely blonde as she walked toward the small counter serving as a bar. Before she reached it, four of the men were on their feet, offering to buy her a drink.

"What's your name, honey?" one of them asked.

"Tiffany," Jennifer said with a sultry smile, accepting the drink.

"Hello, Tiffany. My name's Brad. This here's Al, and Ron, and Jerry. It's a pleasure to meet such a lovely lady," he said, peering at the cleavage above her tight-fitting blouse. "Why don't we sit down and get acquainted?"

"That's very neighborly of you," she said, settling into one of the plastic chairs lining a covered folding table.

Before long, the men had accepted her presence without question, trying to impress her with their boozy banter, steering the conversation to a topic they found endlessly fascinating—themselves. *It's exactly what Margaret told me to expect*, she assured herself.

Jennifer had never done anything like this before. Since reaching puberty, she had ignored the male interest lavished on her, concentrating instead on her true love: acting. *This is acting, too*, she reminded herself. *It's just not a role my family would be proud of.*

She had not called or written her family since arriving in Los Angeles from Pea Ridge, West Virginia, four years ago. What was there to say? She'd been to countless auditions without once being offered a part. But her role tonight would put an end to that. Margaret Zane had explained how important it was—and how it would open a new world for her in the movies.

The men inside the trailer were police officers and sheriff's deputies conscripted into guard duty around the Quarantine Zones. Shortly after the creation of their temporary quarters in the vast empty areas around the zones, the barracks had attracted an assortment of trailers that discreetly offered vices men away from home often fall prey to: liquor, gambling, and women. The small number of female police officers called up for guard duty were assigned to separate billets and had not drawn the same kind of camp followers, Margaret had explained.

Jennifer understood most of the folks back in Pea Ridge would say she was doing something wrong. What did they know? Those poor Hispanics were locked up and being starved to death. Besides, no one would ever find out—Margaret had promised her that. The goal of her part tonight wasn't difficult. All she needed to do was learn the time and place the cops guarding the south side of the zones went on duty.

The men around her laughed and ordered another round of drinks.

This was going to be easy.

---

Hank Evans finished reading the report and handed the document back to his deputy. "This is good work, Bill."

Perkins beamed as he took back the manila folder. "First time you've ever read one of my reports all the way through. It *must* be good."

The report was a printout of the latest e-mails between Ramon Garcia and his ex-wife, Margaret Zane. The messages made it clear the rebels had hired an actress to infiltrate the police details on guard duty around the Los Angeles Quarantine Zones.

"You have to hand it to them," Evans said, leaning back in his chair, rubbing his jowls. "They managed to find the weak link in the security around the zones. You know, I always thought drafting cops to guard the zones was going to backfire."

"Yeah, the cops were pretty pissed about giving up their days off from the very beginning."

"The sad part is, after a couple of drinks, one of them will probably tell that actress just about anything she wants. Some guys just can't resist trying to impress a good-looking woman," Evans said, shaking his head. "The Panchos in Geneva are playing this one smart. Once they learn the cops' deployments and duty schedules, they'll find a way to supply their friends inside the walls."

Perkins adjusted the thick glasses sliding down his nose. "I'm surprised Washington hasn't cracked down on the cathouses."

"I'm not," Evans answered. "The cops are pissed off enough as it is. The folks in Washington aren't going to take away one of their main sources of entertainment."

"I guess after they find out about the Panchos' Mata Hari, they won't have much choice. The cathouse is going to be out of the bag," Perkins said, snickering at his own joke.

"Oh, I think the pony rides may be around for a little while longer."

"What are you saying, Hank?"

"I mean we're not going to tell Washington anything just yet."

Perkins looked puzzled, then his eyes widened. "I get it. You're going to let Garcia and Zane guide us to the Pancho leaders in the zones."

Evans smiled. "You don't wipe out a colony of ants by killing the ones outside. You let them take the poisoned food back inside their nest."

Perkins laughed. "That's good, boss."

"One more thing, Bill...Carol Phelps cannot find out about this, understand? She'll steal all the credit if it works...or roast our asses if it doesn't."

# THE MARCHA OFFENSIVE: *MONTH 5, DAY 26*

**T**en minutes before the start of the U.N. plenary session, Ramon and Octavio entered the Hall of Steps, making their way to one of the couches lining the wall. A handful of tourists were wandering through the cavernous room in the aging Palais des Nations, their footfalls echoing on the marble floor.

"So what's next?" Octavio asked as they sat down.

Ramon glanced toward the tourists, making sure they were out of earshot. "Now that we know the guards' rotation schedule, we can slip a courier into Zone B during the shift changes."

"Your wife has someone we can trust?"

"Yeah, we've lined up a guy from New Zealand who's worked for her studio before."

Octavio's eyebrows rose in disbelief. "Somebody in show business?"

"The studios spy on each other constantly. You think it's a coincidence when similar movies are released at the same time? This guy's a pro."

"Okay, suppose your little movie spy can get inside the zones in Los Angeles. What about the rest of us?"

"If this works, we can use the same methods to get supplies into the other zones."

Octavio snorted derisively. "So California goes to the front of the line once again."

"Los Angeles is the hub of all our communications."

"I told you from the beginning that linking all our communications through one place was a mistake."

"Maybe you were right about that, but don't forget, once our network is back up in L.A., we'll be linked with all the zones again. Jo's reason for a central hub was to maintain security...and it's worked."

"So you admit you were wrong, but you still want to call the shots?"

Ramon sighed, his frustration mounting. "Look, Octavio. It's my own money I'm putting into this."

"I see," Octavio said bitterly.

"Please, Tavio. I need your support. You know I can't do this alone."

Placated by Ramon's flattery, Octavio's face softened slightly. "So how are you going to get the weapons in?"

"Weapons? I'm sorry, hermano, but I think our first priority should be establishing communications, not weapons."

Octavio was suddenly livid. "The reason our people have stopped fighting is because they're out of weapons, ammunition, and explosives," he said through gritted teeth.

"The people in the zones have been isolated for over three months. We need to find out what they need, set priorities, and coordinate our efforts before we can fight again."

"They have to fight *now*, goddammit! If we don't get some headlines soon showing we're still united, these fucking blabbermouths around here are going to figure out we're not representing anybody at all!"

"Keep your voice down," Ramon said, glancing around

nervously. "Look, how can we be united if we can't communicate with each other? We need to let our people in all the zones know they're not alone—and provide them with supplies. They can't fight the Baldies when they're fighting just to stay alive."

"Oh, that's a very nice little speech," Octavio sneered. "Of course, it would sound a lot more convincing if you weren't living it up at dinner parties with these puto Euros and their fancy fucking wines."

"What would you like me do? Wear a hair shirt? Our job here is to get full U.N. recognition and gather support for our cause. Schmoozing with diplomats is part of the job," Ramon said, trying to control his anger. "This is the first chance we've had to do something for our people, but you're turning it into another opportunity to bicker. We can't keep doing this."

Octavio rose to his feet. "Está bien. Do whatever you want," he said coldly. "As you said, it's your fucking money." He then thrust a finger in Garcia's face. "But remember, Ramon...you don't own this movement."

# THE MARCHA OFFENSIVE:
## *MONTH 5, DAY 27*

**H**ank Evans put down the jelly donut when he saw Bill Perkins approach his table at the officers' mess hall. The kid looked nervous, his gait unsteady as he crossed the near-empty dining room.

"It seems I have no fortress of solitude where I can escape the pressures of rank," Hank said with mock seriousness when Perkins reached him.

"Sorry to bug you on your coffee break, Hank," Perkins said, brushing the hair from his forehead. "You got a minute? It's important."

"Sure, sit down," Evans said. "What's up?"

"You know I've been keeping an eye on the e-mails between Garcia and his ex, right?"

"Yeah."

"And you said to keep you posted if anything turns up."

"That's right."

"Well, I've got something big, Hank...I just found an e-mail saying they're going to sneak a courier into Quarantine Zone B sometime this week."

"I told you this was coming," Evans said with an air of satisfaction.

"You were right, Hank," Perkins said, grinning. "That courier is going to lead us right to the top of the Pancho command in Zone B. You want me to put a military team on standby to crash the party?"

"Not yet."

"You want to let Carol know first, is that it?"

"No, we're not going to tell anyone at Langley yet."

Perkins's smile faded. "Hank, that is like *way* over the line on protocol. We should have reported this to Langley back when—"

Evans raised his palm, cutting Perkins off. "Look, Bill. I've already thought this through." Hank lowered his voice, although the only other people in the mess hall were two officers out of earshot in the far corner. "Rounding up the Pancho leaders would be the safe thing to do right now. Hell, Carol might even give us a little pat on the back. But there's a bigger prize at stake here and I'm not going to pass it up."

Perkins squirmed in his chair. "What do you want me to do?"

"Let's have one of our field teams tail the courier. I want to locate the Pancho leaders inside Zone B, but listen to me carefully...I don't want the Pancho leaders taken out yet."

"Why not?" Perkins said, eyebrows rising high above his glasses.

"It's simple. Now that we've broken the Pancho encryption code, we can round up the leaders of all the other zones as well once they start communicating."

Perkins nodded, evidently impressed. "Okay, but why not tell Carol?"

"If we bring Carol in on this now, you think she's going to share the credit? Hell, no. She'll steal all the glory and we'll still be stuck in this Army rat hole eating stale donuts."

"This is way risky, Hank. If your plan doesn't work, we'll lose the chance to nab the top bad guys from the biggest QZ in the country."

"I'll give you cover on this, Bill. If the shit hits the fan, you were just following orders, okay? On the other hand, if this pans out, our careers at the Agency are going to hit the after-burners," Evans said, his eyes gleaming. For the first time since his divorce, Hank Evans felt energized and alive. Look-ing back, he realized the change had started with the Marcha Offensive. Their work with the rebel mole had paid off. They'd been prepared for the insurgent attacks and had dealt the Panchos a serious blow. After years of fruitless tedium, long hours, and bureaucratic infighting, he'd produced a win. The taste had been exhilarating. Now he wanted more. "I've been waiting for a break like this for a long time, Bill."

Perkins chewed his thin lips, wavering between terror and triumph. "You're the boss," he said, almost whispering.

"Good man." Hank slapped his back. "This op is totally black. Are you up to it?"

Perkins swallowed hard. "You can count on me, Hank," he said weakly before heading back to his cube.

Evans looked down at the half-eaten donuts on his plate. He rose from the table and tossed them in the trash. Tomorrow, he might even start working out. Evans was bet-ting his career on this move, but if it worked out, who knew how high this might take him.

---

Edward Jocelyn slithered through the arundo growing out of the cracked concrete bed of the Los Angeles River, timing his movements to match the breeze stirring the tall reeds. Jocelyn had waited nearly a week for the night winds to pick up before making his entry into the Quarantine Zone. Now, with a crescent moon hidden by clouds, conditions were nearly perfect. Despite the stealth-suit that would shield him from infrared detection, Jocelyn knew there was always a chance of being seen with the naked eye.

After crawling with a heavy backpack for more than a mile along the dry, plant-choked riverbed, Jocelyn spotted the landmark he'd been looking for: a large storm sewer drain below a defunct railroad bridge. He entered the concrete tunnel and followed the directions he'd been given, carefully pacing off the distances.

Jocelyn emerged from the storm drain near an abandoned restaurant and made his way to the meat locker deep inside the store. Producing a key, he unlocked the heavy steel door. Inside was a carpeted, book-lined room with two large leather chairs. Jocelyn placed his backpack in the center of the floor and left, locking the steel door behind him. Once outside, he disappeared into the storm sewer, his mission complete.

---

Evans picked up his desk phone's receiver after the first ring. "Hank Evans," he said brightly, still amazed at how cutting out junk food had boosted his mood and vigor. He planned to start running in the mornings soon.

"It's Perkins...Look, Hank...I, uh, can't explain it, but I think we missed the courier."

"What?" Evans shouted, rising from his chair. "For chrissake, Bill! I had to call in some chips with the DOD to get those IR sweepers. What the hell happened?"

"I dunno. I mean, they had the southern side of the zone covered with the infrared sweepers all week."

"Is there a chance the courier hasn't gone in yet?"

"He got in, all right. I just intercepted a message from Zane to Garcia confirming the courier made his delivery."

"Goddammit!" Evans said, pounding the desk. The situation was starting to unravel. They could not arrest Margaret Zane now without raising some sticky questions about his judgment. Even worse, he'd lost the chance to locate the Pancho leaders inside Quarantine Zone B. The only way out was to see this thing through. "Okay, look. Let's not panic," he said feebly. "We're still inside Garcia's network. Let's work that, Bill. But for God's sake, don't tell anyone else about this. Both our asses are on the line on this one."

# THE MARCHA OFFENSIVE:
## *MONTH 5, DAY 28*

**M**ano made sure no one was in sight before entering the alley door into the onetime restaurant. The placas painted on the building by the Verdugos to ward away intruders were better security than Brinks in the barrios. Nonetheless, he checked around inside before moving through various rooms to the large steel door that protected Ramon's library.

Having finished *Crime and Punishment* and *1984* over the last week, Mano was returning for more books. The onetime meat locker Jo had refurbished for Ramon as a seventy-fifth birthday gift held over two thousand titles—books that had opened up a world Mano had never known. Although he still borrowed frequently from Ramon's eclectic collection, the place was not the same without Ramon in one of the leather chairs, sharing ideas Mano didn't always agree with but always found stimulating.

After unlocking the steel door, Mano was startled by a strange black backpack in the center of the small room.

*Could it be a bomb?*

Mano's mind raced through the possibilities.

The door showed no signs of forced entry. Clearly, someone

with a key had placed the backpack in the room. Anyone with that kind of access who wanted him dead would have succeeded already.

He opened the backpack's watertight seal and read the note folded atop its contents.

Hermanos y hermanas,

Sorry I have not been able to reach you sooner. The satellite phone inside this pack is programmed with a secure connection. Just hold down the Send key. Call me as soon as you can and I will tell you more about the rest of the material.

El Viejo

"Thank you, Ramon. I knew you wouldn't forget us," Mano said under his breath as he dug into the backpack. In a plastic bag at the top was a satellite phone, a laptop computer, and a black iridescent jumpsuit with a masked hood and foot covers. Next he found a money belt with fifty American Eagle gold coins—nearly forty thousand dollars. Lining the bottom of the pack were spare batteries and chargers for the electronic devices.

Mano stared at the silver phone only half believing he could actually speak to Ramon with the touch of a button. *What time is it in Geneva?* he wondered. His deployment to Afghanistan had taken him through the U.S. air base in Ramstein, Germany—nine hours ahead of Los Angeles as he recalled from his first overseas call home. His guess was the two cities were in the same time zone, making it midmorning in Geneva. Not a bad time to call.

Mano pressed the key and waited, holding his breath as the vu-phone rang.

———

When Ramon saw the number calling in on his vu-phone, he ordered the limo driver to stop and stepped out of the

Mercedes onto a quiet residential street. "Hello," he said into the receiver, his heart suddenly racing.

"Hello, Ramon."

"Mano! It's good to hear your voice, hombre!"

"Is this a good time to talk?"

"I'm on my way to the Belgian consulate, but I can keep them waiting for a bit. Look, I want you to know how hard I've been trying to reach you. Ever since we lost touch with Jo and the command center..."

"With all due respect, Ramon," Mano cut in. "We really don't have a lot of time."

"You're right, amigo," Ramon said, then paused, mustering the courage to ask the question he dreaded most. "Where is Jo?"

"She was killed during the offensive," Mano said softly. "Nesto led the Army to our command post."

Ramon covered his face and quietly wept. Jo had been like a daughter, the child he and Maggie never had. "I was afraid she was gone," he said, trying to compose himself. "But I just couldn't give up hope."

"She brought Rosa and Pedro back from the relocation camp. It took a lot of Jo's money, but my family is in Los Angeles again."

"I know. She asked me to help her arrange it. I was proud of her for doing that, Mano. You had to know she loved you."

"Look, Ramon, someday we'll have time for all this. But right now, we've got a lot of people still alive who need us, too."

Ramon wiped his eyes. "You're a rock, Mano... If I wasn't an atheist, I'd thank God our movement has you," he said, a slight smile returning to his face.

"Your note said you'd explain the stuff in the backpack."

"That's right, amigo. Our first objective is to get the leaders of all the zones back in touch again. That's what the laptop is for. You can access the other QZs from the wi-fi hub in Jo's house. Call me once you're there and I'll explain how."

"I'll do that. What about the jumpsuit?"

"That's the latest thing in spook wear...a stealth-suit. It makes you undetectable to infrared equipment. They're wickedly expensive—especially in a triple XL size for you. But they're worth every penny. By the way, what's the count on the gold coins?"

"Fifty. You worried about sticky fingers somewhere?"

"I'd like to use the guy who delivered the stuff again and I want to make sure we can trust him. This is just the start, Mano. We're going to get more help to you—and all the other zones, too."

"We need it, Ramon. The supplies Jo stockpiled are running low. I've expanded some of her self-sufficiency programs, but it's going to be months before they make much difference."

"Maggie's recruited an actress who's getting friendly with the guards around you. She's already found a few cops who are willing to look the other way while we bring in supplies. That's where those shiny Eagles come in. People tend not to see so well when they've got a bit of gold glaring in their eyes."

Mano laughed softly. "Thanks, Ramon. We'll put the money to good use."

"I wish I could do more. How are the people inside holding up?"

"You'd be proud of them, Ramon. The siege has turned everyone into revolutionaries. People have pulled together. The drugs are gone and crime has gone way down. They're starving, but nobody's ready to give up. In fact, a lot of them are itching to fight. I've tried to convince Angel that attacking the Baldies now will only prolong the siege, but I don't know how much longer he'll wait."

Ramon snorted in frustration. "I've got the same problem here."

Mano paused. "Do we still have a chance, Ramon?" he asked finally.

"Yes, mi hermano. If we can get full U.N. recognition, a lot of doors will open. But I won't kid you, this is a dangerous time. We need to put this war on simmer until we reorganize and get our strength back. That's why establishing contact with the other zones is so important."

"I understand."

"Good. How soon can you get to Jo's place?"

"I'll have to return Jo's generator to her house so we can have power. We had more urgent needs for it."

"She'd be glad you did that."

"It'll be daylight soon. I'd better wait until it's dark again before I travel. The Baldies have been cutting back on their patrols lately, but they're still frisking anyone who looks suspicious."

"It sounds like the Baldies are feeling pretty cocky inside the zones these days. That's good. We need to lull them to sleep. Listen, Mano, call me once you've reached Jo's house and I'll explain how to get the network running. That laptop is our lifeline right now."

"It should take me about twenty-four hours to get everything ready. I'll call you then. Good-bye, Ramon."

"Take care, hermano. May the God I don't believe in watch over you."

# THE MARCHA OFFENSIVE:
## *MONTH 5, DAY 29*

Hank," Bill Perkins said bursting into Evans's office. "You've got to see the latest e-mail from Garcia to Zane." He handed Evans a printed copy.

Evans read the note, his shoulders slumping with each sentence.

My love,

Mano has finally phoned me! He is going to activate the wi-fi at Jo's house and get us back online as soon as he can. Once I show him how to log on to the network, all the zones will be back in touch again! We need to be ready with more cash. Are the accounts you set up in place? We'll need to move fast. I also have dreadful news. Jo was killed. I wish we had the luxury to grieve right now but we don't. Be strong and try to carry on. It's what Jo would have wanted. Your satellite phone should be encrypted soon and we'll be able to talk.

Tu marido

Evans handed the note back to his deputy. "It kills me that

we missed the courier," he said dejectedly. "He could have led us right to Suarez."

Perkins slapped the sheet with the back of his hand. "We've still got a way to nab Suarez, Hank," he said, smiling slyly. "They're going to be using a wi-fi connection to reach the other zones, right? We can track him down once he powers up their wireless network."

"Haven't the Army patrols already swept the zones for wi-fi hot spots?"

"Sure, but why would the Panchos have a wireless network powered up if they're not using it?"

"I see what you mean, Bill. But we'd need to patrol inside Zone B almost constantly to catch them with their wi-fi fired up. That's going to be damn near impossible with the troop cutbacks."

"Not if you can wrangle a drone for a while from those tight-asses at DOD. We can fly the bird around with an electronic sniffer. Once Suarez is online, bang, we got him."

Evans's eyes widened. "You know, that just might work!" he said, a smile spreading on his face. "Let me check into that drone. We need to make this happen fast. Once Zane gets that satellite phone, she'll probably start calling Garcia instead of using the Web."

"Yeah, the geeks at Langley have been working on a way to crack those new Swiss satellite phones, but right now there's no way. The wi-fi's the only way to track Suarez. You want me to ask the military to put a strike team on standby?"

"No!" Evans said, voice rising abruptly. "I mean, let's make sure we can get the drone first," he added, gathering himself. "In the meantime, get me the dossier on Suarez. There may be a better way to handle this than a military strike."

After Perkins left his office, Evans began racking his brain for a way out of this predicament. Taking Suarez out with a military team would raise a lot of questions he didn't want to answer. Yet coming clean about his blunders would probably end his career—and more important, he reminded himself, remove one of the few rational voices left in the Brenner-controlled CIA. Then he remembered Michael Fuller.

After locating his number in the outpost directory, he called the young officer and arranged to meet that night.

———

Michael Fuller noticed a change in Hank Evans the moment he entered the empty gymnasium. The CIA officer's loose-fitting sweat suit made it clear he'd lost weight, but there was more to it than that. The portly spy chief seemed more confident, too. Evans's request to meet in the officers' gym at 2300 hours had seemed odd—and his new demeanor added to the mystery.

"Glad you could make it, Captain," Evans said, as if a junior officer were free to blow off a meeting with a senior CIA official.

"What can I do for you, sir?"

Evans glanced around the vacant gym and leaned closer. "After our conference with my boss, I got the impression you're an officer who places duty above career."

"I'm not sure I understand you, sir."

"I'll square with you, Fuller. I've got a mission that's totally black…something you'll never get credit for if you pull it off but will probably get you court-martialed if it goes wrong."

Fuller's lips curled into an ironic smile. "You certainly make it sound tempting, sir."

"The only reward of the mission is knowing you helped your country, son," Evans said, placing a hand on Fuller's shoulder. "I think we both agree there are a lot of things we're doing right now that are going to backfire someday. If you don't think this mission is in our nation's interests, you can turn it down. Very few soldiers get that kind of luxury."

Fuller nodded slowly. "I'm still listening, sir."

"I can't tell you how we know, but we're on the verge of locating one of the Panchos' top military leaders. He's somewhere in Zone B. Once we determine his exact location, I want you to bring in the Pancho leader—alive."

Fuller exhaled loudly. "You're not asking much, are you, sir?"

"I think it can be done...and you're the best man to do it," Evans said. "We can pinpoint our target's position and lead you right to him. One of your unit's patrols can shuttle you into the zone inside a Brad and drop you off near the location. After dark, you make your move."

"There are other officers with units patrolling QZB."

"Well, Captain, there's another reason why you're the best choice for this job." Evans paused, apparently trying to find the right words. "I hope you're not offended, but with the right clothes and hairstyle, you can pass for a Hispanic."

Fuller laughed. "My aunt Mildred is probably rolling over in her grave right now. She was in the DAR and would never pass up a chance to tell anyone she met that our line of Fullers came over on the *Mayflower*." Nonetheless, he knew Evans was right. His black hair and dark brown eyes would probably not turn any heads inside the Quarantine Zone. "Why do you want this guy alive?"

"Dead, he's just another martyr. We need to put him on trial, treat him like a criminal. That's going to play better for us in the barrios—and in the world press."

"I see your point. But getting him out alive isn't going to be easy."

"You'll be wired to an extraction chopper. Once you've got your prisoner in a secure location within the zone, we can have you out in minutes. Start to finish, the whole mission should take less than four hours."

Fuller nodded. "When will you need to know my answer?"

"Right now. We'll need time to set up the logistics. So what's it going to be, Captain?"

Fuller looked around the empty gym, unsure of his decision. He wasn't much concerned about his military career anymore. He'd abandoned those dreams months ago. But in accepting this clandestine mission he was, in a sense, betraying his duty as an officer; this was not part of the official chain of command he'd sworn to obey. Yet he'd also vowed to protect his nation—and this mission was vital to that cause. He was certain Evans had no one else better suited for the job. The responsibility was his, and he could not walk away from it.

"When do I need to be ready?" Fuller said at last.

"Within a week. I can give you twenty-four hours' notice. I can't be more specific than that."

Fuller extended his palm. "Call me. I can juggle my duty schedule."

Hank shook the younger man's hand. "Thank you, Captain. I'll be in touch."

Watching Fuller leave the gym, Evans felt a little guilty. He'd withheld a significant fact from the junior officer: Evans wanted no part of a real military operation. Nevertheless, everything he'd said to Fuller was true. The mission was indeed a blow against the Panchos. Taking down Suarez with a covert asset and sparing himself from the wrath of Carol Phelps was simply a bonus of the plan.

"Eggbeater Eddie" Haines, the chopper commander at Outpost Bravo, still owed Evans a favor for overlooking his unit's dismal showing during the Marcha Offensive in his report to Washington. Once he called in his chips with Eddie and arranged for a bird to get Fuller and Suarez out, the operation would be ready.

# THE MARCHA OFFENSIVE:
## *MONTH 5, DAY 30*

**A**fter being accompanied by a bodyguard for the last six months, Octavio felt nearly naked walking outdoors alone. His reasons for dismissing his security for the night, however, were worth the risk.

Octavio leaned on the promenade railing and scanned the faces in the crowd, ignoring the glowing plume of water spouting into the night sky behind him. At the fringes of a Japanese tour group, he spotted Miguel Cardona making his way toward him.

This popular viewing spot for Lake Leman's Jet d'Eau fountain had become the regular meeting point for Octavio and Cardona, his most trusted man from San Antonio. Octavio had been in touch with his Texas cadre since the siege of the zones had started—without telling Ramon. He knew the old fool might try to interfere if he got wind of his plans.

*Politics do indeed make strange bedfellows,* Octavio reminded himself as he thought about his new allies in the operation he'd planned. He had always publicly denounced the Mexican drug lords who ruled the underworld of the barrios on both sides of the border. Now he would use their dirty money and ruthless muscle to help the cause of his people. *But only for this one operation,* he told himself, trying to assuage his guilt.

Their cause needed to strike a dramatic blow, and he was willing to dirty his hands once to make it possible.

Cardona sidled next to him, making a show of staring at the fountain's illuminated mist rising over the lake. "Everything is ready for tomorrow," he said without facing him.

The words filled Octavio with a rush of pleasure. "I've been waiting for this day a long fucking time, Miguel," he said, staring into dark water reflecting the light of the fountain. In that shimmering surface Octavio seemed to see the face of his mother and once again recalled the day burned into his memory thirty-four years earlier when he'd discovered his life's calling.

He was bouncing in the passenger seat of their family's scruffy Ford pickup as his mother navigated the potholes on the desolate Texas road near Brundage. His father's work at a farm there ended today, and his mother would be ferrying his father to Big Wells for another few days of seasonal work. After dropping off her husband, she would take the pickup back to Carizzo Springs to use in her catering business. Although only eight, Octavio helped his mother with food preparation and cleanup.

His mother was driving faster than usual on the rough road that day. Years later, Octavio would realize she was probably trying to stay ahead of the SUV that now pulled up alongside. The man nearest them looked at his mother through the window with an ugly smile and casually let his arm hang outside. It held a gun. "Pull over, señorita," he said, still smiling.

"Don't get out the truck," his mother said sternly after pulling off the road. Putting a shawl over her shoulders, she opened the door and walked back to the other vehicle.

Octavio watched through the back window as she approached the men. He could tell they were drunk as they staggered forward and began pawing at his mother. She tried to fight them off but it was useless. The bigger of the two pressed her against the tailgate, trying to lift her skirt. Octavio saw the man's blue eyes widen for an instant before a sound like a firecracker broke the stillness. The man staggered back, clutching his chest. His companion seemed stunned for a moment, then lunged at his mother. He could see his mother's gun now. She raised it near the man's neck and fired. A geyser of blood exploded behind his head before he fell to the ground.

He would later learn the men were sons of a rich landowner in Dimmit County. After a two-day trial, a county judge sentenced his mother to ten years in prison for manslaughter. "That was the second crime against your mother," his father had said as they left the courtroom.

On that day, Octavio swore he would find a way to avenge the injustice to his mother—and all Latinos. That passion would drive him through law school and into a life as an activist known for his fiery rhetoric and willingness to brawl if necessary.

Tonight, he held the power to launch an attack that would help even the score with the gabachos, something that would shake them out of their arrogant complacency. It was a sweet moment and he wanted to savor it. "Yes, I've waited a very long time," he said to his aide. "Tell them the operation is a go."

# THE MARCHA OFFENSIVE:
## *MONTH 6, DAY 1*

**O**fficer Jimmy Lee Adams weaved his cruiser through the long line of morning traffic backed up along U.S. 81 until he arrived at the Texas 725 overpass. Stepping out onto the gravel shoulder, he heard screams of pain and broke into a run up the man-made hill. Reaching the crest of the knoll that raised U.S. 81 above the crossroad, Adams looked down into the worst accident of his seventeen-year career with the Texas Highway Patrol.

A chaotic pile of cars, SUVs, and trucks lay below the collapsed highway span, crushed into distorted shapes. Bleeding survivors staggered away from the wreckage, calling out desperately, while the torsos and limbs of those beyond help gaped hideously from the flattened vehicles.

The portable radio attached to Adams's chest blared into life. Reports were coming in of similar bridge collapses all along U.S. 81 north of San Antonio. Officer Adams felt his throat tighten as a chilling realization sunk in: This was not an accident.

The news reports that soon followed would prove the highway patrol officer right.

At daybreak on the twentieth of November, six months to the day after the Marcha Offensive, local television news crews began live broadcasts from the scene of a brutal wave of terror in the bedroom communities northeast of San Antonio. During the morning rush hour, bombs had exploded at a series of highway overpasses along a heavily traveled section of U.S. 81. Initial reports placed casualties at eighty-nine dead and over two hundred wounded. Within the hour, news of the bombings had spread across the globe.

A group calling itself the Latino Liberation Front immediately claimed responsibility and warned more attacks would follow until the U.S. abolished the Quarantine Zones. With the words TEXAS TERROR on the screen behind her, a morning talk-show host soberly noted that the Hispanic insurgency had entered an alarming new phase: It marked the first time the rebels had launched deliberate attacks against civilians.

———

Mano was not surprised when the satellite phone buzzed. He'd heard about the bombings in San Antonio two hours ago from a BBC news bulletin on the shortwave.

He opened the silver phone and brought it to his ear. "What's happening in San Antonio, Ramon?"

"I don't know, hermano. I had no idea this was going to happen."

"Maybe it was someone like Angel...somebody angry and frustrated."

"I don't think so. This attack was too well organized. There's only one person in South Texas with the manpower and resources to pull this off."

"Octavio Perez?"

"It has to be. He has a meeting at the U.N. complex in an hour. I'll catch him there and find out. In the meantime, be very careful. The government is probably going to crack down hard. If Brenner doesn't respond to this in a big way, he has no chance for reelection."

"Okay. I'll call you as we planned from Jo's house."

"Good. We need to get our act together—soon."

Arriving at the Palais des Nations a short time later, Ramon dialed up Perez on his vu-phone. "We need to talk right away—privately," he said tersely when Octavio's face appeared on the display.

"Meet me in the courtyard," Perez replied.

Ramon emerged from the white-walled main building into a green space nearly an acre long crisscrossed by pathways and framed by similar-styled structures. He spotted Octavio crossing the courtyard and intercepted him near the arched passageway into an adjacent building.

"Come with me," Garcia said, leading Perez toward a more secluded section of the manicured grounds. "What do you know about the attacks in San Antonio?" he asked once they were alone.

Octavio laughed. "I told you before, Ramon. You may have a rich ex-wife. But you don't own this movement. We did what you didn't have the cojones to do."

"We?"

"You seem surprised that I could find other allies, Ramon. You and your Hollywood gabachos aren't the only people with money, you know. There are others out there who want to help us."

"Who else is behind this?"

Octavio's lips curled in a sly smile. "Let's just say that's my secret for now."

A trio of delegates hurrying between the buildings walked close to them, and Ramon waited for them to pass. "You can't negotiate with another government without clearing it with me."

"Oh? I don't recall you asking my permission when you decided to take care of your California friends instead of supplying weapons to all of our people."

"So you did this just to spite me?"

"No. I did this because it's the right thing for our people."

"That's absurd. Do you realize how bad this makes us look? You killed eighty-nine innocent people."

"Nobody is innocent in this world. Didn't the gabachos decide all our people were guilty when they locked us up and tried to herd us away like animals? Now they can taste a little of their own medicine."

"That's barbaric, Octavio," Ramon said, stepping closer to Perez. "Worse yet, it's stupid. No revolution in history has ever succeeded by committing atrocities."

Octavio's smile never wavered. "So what are you going to do? Rat me out?" he said, his face glowing smugly. Perez knew Ramon could not continue the struggle without him.

"No. But I'll tell the press the HRNA is not behind this."

"Go ahead," Octavio said with a shrug. "Actually, denying it will be good . . . but it won't make any difference."

Perez was right, Ramon realized bitterly. No one would believe him. The scorn of the world was inevitable—and so was the retaliation of the U.S. government. There was nothing he could do now. "I'm not going to let you get away with this," he said, his eyes hard with hate.

"I don't think you've got much choice, viejo," Octavio said over his shoulder as he sauntered away toward the tall white stone buildings.

---

Evans glanced at his desk clock again. Six hours had passed since the U.S. 81 bombings; the call from Langley would be coming anytime now. He'd been through terror attacks before—too many times. After each one, the intelligence community would go into a spasm of finger-pointing that started at the top and worked its way down the chain of command. The bosses at Langley would be called to the White House where aides eager to find a scapegoat would grill them mercilessly. In a crappy mood, they'd return to CIA Headquarters where they would share the misery with their subordinates, perpetuating the eternal government axiom: Shit rolls downhill.

When his desk phone rang ten minutes later with Carol Phelps's number showing in the caller ID display, Hank felt resigned to his fate.

"Eighty-nine dead," Phelps said without preface. "Do you realize the damage this is causing our government?" Evans knew by "government" Phelps meant the president who'd appointed her. "We need to hit back, Hank—and hard. The president's asked me to poll our field offices for ideas. He wants to do something that shows we're still winning."

"I think it would be a mistake to overreact, Carol. It looks like these attacks came from a fringe group."

"Do you have any evidence to support that?"

"Well, they're calling themselves the Latino Liberation Front. That's a new organization as far as we can tell," he said defensively. In truth, Evans was certain the attacks had not come from the leadership of the HRNA. Garcia and his cohorts were trying desperately to unify along a national front again. Their intercepted e-mails would have provided some kind of clue of their role in the attacks. But there was no way to reveal that to Phelps right now without sinking his career.

"All right. Let's suppose it is a fringe group. So what?"

"We might waste a lot of time and resources going after a small rogue group and let the bigger fish slip away."

"So what do you propose we do?"

"Except for these incidents in Texas, the president's pacification strategy seems to be working. Launching indiscriminate attacks might bring the insurgency to a boil again. If the president is willing to bring some of our best troops and equipment back to the home front again, I think we can round up the real Pancho leaders."

"How long would that take?"

"Two to three months. Maybe a little more."

"That's not going to play well in Peoria…and it sure as hell isn't going to play well in Texas." *And the state's thirty-four electoral votes*, Evans added mentally. "We need a win, Hank, and we need it *now*. I can assure you that after this attack, the American public is not going to get squeamish about the way we root out terrorists. Do you understand what I'm saying?"

Evans knew his boss was not a stickler for legal niceties—and there was little sense in arguing with her. He'd been there with Phelps before. "Yes, I do, Carol."

"I'll tell you straight up, Hank. I don't really expect you to have any worthwhile ideas. But I do expect to see some results. Your region is lagging behind the rest of the country in Pancho detainees and body counts. Either your performance improves soon, or you're going to find yourself back in fieldwork charting caribou migration routes in Nome," she said before disconnecting.

Evans slowly placed the archaic receiver back on its cradle, certain that his future now rested on the operation to capture Manolo Suarez.

---

Octavio drained the last of the Cutty Sark, wiped his lips with the back of his hand, and belched with satisfaction. The warmth spreading in his belly came from more than the whiskey. Reports of the U.S. 81 attacks were leading the news all over the world—exactly as he'd dreamed.

Since returning to his apartment from the Palais des Nations five hours ago, Octavio had planted himself on the couch in front of the TV, reveling in the succession of newscasts and commentary shows reporting on the Texas bombings.

He refilled his glass from the near-empty bottle on the coffee table and switched to the Fox News international feed. Five talking heads behind a long desk were discussing the attacks.

"Sylvia, you've covered the U.N. in Geneva," the raven-haired host in the center said to a woman on her right. "Do you believe the denial by Ramon Garcia of the so-called Hispanic Republic of North America? He said, and I'm quoting here, 'These attacks are barbaric and without our consent.'"

The blonde with a perfect pageboy grimaced. "What would you expect them to say, Joan? These terrorists are trying to have it both ways. They want to instill fear in the American people but still curry favor with the international community."

"Marvin, what's the reaction been in the African-American community?" the host asked the man beside Sylvia.

"I think reactions have been mixed. Just as you'll find among whites, some African-Americans feel very threatened by this insurgency; others are more sympathetic. I think it's dangerous to assume people of the same skin color think alike on any complex issue."

"Complex?" Sylvia said, arching her penciled eyebrows. "What's complex about it? You have a bunch of foreigners who have come into our country illegally and now they want to create their own government. How could anyone who calls himself an American be sympathetic to these invaders?"

"I think we're straying off the subject here, Sylvia," the host said apologetically. She then turned left, addressing a craggy-faced man in a tight suit. "Carl Rogers, you're a retired Army general, what's your take on the possibility of a military response from the White House?"

Carl cleared his throat and adjusted his tie. "Well, Joan, as we saw after the Marcha Offensive, the White House and Congress have been flooded with messages calling for punitive strikes against the zones. The attacks today killed three times as many civilians as the Marcha Offensive, which was limited to military and infrastructure targets. Those casualties are going to put pressure on our elected officials to respond. So I wouldn't be surprised to see the president take some type of military action."

"You're saying it's possible the president may order air strikes on the Quarantine Zones?"

"I think with public reaction this intense, everything is on the table."

The host turned left, facing a portly man with a salt-and-pepper beard. "Tom, how are these attacks going to play politically in Washington?"

"I think the bombings have the potential to change the landscape of American politics. Look, Joan, the public is disappointed by Brenner's handling of the whole Hispanic issue. Gallup ran an online poll today that showed the president's approval ratings way down since the attacks. What that means is a huge opportunity for candidates who represent some kind of change."

"Who do think stands to gain from this?"

"I'd say the political stock has really gone up for Melvin Bates of the Nationalists. Not too long ago, Bates was losing popularity for the alleged failures of the Quarantine Act. But after today, hard-liners like Bates are going to start looking good to voters. I'll tell you, Joan, I would not be surprised if Bates mounts the most serious third-party presidential run since Ross Perot."

"Any other politicians who stand to gain from this tragedy?"

"There's some serious talk now that George Nixon could challenge Brenner for the Republican presidential nomination. This will certainly put some momentum behind that."

The host turned to face the camera. "For our viewers who may not be familiar with Nixon, he's a Republican from California and a great-nephew of the thirty-seventh president."

"I think Nixon's still a long shot, but his chances to take the nomination from Brenner just got a whole lot better," the bearded analyst concluded.

"What about these peacenik demonstrations we're seeing in a few cities?" the host asked Sylvia.

"I think it's another case of the liberal media showering unwarranted attention on a handful of geriatric hippies. What you'll find—"

Octavio turned off the set, finally sated with the media stir. They were back in the headlines. That would mean more foreign governments willing to help with money and weapons. Just as important, they'd put fear into the gabachos. A few more operations like U.S. 81 and they'd be ready to make a deal.

He stretched his feet on the coffee table and laid his head back on the couch. *Before long, Ramon will have to admit I was right,* he told himself before falling into a contented sleep.

# THE MARCHA OFFENSIVE:
## *MONTH 6, DAY 2*

**M**assaging the laptop's touchpad with his bulky index finger, Mano steered the cursor over the Network Connection icon and double-clicked. A now-familiar message popped up on the screen: UNABLE TO ACCESS WIRELESS NETWORK.

"No dice, Ramon," Mano said into the vu-phone. "Powering down and rebooting didn't work, either. Got any other ideas?"

Ramon's sigh was audible over the line. "I'm fresh out of options, amigo. How's the charge on the generator holding up? We've been at this awhile."

Mano looked at the satchel-size device. "I've got about an hour of battery power left before I have to recharge."

"Okay, I'll try to recruit some technical help and call you back. Same time tomorrow?"

"I'll be here," Mano said, ending the call.

After turning off the wi-fi system, Mano gazed around the modest home. He'd removed Jo's personal items and had buried them in a metal case in the cemetery. Someday they might wind up in a museum—he hoped. Her clothes and other household goods with any practical value, he'd distributed to the needy. The place was empty, yet in the hazy light of the gas lantern, Jo's presence still seemed to permeate the space... elegant and earthy, kind and ruthless, smart and naive—such a contradiction. His infatuation with Jo was over, but the sorrow of losing a friend and comrade still lingered.

Mano caressed the door frame gently before leaving the house.

———

The telephone was ringing when Hank Evans entered his office, briefcase and coffee in hand. Without sitting down, he answered.

"Our bird found a wi-fi transmission!" Bill Perkins said.

Evans's face widened into a grin. "What time?"

"The transcript from the drone says the network was active for three hours last night. We've got the exact location inside Zone B."

"Excellent work, Bill. E-mail me a map of the location. I'll take it from here."

"You want me to alert the military?"

"Not yet."

"You sure about that? They might slip away if we wait too long."

"I know what I'm doing, Bill."

"Whatever you say, Hank."

Evans hung up and dialed Fuller's number. With any luck, Manolo Suarez would be in custody by this time tomorrow.

# THE MARCHA OFFENSIVE:
## *MONTH 6, DAY 3*

**F**uller peered through his periscope over the man-high wall and saw a faint glow behind the curtains of the ranch house inside the enclosed compound. After stowing the collapsible scope into his jacket, he scrambled over the graffiti-covered wall, carefully avoiding the broken glass cemented into the top of the six-foot barrier.

Circling the house, he found a gap in the drapes of a picture window. A man in the living room was huddled over a laptop, a phone held to his ear, working by the yellow light of a gas lamp. Fuller's excitement rose as he recognized Manolo Suarez from the dossier photos. There were no guards posted outside the house. If Suarez was alone, it would be an unexpected stroke of luck.

Fuller tried the doors. They were both locked. Bursting into the house with no idea how many Panchos were inside was out of the question. He would have to wait. He had about four hours of darkness left, but even in the dim light, someone walking up to the house would easily spot him standing in the glow of the picture window. So he settled into the shrubs outside the window, extending his telescope to keep an eye on his quarry.

Suarez was repeating a pattern Fuller quickly recognized: The rebel leader would speak on the phone, peck away at the laptop, and then grimace. Clearly, whoever was on the other end of the line was helping Suarez troubleshoot a technical problem. *If it's anything like our tech support, this could take a while,* Fuller thought ruefully.

Squatting in the dark, in the middle of a hostile area, Fuller found himself asking the question that haunted many warriors during a momentary lull in combat: *Is this mission worth my life?* Most tried to avoid the question, to think of something else. A soldier could lose his nerve dwelling on that. But Fuller knew the answer. Yes, he was risking his life for his country. The truth, however, went deeper than that.

It began on the day seven years ago that had changed his military career.

Every grad in his class at the Academy had jockeyed to become an aide to General Charles F. Brock. A stint under the one-star leading the development of the Army's next-generation battle tank was a running start up the military ziggurat. In hindsight, Fuller realized why Brock always picked shavetail lieutenants fresh out of the Academy as his aides: They were bright and energetic—but not very savvy. He'd learned that the hard way on the day he found the property deed. The document had been inadvertently included with the packet of contractor specs Brock had given him to review. The deed, which he quickly discovered on the Web had been owned by a subsidiary of the contractor, transferred forty-six acres of prime real estate on the South Carolina coast to Charles Frederick Brock.

After a sleepless night, Fuller entered the general's office and asked for a transfer, saying nothing of the deed. The vanity of Brock's reaction left him stunned. "I've gotten promotions for all my aides, Fuller," he said sternly. "But no one's ever quit me. I promise you'll regret this."

Brock's influence—and his vindictiveness—had proven very real. The general's disparaging evaluation had relegated Fuller to a succession of dog-shit postings. Although he'd fared well when finally given the opportunity to command, Fuller now lagged behind his contemporaries in rank and status.

In truth, this mission was his chance for redemption, to prove to himself he was not the man Brock despised. Huddled in the dark, alone in hostile territory, the thought gave him strength.

Inside the house, unaware of the danger, Mano faced a more mundane test.

Trying to control his anger, he shut down the network and packed away the laptop. They'd failed once again to get the wi-fi operating. Their next step would be to try the hardwired network at Ramon's house tomorrow night—a bigger technical challenge, but a process that might eventually prove more stable.

With the laptop case slung over his shoulder, Mano stepped outside.

"Don't move, Suarez," a voice said out of the darkness.

Startled, Mano saw the outline of a figure holding a handgun emerge from the shrubs. "Put your hands on your head," the man said steadily.

Mano did as he asked. There was no sense in taking chances. An assassin would have finished him by now. "On your knees," the man ordered. "Good. Now down on your belly, real slow, and put your hands behind your back." Mano did as the man ordered and felt handcuffs being slipped over his wrists.

The man's cool, methodical orders quickly convinced Mano this was no ordinary criminal; he'd probably been a cop or a soldier at one time. "I haven't got any money, hermano. But if you need something for your family, I might be able to help."

"Shut up," the gunman said, frisking Mano as he lay on the ground. After taking Mano's gun, satellite phone, and laptop, he said, "On your feet. We're going for a walk."

Guiding Mano from behind, his captor led him several blocks, staying in the shadows until they reached a large empty lot. Pulling Mano into the cover of some bushes along the lot's periphery, the man produced a radio and said, "Foxtrot One, this is Brush Man, do you copy?"

"Roger, Brush Man," a voice from the radio replied.

"I'm ready for extraction."

"Sit tight, Brush Man. We're on our way."

Mano was now certain this was not a heist. His captor was a government agent. When the throb of chopper blades rose in the distance, Mano knew the time to comply was over. Captured, he was as good as dead. Worse. They'd probably parade him through a show trial before they executed him. He needed to make a move—fast.

The helicopter was drawing closer now, the wind from its rotors stirring the bushes around them. When the man stepped in front of him to wave, Mano saw his chance.

He head-butted his captor at the base of the neck. The man staggered to his knees, stunned by the blow. Mano then kicked his kidneys, sending him sprawling to the ground. When he tried to rise, Mano kicked him squarely on the chin, knocking him unconscious.

With the helicopter touching down, Mano dropped to the ground with his back to his captor, searching clumsily for the handcuff key with his hands still bound behind him. A floodlight from the helo began to sweep the area as the man's radio came to life. "Brush Man, this is Foxtrot One. We are at the extraction point. Come in, Brush Man."

Mano found the key and fumbled desperately, finally freeing his hands. He was on his knees over the unconscious body when the floodlight from the helicopter locked onto him, casting a bright circle on the weedy ground. Through the glare of the lights, Mano saw a soldier charge from the chopper, rifle in hand.

"Captain Fuller?" the young soldier called out, moving toward him with his weapon leveled.

Mano wanted to run, but resisted the urge. The soldier's confusion about his identity was the only thing keeping him alive. With the trooper drawing closer, Mano unhurriedly retrieved his phone and the laptop before rising to his feet.

"He put up a fight," Mano said, as the soldier reached him. "Give me a hand."

When the soldier leaned forward to lift the body, Mano shoved aside the man's weapon and smashed a forearm into his chin. The soldier staggered back for several steps and collapsed, out cold.

Mano ducked into the bushes and emerged in an alley beside the open field. After a dozen yards, he darted into an abandoned factory. For blocks he sprinted from building to building until, at last, he could no longer hear the chopper. Breathing heavily, he leaned against the wall, trying to assess the incident. They'd had a major security breakdown. That much was certain. But where?

Mano pulled the satellite phone from his pocket. Its silver skin glowed faintly in the dim light. Could this be how the Baldies tracked him down? Ramon had assured him the line was secure, but they still might have homed in on its transmission signal.

The device was off now, severing any signal that might lead the chopper back to him. But he was still in a quandary. He needed to alert Ramon. Calling him, however, might reveal his location again. He needed to make sure the phone was safe—and that was going to take some time.

# THE MARCHA OFFENSIVE:
## *MONTH 6, DAY 4*

**D**ad? Is something wrong?" Sarah Evans asked as she walked into the apartment's living room, tightening the drawstring on her sweatpants. "I've been yelling, like, forever to get your attention."

Seated in a worn recliner where he'd spent most of the night, Hank Evans raised his eyes from the floor. "No, hon. Everything's fine," he said, trying to sound convincing. Actually, he had not slept at all. "What would you like for breakfast?" he asked, rising arduously from the chair.

"I don't have time," Sarah answered, pulling a hoodie over her yellow soccer jersey. "I've got practice at ten."

"I'm sorry, sweetheart. It slipped my mind."

Divorced nearly seven months and living alone in a two-bedroom apartment, Evans was still not used to chauffeuring his fourteen-year-old daughter during her weekend visits. His ex-wife, Monica, had always taken care of that. But the stress of joint custody paled in comparison with last night's news.

Fuller's failure to capture Suarez had left Evans cornered. If he told Langley about the e-mail pipeline between Garcia and Zane now, Carol Phelps and her desperate cronies would rush in for a quick kill, squandering the chance to nab the Pancho leaders in all the other zones. He couldn't let that happen. There was only one option left.

Evans ran through it again, trying to be sure it would work. Perkins would keep quiet. He had too much to lose. So did Eggbeater Eddie. That left only Fuller—and he was sure a visit with the young officer would sew up that loophole.

"I've got to leave in ten minutes. So you need get to dressed, okay?" Sarah said maternally. The divorce had matured her, much to Hank's surprise—the only bright spot in the split with his wife.

"Yeah, I'll do that."

"Are you sure you're all right?" she asked, tilting her head. "You look awful."

"I'm fine. Listen, I need to make a private call and then I'll be ready to go."

Sarah put her hands on her hips. "Dad...I can't be late again."

"This won't take long, Sarah. I promise," he said, retreating to his bedroom and closing the door.

He'd been trying to screw up the courage to call for most of the night. He had to do it now, before he lost his nerve. After searching through the pockets of his dress suits, he found the card he was searching for and dialed the number.

———

Mano glanced toward the abandoned hardware store again and rubbed his eyes, fighting the urge to sleep. He'd been awake since the arrest attempt twenty-four hours ago, trying to uncover the breakdown in their security.

Shortly after evading his captors, Mano climbed to the roof of a ransacked hardware store. Powering up the satellite phone, he placed it near an air vent and retreated to another building less than a block away. From this spot, he could keep an eye on the phone, yet easily escape. He was certain the Baldies would launch another sortie once they got their injured man out. To his surprise, dawn came and no one returned. Still not convinced the phone was safe, he continued his vigil.

Twice during the rest of the day, he heard the engines of a Baldie patrol in the distance. Neither came within sight of his bait. Even after the sun had set, Mano continued to wait.

Now, with midnight closing in and the battery on the phone surely depleted, Mano was finally convinced the satellite phone was safe.

But that left a mystery that churned in his gut. If the phone had not led the Baldies to him, what had?

# THE MARCHA OFFENSIVE: *MONTH 6, DAY 7*

The story broke as a second-page article in the Sunday *Washington Post:*

Nixon Claims White House Deceiving Public

By Monday, the story was gathering steam. On Tuesday, in response to the deluge of questions from the national media, Congressman Nixon held a news briefing in the Capitol press gallery.

"Congressman, is it true you did not solicit the disclosures from the CIA officer of the alleged Brenner intelligence misconduct?" one of the reporters in the crowded room asked.

"Mr. Evans called my office and left a message saying he had an urgent matter to discuss. I simply followed up."

Another reporter jostled forward through the pack, shoving her recorder toward Nixon. "Why did you go public with these allegations? Wouldn't some say this was politically motivated?"

"I think this administration has shown a pattern of sweeping inconvenient information under the rug. With a disclosure of this significance, I felt the American people had a right to know about it and Congress should be entitled to hold public hearings."

"Did your office check to see if Mr. Evans was a man with an ax to grind?"

"These kinds of questions are an insult to a man who has served his country honorably for twenty-seven years. Henry Evans has an unblemished record with the CIA. What's more, I intend to see that he's protected against smears and retribution by this administration. It's his right under the Whistle-blower Act."

A tall red-haired reporter asked, "Other than Mr. Evans's word, do you have any evidence to support the allegations?"

Nixon knit his heavy eyebrows and answered with the sound bite that would lead every evening news show. "When a senior official within the CIA claims this administration has misled the American people about the extent of our military involvement overseas, I believe that's ample cause for an investigation."

# THE MARCHA OFFENSIVE:
## *MONTH 6, DAY 8*

**M**ichael Fuller looked up from his book and saw Henry Evans's plump figure moving toward him across the hospital garden.

"They treating you all right?" Evans asked, plopping onto a bench beside him.

"I'll be fine, sir," Fuller said drily.

"How long before you go home?"

"The doc says at least a week for a grade-three concussion."

Evans patted Fuller's shoulder. "Don't beat yourself up about this, okay? I know you did your best, son."

"No, sir. I let my guard down and Suarez took advantage of it. I should have brought him in."

Although they were the only people in the hospital garden, Evans leaned close. "Look, I'm sure you've heard the news by now. I want to explain why I went public," he said softly.

Fuller adjusted the bandages on his head and looked Evans squarely in the eyes. "No explanation's necessary, sir. The mission was black."

"Well, it's more complicated than that, Captain," Evans said, wiping at the beads of sweat forming on his brow. "Our office out here in California is close to a breakthrough against the Pancho leadership across the country. It might take us a couple of months, but if we're patient, this could be huge. Here's the thing, though. The Brenner people are desperate for a win against the Panchos right now. If they find out about our break, they'll crash in for a quick score and blow our chances."

"Then why did you go after Suarez?"

"I figured it would get Phelps off my back without compromising our source." Evans glanced around nervously. "Now we're going to have to wait for a change in the White House before we make another move. There's too much at stake to trust this bunch."

Fuller's eyes narrowed. "I think soldiering and politics are a bad mix."

"C'mon, Captain. Spare me the company line. We both believe the Brenner people are mismanaging our conflict with the Panchos, right?"

"My duty as a soldier is to follow orders, not make political judgments."

"You can be a lot more than a soldier, Fuller. If the right man gets elected, I'm going to have my pick of people to run the Agency. I want you to be one of them."

"That's not why I took the Suarez mission."

"I know that. You did it because it was the best way to help our country win the fight with the Panchos. Well, I'm talking about more than a single mission. If the election goes to the right candidate, you'll be in a position to influence how this entire conflict is managed. Isn't that the best way to help your country?"

Fuller looked into the eyes of the portly spook. "I'm not comfortable with this, Mr. Evans. I carried out a black mission for you...and I'll keep my mouth shut. That's all. I'm not interested in anything else."

Evans rose to his feet. "All right, son. Just remember my offer. The next president is going to need men like you," he said warmly before leaving.

Over the next three days, Evans's disclosure to Nixon would spread into a media storm battering the White House.

Editorials across the nation openly questioned the validity of the government's report on overseas troop levels and accused the Brenner administration of doctoring the numbers. When asked about the allegations, the White House press secretary said, "Nixon's assertions are false and politically inspired." Despite the executive branch denials, Congress voted to hold hearings on the charges.

Carleton Brenner watched in dismay as the centerpiece of his presidency—foreign policy—was dragged into a political mudfest. Brenner's reelection bid now faced two major obstacles: the Nixon accusations and the U.S. 81 attacks in Texas. To deflect these political liabilities, Brenner's advisors suggested action that was forceful and highly visible. Soon thereafter, the president created a new position, domestic theater commander, and appointed a fast-rising one-star to the post, General Charles F. Brock.

Less than a week after taking command, General Brock promptly withdrew units from garrisons across the lower forty-eight states and began massing troops around the San Antonio Quarantine Zone in search of the U.S. 81 terrorists. After declaring martial law inside the San Antonio zone, Brock imposed a dawn-to-dusk curfew enforced with armored patrols. More than a dozen curfew violators were killed in the first two days. With the zone locked down, the Army began large-scale sweeps through the area, ransacking homes, seizing weapons, and detaining hundreds of suspicious individuals. To publicize his get-tough methods, for the first time in almost a year Brock permitted the news media to enter a Quarantine Zone—but only in escorted groups.

"The Panchos are going to learn the consequences of terror," General Brock told his first gathering of reporters.

# THE MARCHA OFFENSIVE:
## *MONTH 6, DAY 11*

**R**amon clenched his jaw as Octavio crossed the restaurant. Perez had sent a courier asking for a meeting in this quiet café in Geneva's financial district.

"What do you want?" Ramon said icily after Octavio sat down opposite him.

Octavio's smile seemed genuine. "I may be a barbarian, but I'm not a fool, Ramon. I need your help."

"Oh? You didn't seem to need my help before."

"Look, I only did what I thought was right. We're working toward the same goal—and we have the same enemy. We've got to bury our differences."

"You should have thought of that before you dragged our cause into the gutter."

"I know you, Ramon. There's no way I would have changed your mind."

"You couldn't get permission, so now you're asking forgiveness?"

"Forgiveness? No, I don't regret what we did. I think all our people will gain from it...including you."

"How can you say that?"

"You think I don't know much about history, but I know enough. Do you imagine Martin Luther King would have gotten the Nobel Peace Prize if Malcolm X and all the other black radicals hadn't been part of the movement? Every cause needs a threat, Ramon. If you want to be the Latino Gandhi, go right ahead. But don't try to stop me from doing what needs to be done."

"I will not support senseless violence."

"Look, I'll make you a deal. If you cooperate with me, I give you my word we won't attack again without informing you. You can even keep denying you support El Frente in public if you want."

"Would you stop an operation if I opposed it?"

"I can't promise that. But which would you prefer? We attack with your knowledge—or without it?"

Ramon studied the glass of cabernet before him and said, "What would stop me from turning you in?"

"Your word."

Octavio's gesture of trust mellowed Ramon—and his argument made sense. Isolating himself from Octavio would eliminate any chance to influence his actions. "All right. Suppose I accept a truce, what do you want from me?"

"Your cooperation."

Ramon gently swirled the wine in his glass, weighing Octavio's offer. "What do you have in mind?"

"Like I explained before, we work in small cells this time. No central command and only one directive: Hurt the gabachos every way we can."

"That's only going to prolong the war, not win it."

Octavio leaned across the table. "Ramon, you won't be able to stop us. Don't you see that? I've got more than two dozen men in Mexico right now, ready to infiltrate the other zones and start the cells. With most of the Baldies massed around San Antonio right now, it's going to be easy getting in. It will go a lot smoother if we have your support. But even without it, we'll still succeed. Don't force me to push you aside. I don't want to do that. You mean too much to our cause. Many of our people still respect you."

Ramon took a sip of wine and stared at his reflection in the glass. "I'll consider it," he said finally.

"Have you heard from Mano?"

"Not for several days."

"Face it, Ramon. Your organization is crumbling and you're going to be all alone soon. You and Jo gave us a good start, but times have changed. You need to change with them, viejito."

———

Mano crouched on the roof, scanning the night sky. His three-story perch had an unbroken view over the low, blacked-out buildings of Quarantine Zone B. Certain that he could spot a helicopter homing in on his location in time to take shelter, he pressed the Send button on the satellite phone.

After two rings, he heard Ramon's familiar voice. "Mano?"

"Can you talk now?"

"Only for a few minutes. I was just heading out the door to a meeting with the French."

"Then we both have a reason to keep this short."

"What do you mean? Why didn't you call me last week as we planned? I tried to call you but your phone was turned off."

"A government agent tried to arrest me outside Jo's house after our last call."

"Que dices?" Ramon said, his voice rising in alarm.

"I think they tracked me by this phone."

"No way, Mano. The signal on this phone is not just

encrypted. It's equipped with a directional diffuser that makes it impossible to track. The Swiss make and operate these phones—and they're just as discreet about them as they used to be about their bank accounts. I'm certain they didn't locate you by the phone."

"Then how did they find me?"

The line was silent for a moment. "The wireless network," Ramon said suddenly.

"The wi-fi field isn't very wide."

"You're right—it might only reach as far as the street. But if the Baldies had patrols scanning for any wireless networks in the zone, they could have detected it. All they'd have to do is ride around with a laptop in..." Ramon stopped abruptly. "Mano, I need to reach Maggie right away. She might be in danger."

"Why?"

"If they know we're communicating by the Web, there's a chance they've cracked the encryption on our e-mails."

"When was the last time you were in touch with her?"

"We spoke on her satellite phone earlier today."

"Don't you think she'd be in jail by now if they'd broken the Web encryption?"

"They can't arrest her, Mano. She's still in Canada—and Canada revoked American extradition privileges after the U.S. pulled out of the U.N."

"Then she's not in danger as long as she doesn't enter the country."

"No, but if she can't enter the States again, it's going to hurt us."

"That's true."

"And that's not the worst part. We can't risk linking up with the other zones until we're sure our network is secure. That would lead the CIA to every one of our people in the other zones."

"Yeah. That's too risky. We'll have to work out something else."

"There's another thing, Mano. Perez offered me a deal. If we don't oppose him, he'll give me advance notice of any attacks. I haven't given him an answer."

Like Ramon, Mano found the idea of attacking civilians troubling. More troubling, however, was the idea of failing their people. "Take the deal. We don't have much choice right now. Our priority is to do all we can to keep our people inside the zones alive."

"I agree. Look, I've got to go. We'll talk again soon." Ramon hung up.

Mano scanned the violet sky, no longer looking for a chopper, but searching for an answer.

His wife was pregnant. He was losing touch with his son. Angel, his most trusted ally, was wavering. And they were short of fighters, weapons, and ammunition. His options for sustaining this struggle were rapidly dwindling.

Then Mano remembered something José Antonio Marcha had written: *The will is the most powerful weapon.*

He hoped Marcha was right. Because the only thing he had left to fight with was his resolve.

———

Hank parked his unwashed Buick Lucerne in the deserted parking garage and waited. A few minutes later, a minivan entered the darkened lot and pulled alongside. Bill Perkins emerged from the vehicle and hurriedly entered the Buick.

"You sure nobody followed you?" Perkins asked, pushing his hair from his face, looking around nervously.

"For chrissake, Bill. This isn't a fricking spy movie."

"I'm sorry, Hank," Perkins said, adjusting his glasses. "Everybody knows you're going to testify before Congress. I figured the Brenner people were keeping an eye on you."

In the car's confined space, Hank noticed the kid smelled like mushrooms and wondered how often he bathed. "I asked you to meet me here instead of the office to avoid any suspicions. As long as we stay cool, everything is going to be fine. We just need to sew up some loose ends."

"What do you mean?"

"It's quite simple. You have to wipe out all the e-mails between Garcia and Zane."

"I don't know, Hank," Perkins said, shaking his head. "I don't want to do anything illegal."

"Look, if the Brenner people get that information, they're going to barge in for a quick score and blow our chance to nab the entire Pancho leadership. We have an obligation to our country to end the insurgency. That's more important than some procedural technicality."

Perkins nervously rubbed his face. "I don't feel right doing that."

"Don't worry. We'll reopen the case when the time is ripe. We both know the Brenner people will ruin all our hard work if they find out about this."

"Destroying intelligence documents is a pretty serious breach of protocol."

"Let me put this another way, Bill," Evans said, meeting Perkins's eyes, his voice tightening. "We're both already in very deep shit. Getting caught destroying the e-mails isn't going to make it much worse."

"Well...I guess you're right. We can't let the big fish get away, can we?"

# THE MARCHA OFFENSIVE: MONTH 6, DAY 17

The surf breaking on the beach was a soft hush from the thatch-covered patio where Simon Potts sat, a Mac notebook in his lap and a scotch in his hand. Costa Rica's remote Nosara coast was one of Simon's favorite retreats. The undeveloped beaches, laid-back locals, and scarcity of tourists were the perfect antidote to his work's stress-filled locales. All the same, he still scoured the Web for news each day. He had no choice. Searching for tragedy across the world was an unavoidable fact of his career.

The news from the U.S. these days left him sadly amused. Six months after the Marcha Offensive, with the presidential election less than a year away, the "CIAgate" congressional hearings had begun.

The first witness before the committee, Southwest Regional Director of the CIA Henry Evans, appeared tense, repeatedly mopping his balding pate under the hot camera lights. Despite his nervous manner, most political experts believed Evans's testimony would soon have the White House squirming.

After a brief opening statement, Evans produced copies of

memos and e-mails from Brenner appointees that revealed a consistent policy of misdirection about America's overseas troop deployments. As expected, several of the Republicans on the panel demanded corroboration to verify Evans's allegations. Seeking more proof, the committee subpoenaed more CIA staffers.

In the week that followed, every evening newscast began with a sound bite from the latest junior CIA staffer appearing before the CIAgate committee. As witness after witness grudgingly revealed a pattern of deception about troop levels, all but the most ardent Brenner partisans realized the charges were undeniable. The suspense now lay in how high the blame would go.

Competing for headlines with the congressional investigation was the continuing violence of the Latino Liberation Front. Each day brought new reports of LLF attacks on civilians. Despite General Brock's high-profile efforts, the Army always seemed a step behind, rushing troops to the site of the latest incident only to see a new attack crop up somewhere else. A late-night TV talk-show host mocked Brock's approach as the "whack-a-mole strategy." Few Americans saw the humor as ethnic tensions escalated.

Violence against all minorities spiked. Blacks, Asians, Middle Easterners, even Hasidic Jews were the victims of random attacks. The ranks of citizen militias swelled to an all-time high. Vigilante groups launched armed forays in search of Panchos in the vast abandoned areas around the zones. Most wound up venting their wrath on the "dregs," the smattering of non-Hispanic indigents still scavenging the vacated areas.

Seeking a scapegoat for the domestic turmoil, many on the congressional panel were eagerly anticipating the subpoenas of the high-level Brenner appointees to the CIA.

Conspicuously absent from the panel was George Whitehead Nixon. The originator of the charges against President Brenner had elected to recuse himself from the proceedings. The move would prove to be quite shrewd.

———

Crossing South McDonnell, Mano noticed another freshly painted LLF placa on the sidewalk. It was the third time he'd seen Latino Liberation Front graffiti in the last few blocks—a troubling sign. Evidence the Latino Liberation Front was growing quickly in the L.A. zones over the last few weeks was hard to miss.

Although many in the barrios were dismayed by the LLF's indiscriminate violence, tales of their attacks spread quickly. The reckless and the young celebrated the LLF's exploits, seeing the clandestine ring as glamorous and defiant. Two days earlier, Mano had overheard a teenager on the street openly boasting of belonging to El Frente, as the LLF was called in the barrios. While Mano doubted the bragging, the sudden popularity of the Latino Liberation Front was a new obstacle for their cause. He hoped his conversation with Angel today would help counter the trend.

When he arrived at Angel's duplex, Isabel answered the door but remained behind the locked iron bars guarding the entrance. "Buenos dias, Don Manolo," she said with a gentle smile. "I hope you and your family are well."

Mano smiled back. "My family is fine, Isabel," he answered. "I'm here to see your brother."

The girl's eyes scanned the street behind Mano. "Please come in," she said, unlocking the iron gate.

As Isabel led him inside, Mano was once again impressed by the fourteen-year-old's maturity. Entering the kitchen at the back of the small house, Mano found her brother seated at a plastic patio table cleaning an AK-47.

"Sit down, Don Manolo," Isabel said, gesturing to one of the folding lawn chairs around the table.

"Thank you," Mano said, gingerly squeezing his large frame into the rickety seat. "Please tell your brother I came to see how his vatos are doing with the water purification project."

The girl translated and after Angel responded, she lowered her eyes and said, "My brother said he wants to talk to you alone."

Once Isabel was outside, Angel spoke. "I no work like peon anymore."

"The Baldies can stop the water to the barrios at any time, Angel," Mano said calmly. "We need to have our own water, comprendes?"

"I get water with *this*," he said, holding up the weapon.

"How?"

"We fight Baldies. Baldies will go."

"We're not strong enough to win yet."

"You say no fight. El Frente say fight."

Mano studied Angel's face. The gang leader's eyes were cold, his jaw set. "Are you with them now?" he asked Angel.

Angel slowly nodded.

"The LLF will not bring water or food," Mano said. "The LLF will only bring death."

"I no afraid."

"What about the danger to our people?"

"Dead from hungry? Dead from bullet?" Angel said with a shrug. "Dead is dead."

Mano rose to his feet, shaking his head. "I thought you were a man, Angel. I hope you live long enough to grow up."

The gang leader turned his eyes away from Mano and went back to cleaning the rifle.

Mano walked out of the kitchen, said good-bye to Isabel, and left the house.

Outside the weathered duplex, Mano began his trek home wondering how he would replace his most important ally.

———

Outside Angel's house two days later, Pedro broke into a run when he saw the gang leader emerge from the house. "Oye, Angel," he called out.

Angel smiled as Pedro approached. "Y que, ese?" he said, extending his fist in greeting.

Pedro bumped his fist against the mero's tattooed knuckles. "Y que," he replied, falling into step beside Angel.

A short distance ahead of them on the sidewalk, Pedro noticed a group of young men step out of their way as they approached. "That's Angel Sanchez," he heard one of them whisper in awe as they passed. The gang leader coolly ignored the gesture of respect.

"I haven't seen you around mi casa," Pedro said once they'd passed the teens.

"Tu papá and Angel...mucho trouble."

"Yeah, I heard him tell Mamá you're with El Frente now."

Angel stopped walking and faced the boy. "You no talk this," he said, suddenly serious.

"No, no, Angel. I won't tell anybody. It's just that...well...I want to join you."

The mero studied Pedro's eager face. "Why you want join El Frente?"

"I want to fight. I'm not afraid like my father."

Angel stared into the distance for a moment, weighing the boy's offer before answering. "In El Frente, new vato for watching only. No fight."

"Sure, I'll start as a lookout," Pedro said excitedly.

"You want watch for El Frente?"

"Yes, I'll follow the Baldies and tell you where they go."

"No, you watch tu papá. Tell me what he do each day."

From the doorway of the duplex, Isabel watched her brother and Pedro disappear into the crowd. It was the first time she'd seen Pedro near their house, and his presence made her pulse race. Her heart had belonged to the tall, quiet boy from the first time they'd met.

Pedro's manner was so different from Angel's vatos, who tried to impress her with their coarse advances when her brother wasn't around. Pedro was kind and polite, almost shy. All the same, he made her feel safe.

Isabel made the sign of the cross and said a silent prayer, asking God to somehow bring Pedro into her life.

———

Jammed between the ruins of an ancient movie house and a boarded-up beauty parlor, Tavo's Bar & Grill was one of the few businesses still operating along this palm-lined section of Whittier Boulevard. Approaching the windowless building, Pedro knew Tavo's had survived for a reason: It was the gathering site for Angel's gang, Los Verdugos. For more than a week, the bar had also been Pedro's noontime destination to report on his father's actions to Angel when Mano went home for lunch.

Nearing the tattered, leather-covered door, Pedro gave the thumb-and-pinkie sign to Chico Mendez, the young vato on duty as a lookout leaning against one of the palms.

Stepping inside, Pedro squinted trying to adjust his eyes to the gloom. He knew Angel would be in the back room, holding court on a bar stool behind the pool tables. Although Pedro admired Angel, truth was, his first assignment as a vato had been a total downer.

Spying on Mano not only made Pedro feel guilty, it embarrassed him to report his father's timid agenda to Angel. Since Pedro had begun his surveillance, Mano had spent dawn to dark on most days visiting the homes of people with gardens and chickens, or stopping to talk to plumbers, carpenters, and shop owners, trying to get them to share their skills for self-sufficiency. Yesterday had been no different, with Mano spending the day at a metal shop working on some kind of pipe fixtures.

Walking through the dimly lit bar, Pedro dreaded facing Angel once again.

Angel saw Pedro enter the room, his head bowed and shoulders slumped. He understood the boy's shame. His own father was a peon without the cojones to cross the border and do something to feed his family after the drop in corn prices had cost them their farm in Coahuila. Not that Mano was a coward. He'd just grown soft since his family had returned. *At least his son is willing to take up the fight*, he told himself.

Making his way toward Angel, Pedro nodded somberly to the vatos at the pool tables. "Y que, Angel," he said softly after reaching the gang leader, his eyes on the floor.

"Y que, ese," Angel answered, holding out his fist.

Pedro touched his knuckles to the mero's, then put his hand in his pocket. "My father is still doing the same stuff, going to people's houses and—"

"You no like be vato?" Angel said, cutting him off.

"What?" Pedro said, startled by the question. "No, I like being a vato. It's just that...well, this watching my father...I don't know, it just doesn't feel right."

Angel knew what the boy meant, even if he didn't understand all his words. Being an informer robbed a man of his dignity. If Pedro had done this too willingly, it would have been a bad sign. In any case, it seemed Mano was not going to betray him to the Baldies—his reason for asking Pedro to watch his father. He now had a more important mission for the boy.

"You no watch tu papá."

"Does that mean you...like, don't need me anymore?" Pedro asked softly.

"You are vato, Pedro. I have more work for you."

Pedro's face brightened. "Really? Way large!"

Angel raised a palm, cooling his excitement. "Tu mamá y papá no see you in many days for this."

"That's okay. My father's not too happy with me and my mom is expecting a new baby. They won't miss me."

Angel smiled. Pedro had come along at just the right time. The mission he'd received last night from El Frente would take them outside the zones. The boy's lack of tattoos, confident manner, and flawless English would make it easier for him to blend in.

Angel nodded. "Bien," he said and began to explain their operation.

# THE MARCHA OFFENSIVE: MONTH 7, DAY 3

**O**n the first morning back in the office following his congressional testimony, Hank Evans found a voice mail from Carol Phelps waiting for him. "Until further notice, all your cases have been reassigned," her message curtly explained. Since then, his phone had been silent; no one had entered his office, spoken to him, or even made eye contact. Only Perkins occasionally glanced furtively in his direction, clearly troubled over their pact of silence.

Despite having nothing to do, Evans continued to show up for work, determined not to be fired for negligence. Although his job was protected under the Whistleblower Act, it did not protect him from the disdain of his co-workers. Their contempt soon escalated.

A week later, Evans arrived at his office and found a dog turd on his chair. Days later, he found his office littered with rotting produce. Most recently, someone had hung a dead rat on a string from the ceiling.

Four weeks into the investigation he'd precipitated, Hank Evans moved through Outpost Bravo like an invisible man.

He'd managed to salvage his salary, but it had cost him his career.

---

Mano entered their house, dreading the news he was about to give his wife. "I looked everywhere for him, Rosa. I checked the school, the park, his friends...no one has seen Pedro for days."

"I'm worried, Mano. Pedro's never done this before. He wouldn't stay away without telling us. He's not that kind of boy."

There was something Mano had not told Rosa, fearing it would upset his pregnant wife even more. Days before Pedro had gone missing, he'd discovered the boy was tailing him. Evading his amateur surveillance had been easy. The hard part was accepting the truth. He'd followed Pedro to Tavo's bar several times. That meant his son was involved with Angel—and probably the LLF. Mano's suspicions had been all but confirmed when he'd gone looking for Angel and found the mero missing, too.

"Boys do strange things at this age, Rosa," Mano said, trying not to lie. "It's a difficult time."

"What are we going to do, Mano?"

"I've got to call Ramon at midnight. I'll keep looking for him until then."

Leaving the house, Mano wondered what he would say to Pedro once he found him. How would he win back his son? He'd failed as a parent. That much was clear. Would it help to admit that to Pedro? He would say anything to save his son. Yet part of him was angry—angry that his own blood would fall in with gangbangers and terrorists. *First, I need to find him*, Mano reminded himself. *That's what I need to focus on now.*

After he'd searched the streets for nearly five hours, the

time to call Ramon had arrived. Walking into a vandalized used-car lot, he sat on the hood of a burned-out Malibu and powered up the satellite phone. Since the arrest attempt last month, he'd been calling Ramon at midnight, changing his location each time as a precaution. Before he could press the Send button, the phone buzzed with an incoming call. "You must have something urgent, Ramon," he said into the receiver.

"I've been trying to reach you for hours," Garcia said, exasperated.

"What's wrong?"

"El Frente is planning a strike in your area. Octavio told me late last night."

"Did he give you any details?"

"Only that it would be north of Zone B sometime in the next two days."

"That's not much time. I'll start getting ready."

"I'm guessing the crackdown by the Baldies will start about twenty-four hours after the strike. We need to protect our assets."

"After Angel went over to the LLF, I started burying our supplies. I figured it was only a matter of time before El Frente brought the Baldies down on us. We've got everything but a week's worth of food under the ground already. And don't worry. I've stashed away your library, too."

"Jo always insisted you were smart," Ramon replied, laughing softly. "Sometimes I'm forced to agree with her."

"What worries me is what they'll do to our gardens. Our first crop of beans is coming in."

"Brenner's been letting the media into the zones along with the Army to show he's being tough. The Baldies won't damage the gardens as long as there are cameras around."

"Why not? They're trying to starve us out already."

"Letting people starve and wantonly destroying their crops

play a lot differently on the tube. The Baldies haven't destroyed gardens in any other zones. I think your beans are safe."

"I hope you're right, viejo."

"By the way, I called Maggie and told her to stop the supply shipment this week. Will you be okay without it?"

"Not much choice, is there? Listen, once they start the sweeps I'll have to stay out of sight. I have an underground hideout set up for my family. But the satellite phone might not work there."

"Call me when you can, hermano. I wish there was more I could do."

"You probably saved a lot of lives, including mine. That's not too bad," Mano said, ending the call.

He had deliberately avoided mentioning Pedro's absence—or his connection to El Frente. There was nothing Ramon could do, and every minute was precious now. He needed to find his son—and save their caches of supplies from the Baldies.

# THE MARCHA OFFENSIVE:
## MONTH 7, DAY 5

Thirty-five miles north of Los Angeles, Santa Clarita, California, was at the ragged frontier of the mainstream world. The once-prosperous community that had proudly claimed to be the best place to live in California had deteriorated rapidly during the massive migration northward two years earlier. Swamped by poor families fleeing the violence spilling from the L.A. Quarantine Zones, Santa Clarita had become a place of last resort. Those with money kept moving north. Those without it stayed in Santa Clarita.

Today it was a hardscrabble place, its neighborhoods teeming with people loitering amid the rows of scruffy cars parked along the winding residential streets. Only a small number of Santa Clarita's original residents had remained, clinging to their elegant homes near the city's last redoubt of affluence, the Town Centre mall.

On a December evening, crowded with holiday shoppers, the mall would become the first target in California of the Latino Liberation Front.

Pedro studied the random faces in the mall's crowded food court. Which of them deserved to die? The blond girl with the braces? The young couple with their toddler? The gangsta-wannabes strutting past? The question haunted Pedro, making his insides stir. This was not what he'd imagined in his heroic daydreams. In just over an hour, many of these unsuspecting people would be dead when the pipe bomb in his shopping bag blasted thousands of nails in a deadly hail into the crowd.

Pedro was not afraid. There was little chance of getting caught. His unaccented English and clean-cut looks made him undetectable in the racially mixed crowd. Most would take him for an East Indian teenager. No, he wasn't troubled by fear. He and the two other youths planting the explosives at the mall would have an hour's head start before the bombs exploded.

Pedro glanced at the clock near the pretzel stand. In two minutes, he would activate his bomb and leave.

These people were not the heartless gabachos he'd envisioned. They weren't cruel and evil monsters trying to annihilate his people. They were ordinary human beings—bickering, laughing, posing, talking—clueless to the suffering in the zones.

A wave of remorse washed over him. There was one minute left. One minute before he became a killer. The word reverberated in his head.

*Killer.*

This wasn't fighting. These weren't soldiers. They were just people. Innocent people.

Pedro deliberately recalled the deaths of his brother and sister, trying to goad himself into a rage. Julio had been run down by the Baldies and left to die by the road. His sister had died in a relocation camp. The memories still brought back hurt and anger. But what did these people have to do with that?

The time was up. It was 6 p.m. In a matter of seconds Chico and Felix would be setting their detonators and placing their bombs. *This is a mistake*, Pedro realized. *These people do not deserve to die.*

Then he thought of facing Angel. The mero had warned him this would not be easy, that he might lose his nerve. Yet Pedro had assured Angel he would not weaken—he'd begged the mero to do this. He could not let Angel down now. He'd given his word. His honor as a man was at stake.

Pedro reached into the shopping bag on the floor beside him and triggered the detonator. Rising from the table, he walked to the trash receptacle near the center of the food court. Angel had told him to place the bomb there—where it would do the most good.

But this wasn't doing good. This was wrong.

Pedro kept walking past the trash container until he was outside the mall. There had to be somewhere he could place the charge that would let him keep his word to Angel but avoid killing innocent people. He scanned the outside of the mall, looking desperately for someplace to unload his burden. Then he spotted it among the store signs on the mall's exterior: a U.S. Army recruiting office. The storefront was dark, which would make his task easier.

Moving casually to avoid drawing attention, Pedro reached the glass-fronted office away from the mall's main entrance and looked around. The office was closed for the day, and no one was nearby. Stepping into the recessed entry, he placed the shopping bag against the door and quickly walked away.

Just over an hour later, Pedro was nearly six miles south of Santa Clarita, nearing the empty house where Angel had instructed him to meet Chico and Felix. For the last fifteen minutes, he'd heard the wail of sirens in the distance as one ambulance after another screamed down Interstate 5 toward the carnage at the mall. Pedro stopped outside their safe house and rubbed away his tears before joining the others inside, torn between his shame of being a part of the killings—and for not carrying out his role.

# THE MARCHA OFFENSIVE:
## *MONTH 7, DAY 7*

**G**eneral Brock strode briskly through the door, followed by a cloud of aides. "Atten-*hut!*" someone called out, and the officers of Outpost Bravo rose to their feet. The domestic theater commander stood for a moment, eyeing the men and women hastily gathered for the briefing. "You may be seated," he said stiffly.

From the back of the room, Michael Fuller noticed the general's crisply ironed combat uniform, a contrast with the stained and rumpled CUs of several officers just back from patrols. *Brock's probably got a press conference after this and wants to look like a real warrior,* Fuller mused.

Brock clasped his hands behind his back. "The days of 'business as usual' at this base are over. The heinous crime the Panchos committed in this operational sector two days ago will not go unpunished. We have fought these terrorists with one hand tied behind our backs long enough. Starting tomorrow, Operation Shakedown will go into effect in the Los Angeles Quarantine Zones."

For the next ten minutes, the general outlined his plans: house-by-house searches through randomly chosen areas and the immediate detention of anyone with a weapon or suspicious articles. Fuller recognized the tactics as the same methods that had failed to produce much in other QZs across the country. *The Panchos aren't stupid. They know we're coming.* Fuller was certain that the Pancho leaders—and anything of value—would be safely hidden before Brock's troops arrived.

"There's something else," the general said, his voice turning sour. "I see dirty uniforms in this briefing room. From now on, every soldier in this command will be totally squared away *at all times*. Starting tomorrow, we're going to allow reporters inside the zones. That means people all over the country will be watching us. So you damn well better look like the best soldiers this nation can field.

"Units from my brigade will conduct the sweeps. Combat officers from this outpost are temporarily assigned as my aides. I'm going to need your knowledge of the local terrain."

*Shit,* Fuller muttered under his breath. He'd hoped to stay below Brock's radar, but there was little chance of that now. *You have to hand it to the cagey bastard. By using his own troops while privately picking the brains of the local officers, he can take personal credit in the media for every success.*

"Any questions?" Brock asked.

"Yes, sir," a young lieutenant said, rising to his feet. "What exactly *is* the primary objective of Operation Shakedown?"

"Two words, son...dead Panchos."

---

"We've got to leave for the shelter now, querida," Mano said, carrying the travel bags into the living room.

Rosa shook her head. "No, I can't leave without Pedro. You go," she said, waving him away. "I'll wait here. If we both leave the house, Pedro won't know where to find us."

"You can't stay here, mi amor," Mano said softly, reaching out his hand to help her rise from the couch. "The Baldies know who I am. If they find out you're my wife, you'll be arrested. We can't take that chance."

"I don't *care* what they do to me!" Rosa shouted, pushing his hand away. "I won't leave Pedro behind."

Mano knelt beside her. "Rosita, you know how hard I've been looking for him all this time. Pedro's been gone twelve days, Rosa. We don't know if... if he's still alive," he said, his voice fading to a whisper. "You can't risk your life by staying here."

Rosa stifled a sob. "We've already lost two children, Mano. He's the only child we have left," she said, tears forming in her eyes.

Mano gently rubbed her belly. "You have to think of the baby, mi amor. After I take you to the shelter, I'll come back and watch the house—I promise," he said, rising and extending his palm.

Nodding faintly, Rosa took his hand and rose laboriously from the couch. "I want my statue of Our Lady."

"It's already packed, querida," Mano said, nodding toward the bags.

"Take her out, I want to carry her myself."

Mano unzipped the nylon bag and handed her the statuette.

Rosa pressed the damaged icon against her chest, her eyes closed in prayer. After a moment, she said, "I'm ready to go now," and walked toward the door, her shoulders slumped.

After leaving their house, Mano led Rosa to an abandoned sheet metal shop six blocks away. Near the back of the looted building littered with the remnants of scavenged equipment, Mano pried at a section of the cracked concrete floor with a metal bar, budging the concrete a few inches at a time until an opening appeared. Inside was a small room stocked with food, water, and a chemical toilet.

"It's not swanky, querida, but it sure beats jail," he said, helping Rosa into the shelter. He pointed to a bicycle sprocket attached to a metal box. "Just crank this pump for fresh air every couple of hours."

"I'll be fine. You go and find Pedro."

After laboriously replacing the concrete slab, Mano returned to their house and stationed himself in a burned-out store within sight of the white bungalow. *Will Pedro return, even if he is still alive? And if he is alive, what has he become?* Pedro and Angel's absence and the killings in Santa Clarita were dots Mano did not want to connect. For the rest of the day and throughout the night, he waited for his son, torn by these conflicting thoughts.

At dawn, he heard the throb of a helicopter in the distance. The Army was getting close. He couldn't stay here any longer; he needed to return to Rosa. Without him, she was trapped in a tomb.

Mano was almost at the front door when he saw an infantry squad round the corner. The soldiers advanced silently in a wedge formation, weapons in hand, eyes moving warily left and right along the deserted street. *A recon patrol*, he noted. *The main force won't be far behind.*

Using the rear door, Mano retreated from the soldiers, darting through backyards and alleys, trying to circle behind the recon squad. He had to get to the shelter before the main force arrived.

Running through a narrow passage between two buildings, he heard the throb of a helicopter roar suddenly overhead and froze. In the narrow strip of sky above him, he saw the green belly of an attack helicopter.

For several agonizing seconds the chopper hovered directly over him before finally drifting away. The main force could not be far now. The helicopter was its forward fire support. He pressed on, desperate to reach Rosa.

A block from the shelter, he spotted troops in the distance and took cover in the shrubs around a ranch home. The Army's main force was several streets ahead. Mano watched in dismay as the soldiers systematically entered each house along the street, one squad dragging the occupants outside for questioning while another squad searched the home. A convoy of armored vehicles crept along the roadway beside the soldiers, their turrets rotating menacingly.

One of the civilians on the street protested angrily when a soldier shoved his wife. The soldier clubbed the man to the ground with his rifle then kicked him repeatedly. Mano felt a surge of anger. *You can't help now*, he told himself. *Rosa is depending on you.*

Still seething, Mano reached the metal shop and began prying at the concrete slab. He worked feverishly as the rumble of the vehicles grew in the distance. The soldiers were getting closer. Mano pried desperately at the slab, grunting with exertion, until the opening was finally wide enough to enter. With his foot, he jammed a fist-size stone into the crack, propping it open. Signaling Rosa to keep silent, he crawled inside.

The sounds of the soldiers were getting louder now. "Kendricks, take your squad and check that factory," someone said. "Roger, LT," a voice much closer replied. Mano placed his back against the slab and pushed upward with all his strength, his body quivering with the effort. "Pull out the rock," he whispered hoarsely to Rosa. She removed the stone, and Mano slowly lowered the mammoth slab back into place. As the darkness enfolded them, Mano collapsed, sweat-drenched and exhausted.

Their whole world was now the sound of boots on the concrete floor above them. They waited, breathing shallowly, afraid even the sound of their lungs might betray them. After a while, the footsteps faded. Mano and Rosa hugged in relief, then abruptly ended their embrace. They were safe, but Pedro's fate hung like a presence between them in the darkness.

# THE MARCHA OFFENSIVE: MONTH 7, DAY 8

General Brock stood before the phalanx of cameras and reporters, his foot propped on the tread of a Bradley. Half a kilometer behind him, a company from Brock's brigade was methodically rousting people from their homes and searching each house. "What you're seeing is the most effective tactic we have to suppress an insurgency," he said, gesturing over his shoulder. Dressed in combat fatigues, the embedded correspondents pressed close to the general, taking in every word.

"General, this treatment of civilians might appear harsh to some," one of the reporters asked. "Can you explain why it's necessary?"

Brock smiled, flashing prime-time teeth. "We're trying to find Panchos in these searches, of course. But if we can't," he added with a knowing wink, "maybe we can make them mad enough to come out and fight."

A ripple of laughter spread through the reporters.

Standing beside a line of Humvees parked nearby, Fuller watched the general's media show. He knew a week from now Brock would be off to another hot spot, once again posing before the cameras and lecturing about the need for his heavy-handed tactics. Meanwhile, back here in Los Angeles, the hundreds of new Panchos he'd created with his tough-guy methods would be itching to kill Fuller's men.

After concluding his media briefing, Brock walked unexpectedly toward the Humvees. Surprised by the general's approach, Fuller lowered his eyes and saluted. He'd avoided Brock's attention so far and hoped to remain unnoticed. The general returned the salute and walked past Fuller—then stopped.

*Shit*, Fuller said to himself.

Brock turned to face him. "I see you're still soldiering, *Captain*," he said, making his rank sound like an insult. "Quite frankly, I'm surprised. Are you commanding a company?"

"Yes, sir," Fuller said, his mouth suddenly dry.

Brock mulled over this information for several seconds, leaving Fuller standing stiffly at attention. "Well, then. I've got a detail for someone with your special talents, Fuller," Brock said icily. "I'm transferring you to security duty for the detainees."

# THE MARCHA OFFENSIVE: MONTH 7, DAY 10

Pedro heard footsteps in the darkness and held his breath, afraid to make a sound.

Not until Angel's two-tone whistle echoed through the sewer tunnel did he exhale in relief. Turning on the flashlight, Pedro moved aside the sheet of plywood affixed with debris that camouflaged the entrance to the maze of tunnels where he'd been hiding for the last three days.

"Baldies gone. Vamos," Angel said and then led him wordlessly out of the sewer.

Pedro squinted as they climbed outside. After three days in the dark, even the fast-fading dusk seemed painfully bright. Walking along the street, the mero related in pidgin how the Baldies had swept through the barrios for days, killing dozens and detaining hundreds of others. No one from El Frente had been lost—Angel's plan to arrange a separate refuge for each member of their cells had worked.

"Isabel want you come mi casa. She make you food."

"No gracias," Pedro answered. "What do you know about my family?"

Angel shrugged. "Nada."

"I want to find them. I'll hook up with you at Tavo's," Pedro said before heading home.

Pacing quickly along the rubble-strewn streets, Pedro fell back into the thoughts that had plagued him since his decision at the mall.

The two-day journey back from Santa Clarita had kept his mind occupied as he moved warily through the abandoned landscape. But during his three days of solitude, he'd been torn by a war inside him. He had let Angel down—and his father. It was painful to admit it, but each of them had been right.

Angel had predicted he would lose his nerve, and his father had warned him there was nothing heroic about senseless deaths.

He held back the truth from Angel and pretended he'd placed the bomb as he'd been ordered. There was not much chance Angel would find out—as long as no one from El Frente was caught. He'd watched enough detective shows to know the cops would not give out details to the media on where the bombs had been placed. They'd save that as evidence for convictions.

All the same, it shamed him that he had not told Angel the truth. The thought of facing Mano and admitting his father had been right shamed him just as much. After days of torment, he was still unsure how to resolve these conflicting thoughts. He hoped going home and getting away from El Frente for a while would help.

With the last glow of sunlight lingering in the sky, he arrived at the familiar white bungalow and anxiously scanned the darkened house. At that moment, Pedro was struck by another realization: He should have warned his parents about the chance of an Army crackdown. His actions had put them at risk.

Pedro unlocked the door and peered inside. The changes in their living room shocked him. The cushions on their

prized upholstered furniture had been ripped open, exposing the woolly padding inside; ugly gouges violated the
walls—signs the soldiers had searched the house. A silent
figure suddenly appeared in the corner of his eye. Snapping
his head toward the movement, Pedro saw his father emerge
from the hallway holding a pistol.

Mano sighed in relief. "Pedro...Thank God it's you," he
said as he uncocked the Glock and put the weapon in his
pocket. "With the Baldie sweeps, we didn't know what to
expect when we heard someone at the door."

"I'm sorry, Papi. I should have—"

"Pedro!" his mother called out as she rushed into the living room, holding her belly as she ran. "M'hijo! Thank God
you're alive," she said, hugging him tightly, tears welling in
her eyes.

"I'm glad to be home, Mami," he said, squeezing her
gently.

Rosa leaned back, still holding her son, and looked into
his eyes. "We've been worried sick about you. Tell us what
happened, Pedro." She stroked his head. "Where have you
been?"

Pedro stepped away from his mother. He wanted to tell his
parents the whole truth, but the humiliation of admitting
he'd been wrong held him back. There would be time to
explain things later. "I...I was hiding from the Baldies," he
said, lowering his eyes.

"You were gone for days before the troops started the
sweeps," Mano said softly. "What were you doing, m'hijo?"

Pedro shrugged. "What does it matter?"

"You're our son," Mano said. "What you do matters to me
and your mother."

"Just forget it, okay?"

"Why won't you tell us?" Rosa insisted.

"I don't want to talk about it."

Mano stepped closer. "What are you keeping from us, m'hijo?"

Pedro rolled his eyes. In the darkness of the storm sewer, he'd begun to appreciate his father's wisdom. But now, being questioned like a toddler, his tolerance evaporated. "I'm not a child, Papi. What I do is *my* business. I don't have to tell you everything."

Mano remained calm. "I'm not a child, either. But I tell your mother when I'm going to be gone so she doesn't worry."

Pedro's eyes narrowed. "That's a lie and you know it! When I was little, you used to stay out late all the time. I remember Mami crying because she was worried about you. She tried to hide it. But I heard her."

"You will *not* speak to your father like that," Rosa said sternly.

"Oh, I get it. Papi can get away with whatever he wants. But if I try to be a man, you won't let me."

Mano slowly shook his head. "M'hijo, you're still too young to understand."

"That's what you always say. Well, you know what? I'm *not* too young. I've been helping Angel fight the gabachos. That's more than you're doing, Papi."

Mano slowly closed and opened his eyes. "Pedro, did you have something to do with Santa Clarita?" he asked, his voice tight.

Pedro felt a pang of guilt. He regretted that innocent people had been hurt at the mall, but his anger and shame overwhelmed his qualms. "What if I did? It's something you should have done . . . if you had the cojones."

Rosa gasped, covering her mouth. "Pedro, how could you do such a thing?"

"I'm a man now," Pedro said, tapping his chest. "I do whatever I want."

Lowering her head, Rosa said, "I'm ashamed of you, Pedro."

The words stung Pedro, swelling his rage. "Yeah? Well, I'm ashamed to be his son," he said, jabbing his finger toward Mano, "and I'm not going to stay around here anymore and let people say I'm a coward, too," he added bitterly, walking toward the door.

"Wait, m'hijo," Rosa called out.

"Let him go, Rosa," Mano said, his voice heavy. "He's made his choice."

Rosa looked at Mano, wanting to protest—but couldn't. Although Pedro was nearly grown, their habit of not arguing in front of their children was too strong.

His hand on the doorknob, Pedro turned back to his father, lips trembling, close to tears. He then opened the door and walked out.

"Why did you let him go, Mano?" Rosa asked, her cheeks wet with tears.

Mano bowed his head. "Death isn't the only way to lose a child. This war has taken all our children now."

# THE MARCHA OFFENSIVE:
## *MONTH 10, DAY 5*

It was not going to be an easy birth.

Rosa had been in labor eighteen hours with Celia Alonzo and Mano's sister Teresa at her side. Pacing in the tiny living room, Mano heard every groan and scream coming from the bedroom, his sense of helplessness growing as Rosa's cries became louder and more frequent. All their other children had been born in a hospital where Mano had been allowed into the delivery room to comfort his wife. Celia, however, had banished him.

Around three in the morning, the curandera emerged from the room and brought back a brass platter of hot coals from the cooking fire in the kitchen. Moments later, Mano noticed the powerful scent of lavender drifting into the living room.

Within the hour, Rosa's cries stopped and a new sound filled the air—the unmistakable wail of a newborn.

The bedroom door opened and Teresa waved him inside. "Come see your new son."

Lying on the bed, Rosa was holding the bundled infant, his still-damp head pressed against her cheek. "He's like his father," she said, smiling weakly. "Doesn't like being told where and when to go."

Mano laughed softly, bending to kiss the child. "Welcome to the world, Carlos."

"You already have a name for him?" Teresa asked.

"Yes," Rosa answered. "We agreed that a boy would be named Carlos Vallejo Suarez, after my great-great-grandfather. It was Mano's idea."

"I want Carlos to know about his ancestors," Mano explained. "Carlos Vallejo was from a family of Californios."

"Californios?" Teresa said, yawning.

"The Vallejo ranch covered much of San Luis Obispo—before the Anglos came. Maybe ours will be the last generation that's ignorant of our roots in this land."

Teresa hugged her brother. "You've become quite a historian, mi hermano," she said wearily. "I'm going to lie down for a while. Call me if you need something, Rosa."

"I should go, too," Celia added, patting Rosa's arm. "These old bones are starting to ache."

Mano pointed with his chin toward the nightstand where the brass platter Celia had brought into the room still smoldered with lavender. "Can you take that stuff with you?" he said to Celia. "Strong smells give Rosa headaches."

"That should stay, Don Manolo." Celia stepped protectively between Mano and the nightstand. "Lavender relaxes the mother and purifies the room for the baby," she explained. "I should go now. But please...leave the lavender."

"It hasn't bothered me, Mano," Rosa added.

The rebuff irritated Mano, but he knew the curandera's presence had been a comfort to his wife. "Thanks for your help with the delivery, señora," he said respectfully.

Rosa weakly waved good-bye as the curandera made her way to the door. "Que Dios te bendiga, Celia."

Celia returned the wave and smiled. "And may God bless

you as well, m'hija. I'll be back in a few hours to see how you're doing."

After the midwives were out the room, Rosa said, "Pedro should know he has a new brother."

Mano was silent. They had not seen Pedro since their quarrel following the Army sweeps three months ago. While Mano understood his son's anger, he had not forgiven his actions. It made no difference that Pedro was his own blood. The boy had taken part in the slaughter of innocent people—and been proud of it. "He stopped being a part of this family when he joined a pack of killers," he said finally.

"What the boy did was wrong. I know that. But even a convict would deserve to know he has a brother. Please, Mano. Do it for me."

Mano exhaled slowly. Rosa's delivery had been difficult, and she needed to rest. "All right, querida," he said, patting her hand. "I'll try to find him in the morning. Get some sleep now."

———

Shortly after daybreak, Mano started for Angel's house in search of Pedro. He had not spoken to the mero since he'd gone over to the Latino Liberation Front—and taken Los Verdugos with him. El Frente's presence in the barrios had grown significantly since then. An uneasy marriage now existed between the insurgent factions in Southern California. The Latino Liberation Front had become the shock troops of the cause, exporting violence outside the zones, while La Defensa Del Pueblo provided food and aid. Mano knew that in the macho world of the barrios, the DDP was seen as the inferior partner in the marriage—passive and feminine.

When Mano arrived at Angel's house, Isabel answered the door.

"I'm looking for my son," he told the girl.

"You'll have to ask my brother. He's not here."

"Do you know where Pedro is, Isabel?"

"Con permiso, Don Manolo, but you'll have to ask Angel," she said respectfully.

"When will Angel be back?"

Isabel lowered her eyes. "I'm sorry, I don't know."

"Tell Angel I want to see my son."

"I will, Don Manolo."

"One more thing, Isabel. If you see Pedro, tell him his mother would like him to see his new brother."

"Yes, Don Manolo," she said and closed the door.

Uncertain where to look next, Mano began walking. After several blocks, he reached an area near the South Gate hit hardest by the fighting. The street was lined with gutted buildings, their walls and roofs collapsed into jagged piles spilling onto the pavement. A pair of naked toddlers squatted in a crumbling doorway, their bellies swollen with hunger. They scurried away in fear as he walked closer and a bleak vision overwhelmed Mano. *Is this the world where Carlos will grow up?*

They seemed trapped in a bloody quagmire. La Defensa Del Pueblo was working feverishly to keep their people alive. Yet the attacks of the Latino Liberation Front were keeping the Baldies at their throats. There had to be some way out.

# THE MARCHA OFFENSIVE:
## *MONTH 10, DAY 8*

**P**edro peered through the sagebrush, his eyes locked on a rise of the deserted highway more than half a mile away. At any moment, the Baldie convoy would appear and the eight fighters hidden in the brush along the highway would face their first test against an armed enemy.

As he waited silently, the shame that had plagued Pedro welled up again. He glanced at Chico crouching in the bushes ten paces to his right. *Why can't I be more like him?* Pedro asked himself. At least a year younger, Chico showed no qualms about his role in the mall bombings. In fact, Chico seemed proud of their deed. Pedro's constant remorse made him feel weak. *Why am I different?* he wondered.

The truth was, he knew nothing about Chico. Angel had kept them apart from each other as much as possible. It was for their own good, Angel explained. If anyone was caught, the less he knew about the others, the better. For the same reason, Angel had also forbidden the new recruits to tell their families anything about El Frente.

Pedro had no worries there. Angel had taken him into his home after Pedro's break with his parents. Although El Frente had no titles or ranks, his special relationship with Angel separated him from the others. Pedro enjoyed his elevated status—but most of all, he was grateful for the companionship. He dreaded the shame that sometimes overcame him when he was alone. *That's not how a man should feel*, Pedro scolded himself. He wanted to prove to Angel he was not afraid to fight like his father. To keep his mind occupied, Pedro had started carving wooden figurines, mostly animals. Creating something helped fill the emptiness and chase away the guilt.

A distant drone caught Pedro's attention. A Humvee was cresting the rise in the roadway. Trailing a good distance behind was a line of military trucks. After six trucks cleared the ridge, Pedro saw another Humvee bringing up the rear.

The sound of vehicles was a distinct roar now. Pedro's heart began to pound as they drew nearer. This was the critical moment. If the lead vehicle spotted any of the eight young men concealed in the bushes, it would spoil their attack—and possibly cost their lives.

The sagebrush around Pedro shuddered in the wake of the lead Humvee as it sped past.

He sighed in relief as the vehicle continued up the hill to his right. When it neared the crest of the slope, the bluish white trail of a rocket-propelled grenade shot out from the undergrowth, striking the vehicle. After a blinding flash, the Humvee disappeared in a billowing black cloud. The concussion of the blast rocked the air. Pedro pressed himself against the ground and covered his head.

The squeal of brakes drew Pedro's eyes back to the road in front of him. The rest of the convoy was pulling over—right into their trap. The trucks came to a stop along the roadside, reluctant to move into the RPG's range. Over the roar of the idling trucks, he heard Angel's shrill whistle—their signal to attack.

His hands trembling, Pedro picked up one of the gasoline-filled bottles on the ground beside him and threw it toward the closest truck. Without waiting to see where it struck, he reached for the second bottle and hurled it as well. From the corner of his eye, he caught the red streak of a flare thrown by Chico arcing toward the truck. Pedro watched in awe as the other three teams flawlessly executed the same procedure. With a deep *whoomp*, flames engulfed four of the trucks.

Pedro scuttled away, remaining under the cover of the sagebrush as long as possible. Then he broke into a run. Looking back, he saw the other seven members of his group striding hard behind him. Everything was going exactly as Angel had planned.

The group retreated into a ravine that ran alongside the highway for more than half a mile. Angel had chosen the ambush spot well. To cross the steep-walled ravine, the soldiers would have to pursue them on foot. Any undamaged vehicles would be useless.

Over the crackle of the flames, Pedro heard shouts from the soldiers. "Over there! They went into the gully! Grenades! Grenades!"

Pedro was scrambling out of the ravine when he heard a metallic *thud* against the wall of the gully behind him. He did not look back. Three strides later, the ground below his feet heaved in a teeth-rattling blast, hurling him onto his belly. Like a slow-motion film, a gray cloud enveloped the sky and he caught a glimpse of a strange shape cartwheeling past him overhead. The acrid smell of cordite filled the air.

Pedro lay on the ground, stunned, unable to see through the smoke and dust. A hand grabbed his shoulder. It was Angel. *"Vamos! Vamos!"* he said, dragging Pedro to his feet. Running through the dissipating dust toward the abandoned plat of houses ahead, Pedro discovered the strange shape he'd seen hurtling past him. He stopped, staring in disbelief at the lower half of a body, shredded and burned. On its feet were Chico's familiar Nike high-tops.

The barking of rifle fire broke his trance. Two vatos Angel had stationed in the houses to cover their retreat were firing their AK-47s from the windows. Pedro looked behind him and saw the soldiers duck for cover on the other side of the ravine. He was the last one out in the open. Pedro ran for an open doorway and dove inside as bullets from the soldiers struck the brick wall behind him. Crouching behind the wall, his chest heaving, Pedro knew he was out of the line of fire, but not out of danger. Now he would have to evade the soldiers' pursuit.

Two blocks away, he found Angel at their rendezvous point, an empty tri-level home at the end of a cul-de-sac. The mero wordlessly led him into the backyard to begin their trek back home through the deserted suburb. The others had already dispersed, each taking a different route back, but he and Angel, sharing the same destination, would travel together.

For the first time following a mission, Pedro felt a surge of pride.

———

From a pot Angel had fashioned from a spent RPG casing, Isabel ladled oat porridge into two bowls and carried them to the dining room where her brother and Pedro waited. Her eyes lingered on Pedro as she placed the bowl before him on the table. She should have told her brother about Don Manolo's visit three days ago. But she did not want Pedro to return to his family.

Angel caught Isabel stealing a glance at Pedro. He knew what the look meant. His sister's interest in Pedro was hard to miss. Oblivious to her attention, Pedro nodded in thanks and began to eat.

"Gracias, hermanita," Angel said and gestured for her to return to the kitchen. He then gently slapped Pedro's arm. "Bueno, eh?"

"Sí," Pedro answered flatly and continued eating.

Angel had been impressed by the boy's silence on the way back from the raid. Pedro was maturing. This was not a party and there was no reason to celebrate.

The raid had gone well enough. They'd hurt the Baldies and lost only one of their own—for certain. Tomorrow, he'd take a head count to see how many made it back.

Most important, they were fighting. It was like the turf wars against rival gangs years before. *They need to fear you. That's how you hold your turf.* Still, this was not going to be easy.

El Frente had promised them weapons. So far, it was just empty talk. He was fighting with the most plentiful weapon he had right now...people. They had more volunteers than guns, but he'd accepted the eager recruits anyway and given them tasks to keep them busy...spying on troop movements, carrying messages, scrounging for weapons and supplies. It was risky, bringing so many in. Someone might talk—especially if he was caught. But keeping people involved was more important. They wanted to fight. That strength must not be wasted.

Isabel returned with the cooking pot. "Would you like some more?" she asked Pedro, gently putting her hand on his shoulder. The boy shook his head and rose from the table.

Isabel's attraction to Pedro worried Angel. He wasn't sure which would be worse: if Pedro returned her affection, or if he didn't. And that wasn't the only problem circling Pedro like a vulture.

He was surprised Mano had not come looking for his son—but that could change at any time. Angel wondered once again about the wisdom of bringing Pedro into his house. The boy was sincere and brave. He had the makings of a good vato. But Angel was not sure how much longer this arrangement could last.

Sooner or later, the boy would bring him trouble. Then again, Angel had never backed down from trouble.

"Did you hear about the raid on the convoy yesterday?" Mano said into the satellite phone.

"Yeah, but the reports were sketchy. Stories about dead soldiers don't get much ink anymore," Ramon replied. "I asked Octavio why we weren't told. He said it was news to him, too."

"I think he's lying."

"Actually, it might be worse if he's telling the truth. It means El Frente is losing control of its cells."

"Not being warned about the raid hurt us, Ramon. The troops chasing them into the zone stumbled across one of the supply caches we'd just dug up. We lost a week's worth of food."

"Dammit!"

"I'm not sure what we can do. The LLF is getting bigger every day. It's mostly kids, but they can still hurt people."

"I don't like this, Mano. They're short on weapons and long on manpower. That's a scary combination. If this keeps up, I think it's only a matter of time before some loose cannon out there decides suicides are a good idea."

A chill passed through Mano. His own son might be one of them. He'd yet to tell Ramon about Pedro's defection. When it had happened, there wasn't time. Since then, Mano had to admit, it was mostly shame that kept him silent.

"Mano...Are you still there?" Ramon asked after several seconds.

"Yes, I'm here," Mano said, his voice hoarse.

"What's the matter? You sound upset."

"There's something you should know...my son Pedro's joined El Frente."

# THE MARCHA OFFENSIVE:
## MONTH 11, DAY 2

After four months of undercard matches, the main event of the CIAgate hearings had finally arrived. Carol Phelps, the assistant director of the CIA, was about to face the congressional panel. Anticipating a bare-knuckles clash with the flinty Phelps, the networks were broadcasting her testimony live. Surprisingly, Phelps was grim and glassy-eyed, like someone facing execution, when she began reading her opening statement into the array of microphones on the fabric-covered table.

"Mr. Chairman, members of the committee, my fellow Americans, these hearings have occupied our government for the last five months and, I believe, distracted our nation from more pressing issues facing us around the world. The time has come for this to end.

"The question before this panel is whether the CIA was used to obscure our level of troop deployments overseas. As a number of expert witnesses have pointed out, revealing the full extent of our troop deployments aids our nation's enemies in countless ways. However, since this panel has insisted on treating prudent security policy as some type of crime, it seems the only thing that will stop this incessant and detrimental process is for you to know the person responsible for this policy.

"Shortly after I began my duties as assistant director of the CIA, acting solely on my own initiative, I instructed my staff that it would be in the nation's best interest to misdirect our enemies about our overseas troop levels. This policy…"

Phelps stopped, distracted by the sudden commotion of reporters rushing out of the chamber. One newswoman brazenly filed her story right from the hearing room. "Here's your headline," she said into her vu-phone. "Phelps takes the bullet for Brenner."

———

While Carol Phelps's public confession had probably averted a resolution of impeachment, it did little to bolster Brenner's sagging polls. At the same time, the divisive behavior of the congressional panel had dismayed most Americans, tainting everyone who'd been a part of the long and bitter squabble. Safely outside the CIAgate fallout zone, Nixon's popularity rose, his disclosure that had sparked the hearings now nearly forgotten.

With the Republican convention less than six months away, many were openly wondering if the party would abandon Brenner and embrace the fast-rising Nixon. No clear front-runner had emerged among the Democrats, who seemed preoccupied in a bitter fight within their party for the chance to face a weak opponent. The Nationalists, solidly behind Melvin Bates, were making steady gains among the nativist wing of both parties.

Although Brenner's political advisors felt he'd weathered the CIAgate storm, the Hispanic insurgency would not go away. The low-level but unrelenting attacks by the LLF had become a political tar baby for Brenner, an issue that seemed to stain the president regardless of how he handled it. Nixon, in a tactic reminiscent of his great-uncle, announced he had a secret plan to resolve the insurgency. However, he could not unveil it without tipping his hand to the rebels. Nixon promised that if elected, his approach would quell the rebellion. No other presidential candidate had yet articulated a solution for the constant violence—except to denounce the actions of the administration.

Adding to the political turmoil were growing protests and boycotts by Asian Indians angry over the racial profiling that made them frequent targets of detainment by security forces looking for Hispanic infiltrators.

———

Fuller walked past the holding compound and looked into the sullen faces on the other side of the razor wire. How many of these captives would be shooting at his men soon? Intel and psyops teams had questioned the thirty-four men many times over the last four months. The grilling had produced nothing. If these men hadn't been Panchos when Brock's troops brought them in, after months of brutal interrogations, they probably soon would be.

And now they were going to be released.

Fuller wondered if the Army's policy of releasing these men into a different Quarantine Zone would cut them off from any possible sources of support—or simply alienate them further.

This batch of detainees was among the first brought in during Brock's sweeps. Hundreds more remained in the interrogation pipeline. *When it's over,* Fuller wondered, *how many LLF members will we find? How many more will we create?*

Perhaps worse, Fuller's company was one of the three units sharing round-the-clock guard duty at the Internment Facility—a task diverting almost eight hundred soldiers from patrols inside the zones.

Fuller stared at the hard, dusty ground outside the razor wire. *This is the legacy of General Charles F. Brock.*

# THE MARCHA OFFENSIVE: *MONTH 15*

Fifteen months had passed since the Marcha Offensive. In that time, the Hispanic uprising had descended into a seemingly endless morass of petty terror and retaliatory government skirmishes. The attacks had become so common, they were no longer front-page news. The relentless pressure of the turmoil, however, was slowly threatening to fracture the nation's brittle mosaic of culture and race.

Other minorities were pressing for more power and autonomy. Asians, African-Americans, Native Americans, Pacific Islanders...it seemed every group outside the Anglo mainstream now clamored for a greater voice. Fueling the turmoil was the Hispanic quest for independence, the thorny central issue of the presidential election less than three months away.

For the first time in over half a century, both major parties were approaching their national conventions without a clear nominee. President Brenner had the support of Republican Party leaders, but polls showed Nixon with an edge among voters. A grueling primary season had left the Democrats almost evenly split among three candidates in a fratricidal battle filled with smears, innuendo, and attack ads. One of the candidates, Valerie Dent, a congresswoman from Minnesota, was the first to voice a radical approach to the Hispanic insurgency: a political settlement that included the repeal of the Quarantine and Relocation Act. A bitter clash at the Democratic convention seemed inevitable.

Scheduled last, the Nationalist convention held no suspense. Everyone expected a carefully orchestrated coronation ceremony for Melvin Bates. Polling steadily at fourteen percent of the voters for the last six months, Bates had no real chance to become president, but he would certainly be a spoiler. The question was: Whose chances would he spoil?

———

Ramon raised the volume on his earphone. In less than ten minutes, the music on the cordless device would be replaced by the live translation of a speech by China's prime minister, Jun Ai Guo, the main speaker at today's U.N. General Assembly.

Like all U.N. delegates, Ramon spent most days in conference rooms, legations, and private offices. After nearly two years in Geneva, he'd witnessed the awe-inspiring spectacle of a plenary session only a handful of times. The sight of nearly four hundred delegates gathered in the historic Assembly Hall still thrilled him. Since 1929, this high-vaulted room had hosted a number of assemblies from the sovereign states of the world. And now he was among them, sitting at one of the long wooden delegates' benches behind a small white sign that read: RÉPUBLIQUE HISPANIQUE D'AMÉRIQUE DU NORD. The Hispanic Republic of North America. His country. His people. He never tired of seeing it. *Someday, we'll be more than observers in this room,* he vowed to himself. The prospects of that happening anytime soon, however, seemed very dim.

Even his reunion with Maggie three weeks earlier had done little to dispel Ramon's pessimism. The joy of their first

meeting in nearly two years had been muted by a stark setback: Maggie was now an exile from the United States. They
were almost certain the CIA had breached their online network. A return to the U.S. could mean her arrest. Financially,
it could have gone much worse. They'd managed to salvage
much of Maggie's wealth in the United States—and she could
continue to work for Lyon Studios. Most of their films were
shot overseas these days anyway. But their cause had lost
another operative able to move freely within the States.

Ramon bristled when Octavio arrived and dropped heavily
into the chair beside him. They had avoided each other for
months. After an awkward silence, Octavio leaned close and
whispered, "Look, we better talk or something. It won't look
so good if we sit here and ignore each other, you know what I
mean?"

"Fine," Ramon said icily, removing his earphone. "Are you
enjoying the weather?"

Octavio smiled. "C'mon, Ramon. We can do better than
that, hombre. Who's going to take the gabacho election?"

"I'd say it's a toss-up," Ramon answered halfheartedly.

"I'm pulling for Bates but I know he hasn't got a chance."

"He certainly would be the best candidate for us,
wouldn't he?"

Octavio laughed. "Who else could make me look like a
statesman?"

Ramon smiled for the first time. "'God spare us from moderates,' Jo used to say."

"You see, Ramon. Sometimes we're not that different, you
and me."

Ramon did not find the thought very comforting.

———

After two days of intensive lobbying and fiery speeches, the
Republican National Convention had reached a standstill.

The Brenner camp was pressing for an early vote, believing they had enough delegates to clinch the nomination. The Nixon team was trying to delay the first ballot with a number of parliamentary stalls, hoping to rally more support.

Nixon had worked the caucuses tirelessly, glad-handing with dozens of groups over the last two days. Anxious to maintain his presidential mien, Brenner had avoided such flagrant pandering. However, while Brenner's numerous surrogates were no match for the energetic and personable Nixon, they were able to attend more caucuses, neutralizing the congressman's advantage.

As the third day of the convention opened, a buzz spread through the floor. Nixon was going to address the assembly that afternoon. Speculations of a deal swirled among the delegates. Most believed he was conceding to become Brenner's new vice president; others said he was angling for secretary of state. Nixon's brief speech surprised them all.

Standing at the flag-draped podium, Nixon announced he'd selected a running mate and his chosen partner had agreed. His vice president would be Congressman Melvin Bates.

After a moment of stunned silence, the cavernous hall erupted into a frenzy of cheering as the delegates grasped the brilliance of Nixon's move. With Bates on the ticket, the Republicans could not lose.

The following day, George Whitehead Nixon became his party's presidential nominee.

In November, the Nixon-Bates ticket was elected in a landslide.

# THE NIXON ERA II

*God spare us from moderates.*

*Josefina Herrera*

# THE NIXON ERA II:
## *DAY 1*

**R**amon entered the chalet's great room, refilled Maggie's wineglass, and settled next to her on the leather couch. "Any idea who's broadcasting the inaugural?" he asked, retrieving the TV remote.

"Try channel ten. I think LémanBleu is carrying it live," Maggie replied.

The great room's wall-mounted plasma blinked into life, revealing an iconic scene. George Whitehead Nixon stood in a long gray topcoat, his palm raised to take the oath of office, the Capitol dome in the distance behind him. All eyes on the crowded dais were locked on the new president's squat figure.

"Nice staging," Maggie noted. "You can tell Nixon's got California media people."

"Yeah. It gives the little squirt a lot of gravitas."

"You think Nixon's going to unveil his secret plan today?"

Ramon laughed. "His secret plan is going to be the same as his great-uncle's . . . campaign bullshit."

After completing the swearing-in ceremony, Nixon gripped the edges of the lectern and addressed the audience, his heavy features somber. "Fellow citizens, our nation today faces the sternest challenge to its sovereignty since the War Between the States. In those desperate days, a time that could have forever divided this country, a man emerged who kept our nation together. Against a fierce current of divisiveness, Abraham Lincoln fought to keep the Union intact. After winning the fight, Lincoln was also magnanimous in peace. He knew we would need something more than force to keep our nation together. Our country would need compassion before it could be healed. As your president, I will exercise the full power of our nation against the terrorists who bring violence upon our people. At the same time, I will open my arms to embrace Hispanics who seek peace and harmony. Those who prove their loyalty will be returned to full citizenship. In addition, I will lobby Congress for a repeal of the Terrorist Arraignment Act. Following the example set by Lincoln, I pledge to lead our nation out of this crisis with a strong hand, yet a hand extended in a spirit of hope."

At the conclusion of Nixon's speech, the Swiss talking heads launched into their analysis of Nixon's surprising new initiative on the Hispanic insurgency. The pundits all agreed that the restoration of citizenship was a major concession to the rebels.

Ramon turned off the set and stared silently into the blank screen.

"Do you think Nixon really means it?" Maggie asked, the hope in her voice unmistakable.

Ramon took a long sip of his wine. "If he does, it's going to be very bad for our cause."

# THE NIXON ERA II:
## *DAY 8*

**C**arlos began to cry and Rosa brought the baby to her breast, letting him suckle as she sat on the patched sofa. She had no milk left, but hoped the comfort of her flesh would quiet the child.

She heard Mano stir in the bedroom. Although it was nearly noon, Mano was trying to sleep. Rosa was used to her husband's nocturnal habits. Mano usually disappeared at dusk and returned with the sunrise for a meal and some sleep. She never asked what he was doing. She'd learned long ago it was better not to know.

The baby wailed again, a long plaintive cry that Rosa understood as clearly as if he'd spoken. Carlos was hungry.

"I'm sorry, m'hijito," she whispered, gently rocking the ten-month-old. "Mami is out of milk. Hush, before you wake your papi."

The bedroom door opened and Mano stepped into the living room yawning, his eyes red with fatigue. "Let me hold the baby for a while, querida. I can't sleep anyway."

"Go back to bed, mi amor. I'll take him to Teresa's house so you can get some sleep," Rosa said, rising from the couch.

Mano extended his large hands toward the wailing infant. "Let me hold him for a while. I don't get to see my son enough. When one of us is awake, the other one's always asleep." The child quieted as Mano brought him to his chest.

"He loves his papi," Rosa said, smiling. Then her smile faded. "Teresa said she saw Pedro yesterday, coming out of Tavo's. Maybe you should go and talk to him, Mano."

"This is the only son I have left," Mano said, nodding toward Carlos. "It's been ten months and Pedro hasn't come to see you or the baby. He's made it clear he no longer wants to be part of this family."

"Isn't losing one son bad enough?" she whispered, tears filling her eyes. "Julio was taken from us. Don't turn away from Pedro, mi amor. I don't want to lose another son to this war."

"Neither do I, but I can't condone murder, Rosa...even by my own blood."

"He wants the same things you do, Mano. Pedro wants to fight for his people."

Mano turned away from Rosa, facing the wall. "Do you think it's easy for me, not fighting back? I've never forgotten the Baldies killed Julio. I see them every day, treating us like animals. I want to hurt them, too. But I won't kill innocent people to do it."

Rosa laid her hand on Mano's shoulder, drawing him toward her. "I was the one who asked you to stop fighting so that our people wouldn't starve. Most people are feeding themselves from their gardens now. We've learned how to get by without the government's food supplies. Maybe we're strong enough now."

"Food is only the first step, querida. We need to have our own water and energy before we fight again."

"If we wait much longer, there may not be anyone willing to fight. Since the president announced we can become citizens again, some people are saying the trouble might be over soon."

"It won't be that easy, mi amor. They haven't repealed the

needle law yet. Anyone who's resisted can still be tried for treason. Nixon's only trying to divide us."

"I don't understand, Mano. Aren't we fighting to end the quarantine and become citizens again?"

"That's what I thought when this war started. But we'll always be second-class citizens until we can govern ourselves, Rosa. This land was ours once...someday, it will be again."

———

Angel led Pedro and Isabel into his bedroom—a sparsely furnished space without decorations that mirrored its stern occupant. Kneeling on the floor, the mero removed a short section of baseboard from the closet's door frame and extracted a small metal case hidden in the wall. Inside the case was a Swiss satellite phone that Angel held out to Pedro. "Si los gabachos me matan, llama a uno-ocho-siete con este teléfono. Ese es mi contacto con El Frente. Si me pasa algo, tu estas en cargo. Usa el nombre Flaco cuando llames."

Noticing Pedro's confusion, Isabel translated. "My brother said that if he's killed, you are to call one-eight-seven on this phone. It's his contact with El Frente. If anything happens to him, you are in charge. Your code name is Flaco."

Pedro's eyes widened in awe, then he nodded solemnly. "Entiendo."

Angel put away the black phone and returned the case to its hiding place. "No worry. Angel no die," he said jovially, clapping Pedro on the shoulder. "Vamos a comer."

As they entered the kitchen for their evening meal, Isabel was beaming. Although she dreaded the thought of losing her brother, she was delighted Angel had chosen Pedro as his successor. It meant Pedro would be with them for some time to come.

Now that the fighting was dying down, a glimmer of hope arose in Isabel. Perhaps Angel would consent for her to marry Pedro one day.

# THE NIXON ERA II:
## DAY 24

Fuller rose from the plush leather chair and shouldered his travel bag as the co-pilot entered the hangar's VIP boarding area.

"We're wheels up at oh-eight-hundred, Captain," the Air Force officer announced. "Want some coffee before we take off?"

"I'm fine, thanks."

"Then you're ready to board," the co-pilot said before leading Fuller to the tarmac where a military version of an executive jet waited. Stepping aboard the plane, Fuller's eyebrows rose in surprise. All eight seats were empty. "Am I your only passenger?"

"That's right, Captain. Enjoy the flight. We'll be touching down at Dulles around thirteen-hundred hours," the co-pilot said before retreating into the cabin.

Fuller settled into a window seat ahead of the wings, hoping to enjoy the view. As the jet climbed steeply into the morning sky, he smiled at the irony of the moment.

Almost two years ago, he'd written off his chances for advancement. Now he was being transferred to Washington as an Army liaison with the CIA. There were officers his age who'd kill for this posting.

Completing Fuller's vindication was the reassignment of General Charles F. Brock to the command of a parts supply depot in Michigan. Angered at the snub, the former domestic theater commander had resigned his commission. The scuttlebutt was that the retired general would soon enter politics.

Despite his good fortune, Fuller was still apprehensive about Henry Evans. The former regional spy chief was now assistant director of the CIA and had used his considerable influence with the Nixon team to place Fuller in this plum assignment. There was little doubt Evans would expect some favors in return. Fuller was determined to avoid anything that would compromise his integrity—even if it meant returning to a dead-end assignment like Outpost Bravo.

Life at Bravo had been spartan but not without rewards. Since his days as a cadet at the Academy, spare time had been a rare commodity for Fuller. That had changed over his last two years at Outpost Bravo. Combat duty was mostly long periods of tedium interrupted by brief episodes of pulse-pounding stress. Determined to atone for his tactical mistakes, Fuller had used the downtime to immerse himself in a wide spectrum of writings about two crucial subjects—asymmetrical warfare and Hispanics.

Through his study of Hispanics, he'd gleaned considerable detail about their wide diversity of culture, politics, and race—something he'd already understood in principle.

His readings on insurrections, however, had opened his eyes to a fact rarely mentioned in his military classes at West Point: Most rebellions fail.

The Academy's faculty had dwelled on uprisings that had succeeded—or been suppressed—through military force. But as Fuller had learned from reading civilian scholars, most rebellions simply faded away without decisive battles. The core lesson of these conflicts was essentially the same: Government repression was the rebels' best recruiter.

The way to defeat a rebellion was to create secure and prosperous communities—while methodically hunting down the rebel leaders using stealth. It was hardly the kind of glory hailed in the Academy's military annals. Worse yet, Fuller realized Brenner's White House had led the U.S. into the classic trap of responding to the rebels with military might alone.

To cope with this grim realization, he'd found solace in the mind-numbing effects of bourbon—and sometimes even in the cash-and-carry sex of the trailer park brothels near the outpost. That, however, was not his most guilty pleasure.

No, it was the carnal thrill of leading men in battle that would be the hardest vice to give up. In combat, every fiber of your body felt alive, an adrenaline-laced high that was like a drug—deadly yet irresistible. Anyone who'd survived a battle understood its dark seductiveness.

Fuller gazed out the plane's window. On the ground below, the craggy slopes west of Los Angeles were casting long morning shadows toward the Quarantine Zones. Inside the walls, random clusters of buildings were interspersed with the brown corduroy rectangles of cultivated fields. As his eyes drifted over the familiar landscape, he was stung by a painful recollection.

Manolo Suarez was down there somewhere. Leaving for Washington with the rebel leader still roaming free was his only real regret.

---

Hank Evans's executive assistant silently entered his office and lowered the blinds on the large window overlooking the central courtyard. It was something she did unbidden each afternoon as the sun began to creep into Hank's seventh-floor office at CIA headquarters in Langley. "Thank you, Gita," he said absently, absorbed in the e-mails on his PC.

The svelte young woman paused at the door. "Another Diet Coke, sir?"

"Yes, that would be nice," he said looking up from his monitor, noticing the long slim legs peeking provocatively along the slit of her tailored skirt. "By the way, will you let me know when you hear from Captain Fuller? His flight's due at Dulles this afternoon."

"Of course, sir," she said before softly closing the door behind her.

Hank watched Gita leave and felt something absent from his life since the divorce...a surge of lust. *Better watch it, you old dog,* he chided himself. *That's a harassment lawsuit waiting to happen.* Still, it was good to feel *something* again. Evans's move to Washington three weeks earlier had reawakened the ambition and vigor that had driven him in the early years of his career. Now, despite the breakneck schedule, he'd managed to lose some weight. To Hank's surprise, he would reach the end of the day and realize he'd been too occupied to snack, too busy even to crave food.

It hadn't all been easy, especially leaving Sarah. He'd no longer be able to see his daughter every weekend. But the look of pride in her eyes as he boarded the Air Force jet sent to ferry him to Washington was now a prized memory.

Hank's desk phone rang, and he saw Bill Perkins's extension number on the unit's caller ID display.

Evans had brought his former regional assistant to Langley for a vital mission—to reopen Operation Hollywood Squares, the e-mail link between Ramon Garcia and Margaret Zane. But there was another reason Hank had rescued Perkins from the career hellhole of Outpost Bravo and made him his senior technical security officer: He did not want to leave behind a disgruntled subordinate who knew enough to take him down.

"What's up, Bill?" Hank said into the receiver.

"I've dug up the logs on Hollywood Squares," the TSO said anxiously. "We need to talk."

"Okay, meet me in the courtyard in ten minutes." There was little chance his office was bugged, but this was a topic he could not risk leaking to his bosses.

Entering the courtyard, Evans spotted Perkins on a bench beside *Kryptos*, the abstract sculpture dedicated to the CIA's code-breaking prowess. Perkins had prudently chosen a spot away from the handful of other staffers taking a break in the weak winter sunshine.

"I've got some bad news, Hank," Perkins said softly as Evans sat down beside him. "The e-mails between Garcia and Zane dried up about three months ago."

"Has Garcia tried to reach Suarez?"

"No. The e-mail connection is still active, but Garcia's stopped using it. There's something else...I found out that Margaret Zane has been living with Garcia in Geneva for the last three months."

Evans's shoulders sagged and his face lost its color. The noose he'd been waiting so long to close around the rebel leadership had unraveled. "They know we broke their encryption," he said finally.

"How could they have figured that out?"

"It doesn't matter now." Evans had kept Perkins in the dark about Fuller's attempt to capture Suarez—and he wanted to keep it that way. "Look, Bill, we know Garcia and Zane smuggled a satellite phone to Suarez. That's probably their main contact channel now. We've got to break into their communications again, you understand? Make that your top priority. In the meantime, keep monitoring the old connection just in case. They might use it as a backup."

"I can keep an eye on the e-mails. But how in the hell am I supposed to crack their calls? You know those Swiss phones are impossible to trace," Perkins said, his eyes darting nervously.

"Just figure something out, goddammit. That's why I got you out of Bravo."

"All right, Hank. All right. I'll do my best," Perkins said and walked away.

Evans stared at the pale sky, fighting a sense of despair. He'd lied to his superiors, destroyed classified documents, and risked charges of treason for the chance to round up all the rebels at once. And now that opportunity was gone.

---

After clearing away the dishes, the waiter brought out two fortune cookies in a small, chipped bowl and ceremoniously placed them between Fuller and Evans.

"Can I get another glass of plum wine?" Evans asked, holding up his near-empty goblet.

The waiter bowed and disappeared, leaving them alone in the restaurant.

Evans drained the last of his wine and said, "You're a patient man, Captain. That's a rare virtue these days."

"I'm not sure I follow you, sir."

"You've sat through dinner without asking why I chose to meet you here instead of in my office."

"I can't say that question hasn't crossed my mind," Fuller admitted.

Evans's request to meet in this seedy, out-of-the-way Chinese restaurant seemed incongruous to Fuller after the VIP treatment on his flight to Washington. What's more, Fuller had expected Evans to be enthusiastic about his promotion up the CIA pyramid. Instead, the man slumped into the opposite side of the booth seemed troubled and distracted.

"What I have to tell you is best said privately, Captain."

"Then I doubt it's good news, sir."

Evans laughed weakly. "You're very perceptive," he said and then leaned back, fixing his eyes on the ceiling. "The Nixon people brought me to Washington primarily for one reason, Captain. I told them I was on the verge of an intelligence breakthrough that could identify every Pancho leader in the country." He sighed heavily, his gaze dropping toward the floor. "Today I found out our pipeline into the Pancho leadership has dried up. I'm not really sure what I can do now. We're back to square one."

"I think you're selling yourself short, Mr. Evans. Square one may not be such a bad place to be. We both know there are a lot of things we could be doing better... even without an intelligence breakthrough."

The waiter returned with Evans's fourth glass of wine. After thanking him, Evans downed a long swallow. "Go ahead, Captain. Tell me more. I could use a pep talk right now," he said, smiling grimly.

"You weren't promoted because of a single intelligence lead, Mr. Evans. I heard the president's inaugural speech and I have no doubt you've had considerable influence on his new approach to the insurgency. No disrespect, sir, but those ideas didn't come from Helen Byrne. I suspect the president chose you to shape the Agency's strategy and made Mrs. Byrne the CIA director because of her political connections."

A former U.S. ambassador to Belgium, "Big Hair Helen" Byrne was the widow of a four-term Texas senator and a familiar face in Washington circles.

Evans put down his wineglass, suddenly more lucid. "You surprise me, Captain. I expected you to be a good tactical advisor. I had no idea you paid attention to politics inside the Beltway."

"Wearing a uniform doesn't limit my perspective, sir."

"You're not like most people in uniform, son. Nothing against our front-line warriors, but they tend to see everything in black and white. We need more soldiers like you—especially in Washington."

"I'm glad to hear that, sir. The previous administration missed a lot of opportunities to put the Panchos out of business. I think this president is on the right track."

"He's very impressive, especially up close. You can sense he has a strong vision, but he also has the political skills to get things done. He's managed to get the vice president aboard on handling the insurgency—and Mel Bates isn't known for moderate policies."

"That doesn't sound like someone who's going to dismiss your advice because an intelligence lead slipped away. I'm guessing you recommended the Ink Blot strategy?"

Evans's eyes brightened, his excitement rising. "I suggested a variation on the Ink Blot. We're going to start by pacifying sections of Quarantine Zones along the northeast seaboard."

"I understand. It'll be almost impossible for more insurgents to slip in from Mexico."

"Exactly. Once we've cleared out the Panchos and secured the pacified areas, we'll reestablish public services. Now here's our twist on the Ink Blot strategy: As a carrot for good behavior, we'll offer a return to citizenship for everyone in the pacified areas if they keep the peace for at least a year. Within two years, we hope to expand the pacified areas throughout the country. As our ink blots spread, the Pancho base of support is going to dry up. We're very close to rounding up enough votes to repeal the needle law. When that's done, it'll get easier to find out who's really behind the insurgency."

"That's good, sir. But if we're going to hold out a carrot to Hispanics who reject the insurgency, we need to have a good stick as well."

"What have you got in mind?"

"A few crack regiments to root out the insurgents. We need troops equipped with the latest technology... night-vision equipment, drones, combat robots, anti-RPG defenses. That will mean bringing some of our best troops stateside for a while."

"It's already being done. Anything else?"

"Yes, sir. The Brenner people never tried to drive a wedge between the rebel factions. There are several fracture lines of nationality and race we can exploit within Hispanic communities across the country."

"For instance?"

"Cubans are a good example. They're concentrated along the East Coast and are very different from Hispanics in the Southwest, who are primarily of Mexican origin. Most Cubans are politically conservative. When they could vote, they typically voted Republican—a big difference from most Hispanics. Cubans are very nationalistic and don't like being lumped in with other Hispanics. It wouldn't be hard to get them to break ranks. Besides, most other U.S. Latinos have always resented the preferential green card status we gave Cuban exiles during the Cold War."

"You seem to know a lot about Cubans."

"I grew up around some Cuban families in New Jersey. On the street, they looked like your average white suburbanites. But at home, they had a very different culture."

"You said Cubans are one example. You have any others?"

"Let's see . . ." Fuller extended his hand, counting his fingers as he spoke. "Mexicans look down on Guatemalans . . . Costa Ricans dislike Nicaraguans . . . Peruvians and Chileans have no love for each other . . . Colombians and Venezuelans have a long-standing border feud . . . and most Spaniards believe they're superior to anyone from the New World." He closed his hand into a fist. "Right now, though, they've all got a common enemy . . . us."

"Fascinating, Captain. I never realized suburban New Jersey was such a mecca for Hispanic immigrants."

Fuller laughed. "I had a lot of time to read at Outpost Bravo. You might say I was more than a little motivated to learn about my opponents' weaknesses."

"They say Americans learn their geography from wars. I think that's also true about foreign cultures."

"Other than language, there isn't a lot you can generalize about Hispanics. When you think about it, it's like lumping everyone from a nation that speaks English into a single group."

"I see what you mean. It's hard to picture a lot in common between Jamaicans and Canadians. So why do you think most people picture a swarthy guy with a serape and a sombrero when they hear the word *Hispanic*?"

"Our border with Mexico really skews our perspective. Mexico's population is predominantly indigenous. That's not always the case throughout the rest of Latin America. Hispanics come in every color—and that's important to us, Mr. Evans. You see, I think we could train Caucasian and African-American agents to work inside the zones."

"What about language?"

"Very few second- and third-generation Latinos speak much Spanish. Most people in the barrios know that. With the right kind of cultural training, our agents could blend in. The DOD spends billions researching our foreign enemies. And even most of the public knows the difference between Sunnis and Shiites, or Persians and Arabs. But we know next to nothing about Hispanics. The more I read, the more I'm amazed at the depth of our ignorance about these people."

"That kind of information is worth a report, Captain. Are you up to putting something together for me?"

"I can start on it tonight, Mr. Evans."

Evans smiled. "Tomorrow will be fine. Look, son. I suspect we're going to be seeing more of each other than our own wives—if we had them. So let's drop the formalities. Most people call me Hank. Do you prefer Michael or Mike?"

"Mike is fine with me, sir...I mean, Hank."

"Fortune cookie, Mike?" Evans asked, offering the bowl to the young officer.

Fuller broke open a cookie, scanned the fortune, and wordlessly handed it to Evans. It read: YOUR PLANS WILL MEET WITH GREAT SUCCESS.

Evans laughed. "Let's hope the fortunes here are better than the food."

# THE NIXON ERA II:
## *MONTH 5, DAY 11*

**M**ano wiped his brow with the back of his hand before dialing the satellite phone. A June heat wave had descended on Los Angeles and the temperature was suffocating—even near midnight. Hoping to catch a breeze, he'd gone to the roof of a seven-story parking lot on Broadway for his daily call to Ramon. So far, all he'd gotten out of it was the exercise of climbing the stairs.

"What's your take on the El Paso decision?" Mano asked once Ramon was on the line.

Ramon laughed softly "Saying *Hello, Ramon,* is too much to ask?"

"We pay for this phone by the minute, hermano," Mano said evenly.

"Well, I wish we had more to talk about," Ramon said, his voice becoming somber. "Right now, we're not making much progress anywhere."

"This trial in El Paso might be significant."

The previous November, a Texas sheriff with an eye on reelection had gotten wind of a federal investigation and pre-emptively arrested a cadre of eight partisans from the Latino

Liberation Front, including the defector who'd broken the case. Legal maneuvers by the defense team had stalled the trial for five months. The trial itself, however, had lasted less than a week. Prohibited by the needle law from considering the prosecutor's plea-bargaining with their informer, the jury had convicted all of the "El Paso Eight" of treason under the Terrorist Arraignment Act. The men were now awaiting execution.

"Yeah," Ramon agreed. "If there was ever any doubt, this case proved even snitches will be executed under the needle law. This won't make much difference for us right away, though. We're not doing anything to risk being arrested, are we?"

"How's Perez taking the news?"

"Octavio told me he hopes the sheriff gets reelected," Ramon said with a bitter laugh. "Hate to admit it, but for once I agree with him. We could use some more hard-ass good ol' boys like him."

"I still feel bad for the eight he rounded up—even if they were LLF."

"That's debatable, amigo. El Frente's recruited nothing but thugs and . . ." Ramon paused, his tone suddenly gentle. "I'm sorry, Mano. I forgot about Pedro."

Mano stared into the darkness on the horizon. "I wish I could forget," he finally said.

# THE NIXON ERA II:
## *MONTH 6, DAY 2*

**S**imon Potts finished his scotch, studying the plasma screen high on the wall in the airport bar. The news report on Nixon's latest moves in the Hispanic insurgency made his trip to South Korea look like a good decision. There would not be much drama in the U.S. anytime soon.

Even Nixon's harshest critics were conceding that the president's promise to reinstate full citizenship for Hispanics had been a powerful inducement for peace. In addition, Congress had agreed to suspend the Terrorist Arraignment Act—albeit only in zones that had been declared "pacified." The compromise had come because many lawmakers had been unwilling to appear soft on terrorism. Despite the half measure, the limited repeal of the needle law had reduced tensions inside the zones.

Nixon's military moves were succeeding, too. Unlike the Brenner strategy of chasing the insurgents across the country in retaliation for the latest attack, the Army was now concentrating its forces to create permanently secure areas within the Quarantine Zones. In several Quarantine Zones along the East Coast, a semblance of normal life had returned.

Electrical power, mail delivery, trash pickup, schools, and regular police patrols were once again a part of daily life.

Known as the Ink Blot strategy in national security circles, the ultimate goal of Nixon's policy was to continually expand the pacified areas and choke off the insurgency.

Few could argue with its initial success—especially Simon Potts.

———

Hank Evans raised his gaze from the stacks of printouts collated on the table when Michael Fuller entered the room.

"Do you have the latest casualty stats?" Evans asked.

Fuller patted his briefcase. "I brought eight copies."

"Good. Be ready to pass them out after my initial report. By the way, is that the new domestic theater fruit loop?" Evans said, nodding toward the red-and-blue combat ribbon on Fuller's dress uniform.

"They were issued last week."

Evans smiled broadly. "That's going to play well with the committee."

Evans and Fuller had gathered in a Capitol antechamber to put the final touches on a presentation to the Appropriations Subcommittee for Domestic Theater Operations, the congressional representatives who held the purse strings for the CIA's counterinsurgency.

"You think Collins is still going to be our biggest obstacle?" Fuller asked. "Yesterday he told the media it looks like our pacification plan may be working." Joshua Collins, a four-term Democrat from West Virginia, was chairman of the committee.

"Politicians always hedge their bets, Mike. Collins wants to go on record saying something positive in case things keep going well for us. Don't worry, the minute we start seeing some setbacks, he'll jump down our throats again."

As Evans and Fuller gathered their documents, Helen Byrne opened the antechamber door. "It's time to go, boys," the director of the CIA drawled.

The trio crossed the dim Capitol corridor and entered a conference room where the eight members of the sub-committee sat along one side of a long table. After taking seats across from the lawmakers, Byrne teed up the presentation.

"Honorable ladies and gentlemen, the administration's pacification strategy is widely agreed to be succeeding at curbing the violence of the Hispanic insurgency. As one of the architects of this strategy, Henry Evans is the person best qualified to explain its goals and budget requirements."

For the next hour, Evans presented his case for rebuilding the infrastructure of the pacified areas in the Quarantine Zones. The committee members probed at a number of details, and then Chairman Collins curtly dismissed the supplicants.

"How long before we know?" Fuller asked softly as they walked through the corridor.

"At least a couple of weeks," Byrne answered. "Let's not kid ourselves, boys. This is going to be a tough sell, no matter how good the news has been. If we were asking Congress to pick up the tab for guns and bombs, we'd have a much better chance. But politicians aren't usually eager to appropriate three-point-eight billion unless it lines the pockets of somebody who'll vote for them—and at least for the present, Hispanics can't vote."

---

"Tight, Dad. Very tight," Sarah said, following her father into his office. "This is way nicer than your place at Bravo."

Hank smiled, his pride unmistakable. This was Sarah's first chance to attend Family Day at Langley, a once-a-year event when all classified materials were stowed and relatives could enter the facility. "Check out the view," he said pointing toward the large window.

Watching Sarah walk ahead of him, Hank was again astonished at the changes in his daughter—and how quickly they'd occurred. The spindly adolescent who had flown in for a visit a few months back was gone, replaced by someone with curves and a swaying gait. Sarah would be sixteen next month and like every father, Evans was proud—and terrified—of the changes in his daughter.

"It looks like a college," Sarah said, gazing out at the complex of white boxy buildings.

Evans stared at his daughter as she surveyed the Virginia landscape, someone he loved yet barely knew. He'd seen Sarah only a handful of times since moving east, each visit like a holiday with sightseeing, movies, shopping, but no real intimacy. "Speaking of college," he said, searching for a topic of conversation, "had any thoughts on where you want to go?"

"My soccer coach says Stanford's program is getting better."

"Yeah, I read that, too."

After an awkward silence, Sarah turned her green eyes toward her father, her expression sober. "I wish Mom could see all this, Dad," she said, gesturing to his office. "Maybe she'd understand why you worked so hard all those years and—"

"Let's not go there, hon," Hank said, looking away, his eyes distant.

Sensing her father's distress, Sarah smiled. "So what else can I see? Some kind of secret weapon or something?"

Evans's face brightened. "We've got secret weapons coming out of the woodwork around here. They're no big deal," he said, winking. "How about we head to the cafeteria instead? They've got some great muffins—low fat, too."

"You *are* losing weight, Dad," Sarah said, patting his stomach affectionately as they walked toward the door.

On their way down the hall, Evans saw Mike Fuller approaching.

"Sorry to interrupt your Family Day, Hank," Fuller said, nodding to Sarah. "I thought you should see this." He handed Evans a memo.

Evans skimmed the document and said, "Mike, this is my daughter, Sarah. Would you mind taking her down to the cafeteria for some muffins?"

Sarah's eyes widened. "Dad, what's the matter?"

"Something has come up, hon. Go have a bite. I'll join you in a few minutes," he said over his shoulder, walking back to his office.

Sarah lowered her head. "Don't forget me again, Dad," she said softly as he retreated down the hallway.

Evans never heard her.

Behind his desk, Hank dialed up Helen Byrne and said, "I can't believe this. How could the committee turn us down?"

"The word I'm getting from Collins is he's not ready to raise taxes to make life easier for our enemies."

Evans slammed his fist against the desktop. "Goddammit, Helen! They *know* a military solution is going to cost us more in the long run!"

"Yeah, but Collins says the opposition will beat him bloody if his committee approves the money."

"So what the hell are we going to do? Rebuilding the zones is one of the cornerstones of our strategy."

"Well, there's still a way we can get the money. It's not the prettiest pony in the parade, but it'll get us where we need to go."

"I don't like the sound of this, Helen. What have you got in mind?"

"There's a big construction company in Collins's district

that's been a key contributor to his reelection campaigns. Now, let's suppose that construction firm got a no-bid contract for rebuilding roads and bridges in the zones. Under those circumstances, I think Collins just might be inclined to use his influence as committee chairman to round up some bipartisan support."

"But that takes away jobs from the Hispanics. We were counting on them to rebuild their own communities as part of the pacification process."

"You saying you can't tame this horse unless it eats nothing but oats?"

"Spare me the homespun analogies, will you, Helen? You know this isn't the way we planned the pacification. How in the hell are we supposed to make life normal again without jobs? And besides, the rebels won't dare attack Hispanic construction workers without alienating their communities. Once you bring in outside workers, it's going to be open season on anybody in a hard hat."

"Well now, that's their problem, isn't it? Those boys will be well paid."

"I don't know. This doesn't feel right."

"Look, Hank. This is our best chance to get the money. I'm going to make Collins the offer...unless you can convince me it won't work."

Evans rubbed his chin. "It'll work," he said reluctantly. "Not very damn well, but it'll work."

"Cheer up, Hank. They say politics is like making sausage. It's not a pretty sight—but in this town everybody likes a bit of pork."

# THE NIXON ERA II:
## *MONTH 7, DAY 3*

The thick drone of voices washed over Angel as he rounded the corner into the open-air market. Since Nixon's election seven months ago, this once-bustling commercial section of Whittier Boulevard had made a comeback. The wide street, no longer used by vehicles, was now lined with stands selling vegetables, fruit, eggs, and live chickens, all grown inside the walls. Shoppers jammed the pavement, haggling vigorously as vendors in bike carts noisily hawked tamales, baked goods, and roasted peanuts.

Near the corner of Whittier and Hendricks, Angel noticed that the barrio's only shoe repair shop had reopened. Next door, a resurrected hardware store offered refurbished tools, garden implements, and cooking utensils. A bodega on the same block displayed recycled containers of peanut oil and peanut butter alongside sacks of cornmeal and strings of dried chilies. Angel knew that in the back, out of sight of the Baldie patrols, the owner kept the black-market goods: spices, canned meat, soap, cigarettes, liquor, and other contraband items obtained from the guards surrounding the walls.

Angel crossed the street, stepping around a knot of teens

pitching pennies on the sidewalk. The boys, absorbed in their
boisterous game, did not look up as the mero passed. This minor
renaissance of prosperity had brought a new attitude. After years
of hardship and scarcity, most people seemed in better spirits.

Not Angel.

He was disgusted to find his people were losing the fire in
their bellies, bought off by a few crumbs of comfort. Even
the teens who had once flocked to El Frente now seemed con-
tent to gamble, carouse, and get high on the resurgent supply
of booze and drugs. Worse yet, most of the Verdugos had
drifted back into pimping and protection, leaving him with
only a few vatos he could count on to carry on the struggle. If
this slide continued, Angel knew the people of the barrios
would be back where they started, groveling before the gabachos once again. The deaths, the blood, the pain . . . it would
all have been for nothing.

The move El Frente was planning, however, could turn
that around.

For sure, it would be more dangerous than anything
they'd tried before. But they needed something bold, something that would put fear in the hearts of the gabachos.
Their sporadic attacks had become so common, they no longer made headlines. This new tactic would put them back
on the front page again. The government would be forced to
crack down on the zones . . . and that would put an end to
the soft life that was leading his people back into the yoke.

Rosa placed the steaming cup on the table before Mano and
stepped back, gauging his reaction.

Mano raised the cup to his nose, cautiously sniffing the
inky brew.

"Go ahead. Taste it," Rosa insisted.

Mano took a tentative sip. "Hmmm. Not bad . . ." He took a

deeper drink and smiled. "It's not exactly coffee, but I like it. Thank you, querida."

Rosa beamed with pride. "It's made with chicory from our garden. I learned about it from Celia. Some people have been using it instead of coffee for years."

"It'll be nice to have a hot drink in the mornings again," Mano said, looking at his watch. "It's time for me to call Ramon." He gulped down his drink and rose from the table.

"Say good-bye to Papi, Carlos," Rosa said to their seventeen-month-old.

Perched in a makeshift high chair, Carlos gurgled and waved, flashing his father a gap-toothed grin. Mano kissed the boy and walked outside. Although the satellite phone was secure, Mano still avoided exposing his family to any details of his clandestine work.

Two blocks from home, he crossed an empty parking lot and settled on a low concrete wall where he could keep an eye on anyone approaching. For the last seven months, his calls to Ramon had become dreary sessions with little good news to report. The slow progress toward self-sufficiency in the barrios was matched by the glacial pace toward diplomatic recognition in Geneva.

Mano speed-dialed his mentor and found Ramon unexpectedly agitated. "El Frente is planning a national operation, Mano. Octavio wouldn't give me any details, but he said the government is going to come swarming into the barrios again."

"When?"

"Octavio wouldn't say. I'd guess very soon."

"That's strange. I haven't seen any clues the LLF has anything in the works."

"I'd get ready anyway, amigo. We can't take any chances."

"Will you be able to warn the other zones in time?"

"We're going to try. We've got a blitz planned for Maggie's courier network."

"Good. I'll see what we can do to protect our assets here."

"Is there any way you can camouflage the cisterns you're building?"

"Not really. But we can always build new holding tanks if the government discovers them. I'm more worried about the feeder pumps. We'll need to disconnect the pumps and bury them somewhere else. They're black market and impossible to duplicate."

"How far do you think this is going to set us back?"

"It's hard to say, Ramon. Quite frankly, our projects are way behind schedule anyway. Most people these days would rather try to get what they need through the black market than work free for the common good."

"Look, Mano. I know pumping cash into the zones has its downside. But we're going to have to live with that until we're completely ready. The feds still trying to recruit snitches?"

"You're changing the subject."

"Is there any point in arguing about this again?"

Mano sighed. "No. But it eats at me that so few people want to work at being self-sufficient anymore."

"We need to be patient, Mano. When the time comes, people will get back on the bandwagon. At least they haven't started ratting us out to the government, right?"

"No—and they've upped the bounty to ten grand. Fortunately, nobody believes they'll live to collect it thanks to the sheriff of El Paso."

"Yeah, the El Paso boys have run out of appeals. They've got three weeks left. I hate to say this, but if those men have to die, I hope they broadcast it on prime time."

Mano shook his head. "What kind of war is this when we gain when our own people die?"

"It's no different from any other war, mi hermano," Ramon said softly. "No different at all."

# THE NIXON ERA II:
## *MONTH 8, DAY 1*

**J**ogging past the park's baseball diamonds, Sarah Evans checked her running watch. She'd logged four kilometers so far—not bad for a warm-up. But she'd need to push herself much harder to make Santa Clarita's high school soccer team. Her summer league coach had warned the eighty-minute varsity games were one of the hardest adjustments for a player moving up in class. So today, she planned a real test of her stamina: the hill trail south of the park.

The sound of her footfalls dulled as Sarah veered from the park's paved running track onto the dirt trail that lead to the tree-covered hills about two hundred meters away. She checked her running watch again and smiled. The high-tech device had been a sixteenth-birthday gift from her dad.

*Will Dad come see me play this year?* she wondered, striding over the uneven trail. He'd always encouraged her passion for sports. Too bad her mother didn't.

Sarah knew she was a disappointment to her mother. A high school cheerleader and prom queen hopeful who was still always impeccably groomed, Monica Evans blamed Sarah's sports obsession for her daughter's apparent indifference to her appearance—and for her lack of friends. Sarah even suspected her mother thought she was gay. In reality, she was hit on by guys regularly. *Mom is so clueless*, she told herself, laughing softly.

About fifty meters from the entrance to the tunnel-like trail into the hills, she tightened the belt on her fanny pack, glad she'd left her wallet and vu-phone in her locker. Carrying the extra weight would be a chore today. The weight of her locker key would be enough baggage. She then glanced west. The sun was sliding closer to the horizon and the air was getting cooler, making the sweat on her neck tingle. Her mother had warned her not to run alone—especially late in the day. But when else could she run? After-school soccer practice lasted until five. Besides, her mom never got home from work before seven. She'd never know.

Crouching in the dense fern pines on a rock ledge above the jogging trail, Angel watched the lone runner approaching. He tapped Pedro on the shoulder, who sat dozing against a tree trunk, and pointed to the girl in a blue sweat suit running toward them. After two fruitless days hiding in the heavy underbrush, this might be the moment they'd been waiting for.

Pedro had scouted a number of sites for their operation, and this jogging trail seemed the most promising. Located on the south edge of Santa Clarita, it was only twenty-three miles from Quarantine Zone B. More importantly, the location gave them a path back to the zone with dense cover most of the way—something essential to their mission: El Frente had ordered Angel to capture a hostage.

He and Pedro weren't stalking a particular person. They simply wanted to capture an Anglo in the easiest way possible—preferably a young female. That would generate the most publicity. But finding a target had been far from easy. For the last forty-eight hours, they'd watched in frustration as dozens of joggers passed by. None had been alone and isolated. With their small cache of food and water nearly gone and El Frente's deadline looming, Angel had begun to doubt his choice of sites. Now their luck finally seemed to be changing.

From his hidden perch, Angel scanned the park. No one except the slender blond jogger was in sight. The situation was perfect. Once she entered the wooded trail, the girl would be in their trap.

The gang leader could hear her footsteps now. She would reach their hiding place in seconds. Angel pulled the ski mask over his face and signaled for Pedro to do the same. After two days of waiting, they were about to bag their hostage.

———

The trail began to rise steeply as Sarah entered the woods, the stress of the sudden incline burning her calves. Just ahead, the tree-lined trail wound through an outcropping of rock, cutting a narrow passageway through the hill's beige stone. The footing grew uneven as she entered the gap and she lowered her gaze, stepping carefully over the rocky ground. From the borders of her sight, she spotted movement ahead. Looking up, she froze in terror.

A man in a black mask stood in her path.

She stared at him in shock for an instant—tall, slim, dressed in black—then turned to run away.

Before she'd taken a step, another masked man emerged from the shrubs. This one, shorter than she was, held a gun leveled at her face. "You talk. You die," he whispered coldly.

Her body began to tremble and she closed her eyes. *Oh, my God. Oh, my God. Please don't let this be real.* She was too terrified to resist as the men removed her fanny pack, then covered her mouth with tape, slipped a dark cloth over her head, and bound her hands behind her.

Grabbing the shoulder of her sweat suit, the one with the gun said, "You come, *now*," and began pulling her forward. Trying to keep up, she tripped, almost falling before someone steadied her. "Are you okay?" a different voice said. She nodded, feeling tears flowing down her cheeks.

Stumbling sightless over rough terrain at the mercy of strangers, she quickly lost track of time, her world reduced to a black void where her only thoughts were surviving the next moment.

After what may have been hours, the shock began to wear off, replaced by an overpowering thirst. She'd been dehydrated by the running before her capture and on the move for some time now; her throat felt hot and dry, making it hard to swallow. With her mouth taped, however, she had no way to ask for a drink. The thirst seemed to clear her mind, though. For the first time since her capture, she began to assess what had happened.

Her captors were Panchos, she was sure of that. Besides a thick accent, the one with the gun had dark brown eyes surrounded by olive skin behind the mask—the last thing she'd seen and a sight she wouldn't quickly forget. He was the one holding her and seemed to be the leader.

As they continued at a near run, the exertion took its toll. Forced to breathe only through her nose, her body was starving for oxygen, making her legs rubbery. *They're going to run me to death*, she thought, starting to cry again.

A short while later, they stopped. "Let's give her a drink," she heard the other one say.

"No," the leader answered harshly, pushing her forward. "No hay tiempo."

"She looks pretty shaky. If she passes out, we'll have to carry her."

"Bien," the leader said, pushing her toward the ground. "You sit now."

Off her feet for the first time in hours, Sarah felt her legs tremble then quickly begin to ache. They lifted the cloth covering her face just enough to uncover her mouth. "I'm sorry. This is going to hurt," the nice one said softly before removing the tape.

She ignored her stinging cheeks and said, "You guys don't have to—"

"No talk," the leader growled, pressing what she knew was a gun against her ribs.

"Here. Take a drink," the nicer one said, bringing a container to her parched lips.

As the tepid water filled her mouth, the pleasure was intense, like feeling life flow back into her body. She tilted her head back, gulping greedily.

"Not too much. You'll make yourself sick," he said, gently wiping away the water spilling over her chin. "Look, just relax. If you do what we say, no one is going to hurt you, okay?"

Afraid to speak, she nodded in thanks—then felt her tears start again as her captor replaced the tape over her mouth and helped her stand.

They kept moving, her legs now aching with every step. She had no idea for how long. The leader spoke only to give orders, usually in Spanish. The other talked more often, reassuring her during their sporadic stops for water.

The excruciating pace of their journey ended suddenly when they entered a dank, echoing place—some kind of tunnel, she guessed. The leader pressed something very sharp against her throat. "You walk very soft or you die. Comprendes?" he whispered menacingly.

As the Panchos led her silently through the tunnel, Sarah suddenly realized what this meant. They were taking her inside one of the Quarantine Zones. A wave of panic engulfed her, a terror like someone was dragging her under murky water. *No one will find me once I'm in there.*

She wanted to run while she still had the chance. The point of the blade against her throat squelched the urge. *How far will I get blind and bound?* a voice in her head asked. Despair replacing panic, she kept moving quietly.

After they'd traveled silently through the tunnel for a while, the tension finally ended. "I'm going to untie your hands," the nice one said. "We're going to climb a ladder." After reaching the top, the feel of a breeze told Sarah she was back aboveground.

As they retied her hands and led her away, Sarah could feel pavement under her running shoes for the first time since they'd taken her. A short while later, the squeak of a door hinge told her they were entering a building.

"Sit here," the nice one said guiding her to a chair.

One of the Panchos then removed Sarah's blindfold. Unaccustomed to the light, she squinted in pain at the harsh glare of the gas lantern hanging in the windowless room.

Her eyes adjusting to the brightness, she saw the blurry shapes of her captors, two pale ghosts hovering in the empty room. She did not want to look at their faces. Being able to identify them might be a death sentence. Lowering her eyes to the floor, she felt tears flowing again and was surprised she had any left.

*Keep it together,* she told herself. *They probably aren't going to hurt you—at least not yet.* These Panchos were after something from her dad. She needed to stay calm and figure out what they wanted.

"I'm going to take off the tape," the nice one said.

Sarah nodded and closed her eyes as the man carefully removed her gag. Despite his efforts to be gentle, the pain was searing. Her hands still bound behind her, she rubbed her cheek against her shoulder, trying to soothe her burning skin.

"Your cheeks are a little red, but you'll be okay," he told her, lifting her chin.

Sarah realized it was pointless to avert her gaze any longer. Sooner or later, she would have to look at them. Taking a deep breath, she slowly opened her eyes.

To her relief, the men still wore masks. Able to study them for the first time, she noticed the nice one was considerably taller than the muscular leader. Neither man held a weapon, a sign they did not consider her much of a threat.

"I want to talk to my dad," she said, trying to keep the fear out of her voice. "Whatever you want, he'll give it to you."

"We don't want money. We want the government to release some of our people. The ones in El Paso."

Sarah had heard about the Panchos who'd been sentenced to death. "I don't know what my dad can do about that. He's with the CIA, not the courts."

The two men exchanged glances. The leader said something in Spanish and the other man nodded in acknowledgment and said, "Tell us about your father."

"Don't you know who he is? Isn't that why you kidnapped me?"

"Never mind. Tell us about your father."

How could these men not know who her father was? Maybe they were checking to make sure they had the right person. "My father is Henry Evans...He's the assistant director of the CIA."

Sarah saw the nicer man's eyes widen with surprise inside the mask.

The leader stepped closer, staring hard. "Where father live?"

"In Washington, D.C. Well, in Arlington, actually."

"Why you not there?"

"Don't you guys know all this already?"

The leader leaned toward her, his face menacingly close. "Why you not there?"

"My mom and dad are divorced. I live in Santa Clarita with my mom. I only spend school vacations with my dad."

"What you mother name?"

Sarah frowned in confusion. These questions did not add up. Surely they'd know this, unless... "You guys don't really know who I am, do you?"

After a moment, the nice one said, "No. We were just looking for a hostage and you were—"

"*Silencio!*" the leamder yelled, cutting the other man off. The leader studied her wordlessly, his dark brown eyes giving no clue to his thoughts. Sarah sensed her fate hanging on this moment. *What if he decides there's no way they'll get away with kidnapping the daughter of a CIA boss?*

Suddenly the leader grabbed Sarah, pushed her against the wall, and stepped away. Facing the two men, Sarah felt like a condemned prisoner before a firing squad. "Adelante," he said impassively to his subordinate, who reached into the pocket of his black fatigues.

A wave of terror washed over Sarah. *Oh, God. They're going to shoot me. I'm going to die.* She closed her eyes, her body trembling. Sarah saw her mother's face bursting into tears as she learned her daughter had been killed. The image of her father came next, a look of stunned horror in his eyes. Her knees grew weak and she began to slide downward along the wall. "You don't have to do this. Please. I'll keep quiet."

Sarah felt someone gently lifting her back to her feet.

"Open your eyes, I'm not going to hurt you," the nice one said, pointing an instant camera at Sarah.

As the camera flashed, flooding her retinas with a hot, white glow, Sarah felt an intense rush of joy and relief.

She had been spared. She was alive.

———

Angel turned off the satellite phone and smiled. His contact at El Frente had been pleased to hear about their stroke of luck. The daughter of the number two man at the CIA... surely, God was smiling on their cause.

Angel was relieved his superiors would handle the contact with the media. That would have been impossible for him. Composing the ransom note would fall to someone lucky enough to read and write English like Pedro.

He would never admit it, but Angel envied Pedro's ease with the language and customs of America. It was a valuable asset, but it came with a price.

The boy was smart and brave but, like his father, Pedro had too much pity. Several times during the capture, Pedro showed too much softness toward the girl. Every gabacho was equally guilty of oppressing their people. Man or woman, old or young, it made no difference. They were all the enemy—none of them deserved mercy. If Pedro kept this up, Angel would have to choose another successor—no matter how Isabel felt.

The task ahead of them would not be easy. The girl's father would bring some major heat down on them.

But that was exactly what the leadership of El Frente had been hoping.

# THE EL PASO EIGHT HOSTAGES

*Justice comes from the heart, not the mind.*

*Josefina Herrera*

# THE EL PASO EIGHT HOSTAGES: *DAY 1*

**W**hen the editor of the *San Antonio Sentinel* opened the worn manila envelope, she knew immediately this was the biggest story of her career. The envelope contained Polaroid photos of eight teenage girls and a ransom note from the Latino Liberation Front. The abductors promised to kill their hostages unless the El Paso Eight were released within ten days.

The kidnappers had listed the name and home city of each hostage. Last on the list was Sarah Evans of Santa Clarita, California. Typed below her name was "daughter of Henry Evans, assistant director of the CIA." A Web search by the editor quickly verified the claim.

The editor then checked police blotters in California and discovered a missing persons report filed in Santa Clarita by Monica Evans. Her sixteen-year-old daughter, Sarah, had disappeared four days earlier. Similar searches on the other names produced the same results. This was not a hoax.

Certain that the feds would confiscate the evidence, the editor ran a front-page article with the photos and the ransom note before notifying the authorities—or the girls' parents. A mother herself, the editor had qualms about her decision. But this would be the biggest scoop in the history of the *San Antonio Sentinel*.

Shortly before noon, the *Sentinel* released the story online. Minutes later, it spread like a chain reaction to newspapers, TV, and radio stations across the nation. Within twenty-four hours, news of the El Paso Eight hostages would be the top story of every news source on the globe.

————

Hank's hand was trembling as he slowly hung up the desk phone. *They have my daughter. They have Sarah.* The thought echoed through his mind, an insistent chant trying to convince him of something he did not want to believe.

He remembered the last time he'd seen Sarah, waving good-bye before boarding the plane back to her mother, smiling sadly. *My God, what have I done?* he wondered suddenly. *How could I let this happen?*

The office around him turned blurry as tears filled his eyes. Hank lowered his head onto his hands and wept, his heavy body racked by silent sobs.

Sometime later, his tears spent, a sober voice in his head said, *All right, get a grip. Pity is not going to bring Sarah back.*

Hank wiped his cheeks and sat up straight, trying to clear his thoughts.

She was alive—there was little question about that. Dead hostages had no value. The question now was . . . what could he do to get her home?

Meeting the kidnappers' demands was impossible. A U.S. court would never rescind a death sentence under these circumstances. No, they would have to track these cowards down. That was his only hope of getting back his daughter.

Thoughts of the people who'd captured Sarah now entered his mind. He'd dealt with terrorists during much of his career, but this was the first time their cold cruelty had touched his family. *They'll regret it*, he promised himself. *If they harm my daughter, so help me God, I will—*

Hank stopped himself, trying to control his rising rage.

Anger would only dull his thinking. To save his daughter, he would need to walk a tightrope—a balancing act between fierce motivation and coolheaded decisions. From years of experience, Hank knew somewhere in the resources already at his disposal was the clue that would break the case. He needed to find it—in less than ten days.

Then he remembered Hollywood Squares.

The messages between Garcia and his wife had stopped, but the e-mail connection was still working. He had an inside pipeline to the highest levels of the rebel leadership—if he was willing to break the rules. *I'm way past that now*, he reminded himself. There had to be some way to use this connection to the Panchos, although he was not yet sure how. One thing was certain. He would need to lead the investigation himself. He could not risk revealing the story behind Hollywood Squares.

Hank picked up the desk phone and speed-dialed Helen Byrne. "It's Hank," he said calmly when she was on the line.

"My God, Hank. I heard the news. You must be—"

"I'm okay, Helen," he said, cutting her off. "Listen, I want to head the investigation on the kidnappings."

"That's highly unusual, Hank. You know it's customary for close relatives to—"

"Sure. I know, I know. But I've got an inside lead that could break this case."

"What is it, Hank? Tell me. We'll use it to get your daughter back."

"I can't tell you, Helen. It would compromise my sources."

"You're not giving me much to go on here. What *can* you tell me?"

"It's totally black—very sensitive. That's all I can say."

Byrne paused for a moment. "I'm sorry, Hank. This is way too sketchy. I can't recommend you to the president based on this. I realize you're distraught but you have to understand my position."

"Well, let me put this another way, Helen," Evans said coolly. "If my source on this case ever leaks, it could damage the White House. Now, we both know that would not be good for *any* of us. However, my daughter's life is on the line and I'm willing to accept the political fallout. If you're willing to do the same, then go ahead and appoint someone else."

"Is that a threat?" Byrne asked, an edge to her voice.

"I'm just stating facts, Helen."

"I've never known you to play hardball like this, Hank. You may be out of your league."

"You go ask Mr. Nixon if he wants to take the chance." Hank held his breath, hoping the bluff would work.

The line was silent for a moment. "That won't be necessary," Byrne said tersely. "I'll recommend you."

---

Mano turned off the shortwave radio when the BBC report was over. His noontime meal of eggs and cornmeal cakes sat on the table before him, cold and uneaten.

"I'm ashamed of our people, Rosa," he said, staring at the radio. "Ramon warned me El Frente had something planned. But this..." Mano shook his head in disgust. "They're behaving like animals, preying on the most defenseless." That his son was one of the predators was something Mano would not say aloud. Pedro had become a taboo subject in their home.

Following countless arguments about their son over the last eight months, Mano and Rosa had gradually settled into a strained silence about him. But today's news of the hostages was too terrible for Rosa to ignore.

"Pedro never learned these things from us, mi amor," she said, laying a hand on his broad shoulders.

His eyes downcast, Mano said, "Maybe he did. My example taught him to fight."

Rosa lifted his chin, raising his gaze to meet her own. "No, Mano. Pedro may have taken the same path, but he's not following in his father's footsteps."

Mano looked away, then rose from the table. "I should call Ramon. He might have some more news." After retrieving the satellite phone from its hiding place in the hallway ceiling, Mano headed outside.

Several blocks away, in an alley behind a shuttered strip mall, Mano connected with his mentor in Geneva. "El Frente's hit a new low, Ramon," he said into the silver phone.

"It's barbaric—I agree," Ramon replied. "I've already issued a statement to the media denying the HRNA is involved. How many people will believe it…that, I'm not so sure about."

"Well, at least we're ready if there's a crackdown by the Baldies. Any ideas on what the government will do? El Frente's only given them ten days."

"I know how Octavio thinks. He wants to force Nixon's hand and goad him into something heavy-handed. This isn't about releasing El Frente's prisoners in El Paso."

"Have you talked to Perez?"

"No, I'll meet up with him later at the hall. But I have something important to tell you, some good news for a change…We've finally got a Web link to all the other zones in place."

"Are you sure it's secure?"

"Yes, we've tested it and it's secure."

226    **Raul Ramos y Sanchez**

"I'm sorry, Ramon. I don't completely trust all this cyber stuff," he said, recalling his near capture.

"Our new network is really ingenious," Ramon said, a touch of pride in his voice. "Maggie has connections with a special effects house that constantly transmits huge compressed animation files around the world. She says we can piggyback our messages inside their encrypted system. We're already linked by satellite phone with a lot of the zones. Once our couriers get the connection codes into the rest, our network will be back in business."

"How long before it's all in place?"

"Hard to say for sure, but I think most of the zones will be linked within a week."

Mano rubbed his chin, considering the possibilities. "That's good, Ramon. There's a chance the linkup may help us get the hostages back home alive. I'm sure the girls are being held inside the zones."

"Mano, this hostage crisis could not have come at a worse time. We're on the verge of some huge progress on the diplomatic front. Once all the zones are linked in real time, we'll be ready to coordinate our political and military moves again. The sooner other countries see us acting as a nation, the sooner we'll get more aid—and U.N. recognition. But if this hostage situation ends with eight dead girls..."

"...we look like monsters," Mano said, finishing his sentence.

---

Ramon had been waiting almost an hour near the entrance to the Hall of Steps when Octavio appeared. Gesturing for Perez to follow, he wordlessly led his fellow delegate inside a small conference room. "How are these kidnappings going to help us?" Ramon asked after closing the door behind him.

Octavio grinned, clearly delighted. "We're back on the

front pages, aren't we?" he said, dropping into a chair and putting his feet on the conference table.

Still standing, Ramon said, "Yes, and most of the world now thinks we're ruthless zealots."

"What's wrong with that? You think we can sweet-talk the gabachos into giving us our liberty? Don't be a fool, Ramon. The only thing that works is fear."

"Octavio, this plan is not just stupid...it's wrong. I will not be a party to the deaths of innocent children."

"Well, then," Perez said through gritted teeth. "Maybe it's time you stepped aside."

"No, Octavio. I'm not going to step aside. I'll fight you."

Perez stood up suddenly, sending the chair crashing behind him. "You should think that over carefully, old man," he said icily, stepping forward menacingly.

"I've gone along with you long enough," Ramon said, standing his ground. "You're a dangerous, barbaric fool and I won't let you do this."

Octavio's eyes narrowed with rage. "It's only out of respect for what you've done for our people in the past that you're still alive." He leaned very close, his bulk dwarfing Ramon. "But I'm warning you...unless you're ready to become a martyr, don't try to interfere," he said before walking out, slamming the door behind him.

# THE EL PASO EIGHT HOSTAGES: *DAY 2*

*Drip-drop. Drip-drop. Drip-drop.*

The rhythmic beat of water falling somewhere in the darkness was Sarah's last link to reality. The steady sound gave her a focus, something to distract her from the terror of being alone in total blackness. After her last meal, she'd been blindfolded by the leader and moved to this dark place that could only be part of a sewer. The dank, fetid smell had convinced her of that.

Everything she'd suffered before in her captivity now seemed easy in comparison. Handcuffed by her left wrist to a vertical pipe, she could move only a single step in any direction. On the filthy floor around her were a mattress, a bottle of water, and a wretched-smelling pot for her bodily functions. By tossing pebbles into the darkness and listening, Sarah had determined she was at the dead end of a long tunnel. In the beginning, she'd tried calling out—softly at first, then gradually louder. Her voice had echoed back unanswered.

Alone in a black void, her life before she'd been captured now seemed like a dream, a time and place that had never really existed. Desperate to make her past seem real, she tried to recall the contents of her bedroom...pictures from her last visit with her dad...her collection of sports trophies... schoolbooks from—

A distant scuffling brought the terror flooding back. "Hello?" she called out into the darkness, her voice quivering. "Is somebody there?"

"It's okay, Sarah. Don't be afraid."

At the sound of the nice one's voice, Sarah's fear began to ebb. She knew it was strange to feel safe around one of the men who'd captured her but the nice one's small gestures of kindness were the only comfort she could cling to in this nightmare. All the same, she did not want to show any of her captors how afraid she really was. "I haven't seen you in a while," she said, trying to sound composed as the man walked closer, invisible behind the beam of his flashlight. "Actually, I haven't seen you at all, I guess."

"I didn't know you'd been moved. I brought you some stuff," he said, shining the flashlight onto the mattress. A blanket and a scuffed plastic flashlight appeared inside the cone of light. "It can get cold in here and the dark can drive you crazy sometimes."

"Thanks," she answered. "How do you know what it's like down here?" she asked glancing sidelong at his masked face, hoping to learn where they were holding her.

"You shouldn't ask any questions, Sarah. The less you know, the better it is for everybody," he said gently. "The flashlight's for emergencies. Don't use it unless you have to. We don't have a lot of batteries." He added, "Oh, yeah. Keep the blanket and the flashlight under the mattress, okay? You're not supposed to have them."

"Will I get in trouble?" she asked, suddenly anxious.

"No—I will."

"You're very nice," she said, wondering if his kindness might help her escape.

"I've got to go," he said, standing up. "One final thing. Don't say anything about me being here."

"Why not?"

"Remember, Sarah. You shouldn't ask questions. I'll check back on you when I can," he said before leaving.

Alone in the darkness again, Sarah turned on the flashlight and moved the beam around the room for a moment, studying her surroundings. She then turned it off to conserve the batteries. To her surprise, she felt a strange euphoria.

Her terror of the dark had vanished.

---

Hank watched Bill Perkins walk closer, moving through the early-evening shadows on the tree-lined sidewalk, hands stuffed into his jacket pockets against the chill October breeze.

"You want to come up to my apartment for some coffee or something?" Perkins asked, nodding toward the high-rise behind him. "It's cold out here."

"I'd rather talk where I'm sure we're alone," Evans said, starting down the deserted sidewalk and flicking his head for Perkins to follow.

"You think my apartment's bugged?" Perkins asked, his voice rising in alarm as he scrambled to catch up.

"Why take any chances?"

Perkins stopped. "This is about Hollywood Squares, isn't it?" he asked, the wind tangling his long hair in his glasses. "I'm not sure I want anything more to do with that, Hank."

"Suit yourself," Hank said over his shoulder. He continued walking. "I'm sure the rapists are a lot gentler in minimum-security prisons."

"Wait, Hank! Wait!" he called out, jogging to catch up. "You said you'd protect me, man—that you'd tell them I was only following orders."

Hank stopped and fixed his eyes on Perkins. "That was before the Panchos grabbed my daughter, Bill. Things are different now."

Perkins blinked rapidly behind his heavy glasses. "You've changed, Hank."

"No, I haven't changed. This whole fucking business has changed. Used to be, we didn't go after each other's families," Hank said, his voice suddenly hoarse with emotion. "Not that we were gentlemen back in the Cold War, but goddammit, Bill. This is just...just..." He lowered his head, pressing his hand against his mouth, unable to say more.

Perkins hesitantly put his hand on Evans's shoulder. "I'm sorry, Hank. I'm sure it's tough."

Evans took several deep breaths, regaining his composure. "Yeah, well...," he said, exhaling slowly. "I need your help, Bill."

"Sure. I'll do whatever I can."

"Thanks." He began walking again, Perkins alongside. "I need you to check the Hollywood Squares connection—every hour. If there are any messages at all on that connection, even if it's spam, I want you to contact me right away. I've thought a lot about this. They could be hiding messages in phishing scams for all we know."

"I'll look at everything, Hank. But I don't need to check it every hour. I can set an auto alert."

"No! Those alerts go through the main server, and they can be traced."

"All right. Chill, dude. I'll check the connection manually," Perkins said. "But do you really think Garcia and his bunch are behind the abductions? It doesn't seem like their kind of play."

"Yeah, I've thought about that—and I agree. The HRNA has always hit military and infrastructure targets in the past. Kidnapping teenage girls is not really their MO," he said, then added, "and Garcia has sure as hell denied he supports the Latino Liberation Front after every one of their attacks."

"Most people think that's bullshit."

"I'm not so sure."

"So why are we doing this?"

Hank breathed deeply. "It's a long shot, Bill, but I'm hoping we can find a clue to the people behind this. I have a hunch Garcia knows who they are."

"Well, if Garcia knows who they are, and he's against what they do, why doesn't he turn them in?"

"Would you rat out a fellow American to the Panchos for doing the same thing?"

Perkins was silent for a moment. "I suppose not," he said finally.

"Look, Bill, we've only got nine days. We need to work this. It might be our only chance."

"Don't worry, Hank. If Ramon Garcia gets so much as a Viagra ad, you'll know about it."

"I owe you," Hank said, patting Perkins's arm. "Now get back to your apartment. This is no kind of weather for an El Segundo beach nerd."

As Hank watched his aide disappear into the shadows, a pang of guilt shot through him. Yes, he was doing all he could to save his daughter—but he was also still protecting his career. The time might come when he would have to choose between the two.

# THE EL PASO EIGHT HOSTAGES: *DAY 3*

**F**uller topped off his cup from the self-serve coffeepot at the Langley Mart and glanced at the *Time/WorldReport* on the newsstand. Although long obsolete as a breaking news source, the last of the printed weeklies was still a good bellwether of political trends. This issue's cover featured the hostage photo of Sarah Evans under a stark headline:

Daughter of Number Two at CIA Abducted. Is Anyone Safe?

After paying for his coffee, Fuller slid into his leased sedan, deep in thought. Even before Hank had asked him to join the investigation team, he'd worried that political grandstanding over the case would hurt the government's chances of finding the hostages. Three days into the investigation, the political battle lines had formed.

Nixon's enemies had pounced on the hostage incident, eager to bash the president for being soft on the insurgents. Rushing to the president's defense, moderates noted this was an isolated event. They wanted the president to announce a stay of execution for the El Paso Eight, buying time for a negotiated settlement—and possibly of catching the abductors. Hard-liners insisted that negotiating with terrorists was an invitation to more terror.

Fuller had been only mildly surprised when Vice President Melvin Bates publicly broke ranks with the White House. "Showing tolerance to terrorists is like showing fear to a bully. It only eggs them on," Bates had told reporters. Fuller glumly realized Bates's attempt to appease his hard-line base had weakened the president's position. Without the vice president's support on the right, any bargaining would make Nixon look weak.

Even Nixon's twenty-five-thousand-dollar reward for information on the abductors had been blunted by his vice president. "This is not the time to give quarter to terrorists," Bates had said publicly when the White House had requested a temporary repeal of the needle law so informants would come forward. The emergency repeal bill had never made it out of congressional committee.

With eight missing girls and a raging political debate inside the Beltway, the Hispanic insurgency had moved to the front burner of the national media again. What's more, it was becoming personal for Fuller. Much of the progress they'd made in pacifying the zones was now at stake—along with the fate of a friend's daughter.

Turning onto the wooded drive that led to CIA headquarters, Fuller had a disturbing thought. *Would any of this be happening if I had taken down Suarez when I had the chance?*

───────

Pedro put on his mask, then placed his backpack on the floor of the storm sewer and removed the board camouflaged with litter that concealed the entrance to the tunnels. By the dim glow of his penlight, he made his way through the labyrinth until he reached the alcove that held their hostage.

Crouched against the wall, Sarah smiled weakly under the penlight's beam. "Hi," she said, trying to sound upbeat but not quite succeeding. "Welcome to the dungeon."

The girl did not look healthy, her blond hair matted, her eyes red and sunken. All the same, Pedro had to admit she'd shown courage during most of her ordeal, something he had not expected. The last three days had been the most time he'd ever spent around one of *them*. Even before the Quarantine Zones, everyone in his world had been Latinos—except for a few teachers and merchants. Most of what he knew about Anglos had come from movies and television. So Sarah intrigued him—although he knew his interest was not a good idea. Then again, she was also very attractive, someone whose delicate features, fair hair, and green eyes he found exotic and seductive—even in her weakened condition.

Putting aside these thoughts, Pedro removed the food and water from his backpack. "It's tortillas again. Sorry I couldn't bring you anything different. We don't have a lot of other stuff."

Sarah reached for the bottle and took a long drink. "It's okay. I'm not really hungry."

"You need to eat."

"Now you sound like my mother."

"No, it's not like that at all. When you waste food in your world, there's always more." Pedro handed her the two tortillas wrapped in corn husks. "Here, somebody's going hungry so you can have these."

"If you let me go, someone else can have the food."

"Can't do that. So you might as well eat it."

Sarah slowly unwrapped a tortilla. "Is that why you're a terrorist...because you don't have enough to eat?" she asked, taking a small bite.

"A terrorist?" Pedro stared silently for a moment. Angel wouldn't like him talking to her about this, but she needed to know the truth. "My brother was killed by your soldiers. He was nine. They ran over him with a tank and didn't even slow down. My sister died when she was five in a relocation camp. Is someone who fights because of that a terrorist?"

Now it was Sarah's turn to be silent. She locked eyes with Pedro and finally whispered, "I'm sorry. That must have been awful."

Pedro looked away. "It's been getting colder. I'll bring you another blanket next time. Anything else you need?"

"Can you switch hands? This one's getting really sore," she said, gesturing to her arm bound to the wall.

Pedro examined her wrist. A raw, angry rash had formed under the rusty handcuff. "I'm sorry. I don't have the key. But I'll bring you some salve and a piece of cloth to wrap around your wrist next time."

"Thanks," she said softly, then looked up at him and added, "You don't seem like the kind of guy who goes around kidnapping people. You're way too nice for that."

Sarah's words of praise pleased Pedro—but they also stung him. Looking into her sea-colored eyes, he was once again ashamed of El Frente's attacks on civilians. Making Sarah more comfortable helped him feel better, but there were limits to what he could do. "Look, I've got to go," he said, rising to his feet.

"Wait," she said, lightly brushing his hand. "I don't even know what to call you."

His skin tingling under her fingers, Pedro weighed her question for a moment. "Why don't you pick a name?" he finally said.

"I've never named anyone before. Let me think," she said, tapping her lips. "I'll call you Barry. That's what I called my first goldfish."

Pedro laughed softly. "I don't think I'd like spending all day in a jar."

"Me either," she replied and began to cry.

───

Evans and Fuller rose from their chairs when Helen Byrne entered the high-security conference room.

"Please sit down, boys," Byrne said, taking a seat at the head of the table. "I called you here because the White House is very concerned about the progress of the hostage investigation."

Evans was not surprised. With only seven days left until the LLF deadline, the Domestic Criminal Division of the CIA, once known as the FBI, was using every forensic tool in its arsenal on the high-profile case—and had yet to make a significant breakthrough.

Evans cleared his throat. "We got the final lab results on the evidence, but they're not very promising. The ransom note and the photos were handled by too many people at the newspaper for any usable prints or DNA traces. All we could gather from the emulsion batches on the Polaroids was that they were all produced this year. And the toner signature on the paper shows it was a Canon printer sold in North America. As you already know, the letter was mailed from Vancouver. The Canadians haven't been very cooperative. So we haven't been able to track it back any farther than that."

"Doesn't seem like we're dealing with a bunch of Einsteins here," Byrne said, arching an eyebrow in disdain. "Snail mail...Polaroids...that's caveman stuff. It's been a while since terrorists have used anything but the Web to get the word out."

"I don't think the Latino Liberation Front is quite as well funded as some of the Islamic groups we've faced," Evans explained. "But these bastards still seem pretty shrewd."

Byrne pursed her lips, seemingly unconvinced. "Have we started field investigations in the zones nearest to the abductions?"

"We have. However, this isn't your typical case, Helen. An ordinary investigation relies on a documented society. We track down suspects through a home address, place of employment, rap sheet, prison record—anything we can use to identify and pin down the perp. The problem is, official records no longer exist in the zones. People, homes, busi-nesses, schools—they've all been undocumented since the walls went up. And there's no local law enforcement."

"Sounds like a damn messy haystack to find our needle in."

"It gets worse. Very few people are giving our investigators any help. Law enforcement depends on law-abiding citizens."

"So, bottom line, we haven't turned up a damn thing?"

"For the moment, that's true. But—"

"That's what I was afraid of," Byrne said, pressing her palms together. "Hank, I'm going to advise the president that he order house-to-house sweeps by the Army in the suspected zones. It's pretty clear that police methods aren't going to work in this case."

Fuller looked at Evans, silently asking for permission to answer. Evans nodded his approval.

"Ma'am, I don't think the kidnappings have universal support inside the zones," Fuller explained. "But if we go barging in with military sweeps, they'll close ranks. The LLF has planned this move well. They chose a deadline that might seem reasonable to the media, but they knew all along we don't have enough troops to locate the hostages in time. There are over six hundred square kilometers of walled-in zones across the country. Searching house-to-house is useless. This is really a trap. They *want* us to reinvade the zones."

"Why would the Panchos try to bull-rag us?"

"The LLF is desperate, ma'am. Our pacification efforts are working and they want to provoke their people against us again. That's why they're egging us on to strike back."

Byrne shook her head, unconvinced. "If we can't go in after the hostages, what in the hell *are* we supposed to do?"

"We need time to find allies in the zones, people who are outraged by the kidnappings," Fuller said. "It could be our key to building a network of collaborators."

Evans gestured toward the captain. "Fuller's working on some angles to divide the Hispanics along racial and national lines, Helen. We need the president to buy us more time. He needs to order a stay of execution."

Byrne drummed the tabletop. "I've got a pretty good idea

how Nixon's feeling, boys—and a stay of execution's not exactly going to warm his cockles." She paused, taking a deep breath. "I'll go to bat for you and recommend a stay...but I'm not going to back down on the military sweeps."

"Helen, please..."

Byrne rose from the table. "I'm sorry, Hank. The president's got to look like he's doing more than wringing his hands and hoping. We've got to punch every button we have or the press will eat him alive."

Hank's eyes flashed as a surge of rage rose like hot steam in his chest—his daughter's life was an afterthought to these people. Then an inner voice said, *Steady. Steady. They'll take you off the case if you overreact.* He exhaled slowly. "Look, Helen," he said, trying to sound calm. "I hope you'll remind the president that these recommendations come from a man whose child's life is at stake."

Byrne listened impassively then turned to Fuller. "Can we have the room, Captain?"

"Yes, ma'am," Fuller said before leaving the conference room.

Once the door closed behind the captain, Byrne said, "I'm a parent, too, Hank. I understand how you feel. I'm sure that's why you tried to strong-arm me for this job—to save your daughter. Hell, in your shoes, I'd probably do the same thing. But giving you the lead on this case was against my better judgment. So let me set you straight. I don't believe anything you may have on the president will play any worse in the press right now than if he does nothing about these hostages." Byrne leaned toward him, resting her hands on the table. "So I suggest you get with the program, or I'll get someone else. Do we understand each other?"

Evans's shoulders slumped. Byrne had upped the bet and called his bluff.

Hank nodded slowly, knowing his best chance to save Sarah now rested with Hollywood Squares.

# THE EL PASO EIGHT HOSTAGES:
## *DAY 4*

Eyes gleaming with satisfaction, Angel watched the
Baldie formation slowly work its way down Fairmount
Street—a loud, ponderous beast announcing its approach
with the roar of armored vehicles and orders shouted through
bullhorns. The gabachos were reacting exactly as El Frente
had planned: The Army had launched house-to-house
sweeps.

Peering through the broken window of an empty paint
store, sheltered from the view of the troops, Angel could see
the soldiers rousting people into the street and methodically
searching every building. Deep in hostile territory, the troops
were clearly tense and showed little patience with complaints
from the people they were herding out of their homes and
businesses. Resist too loud and you'd be bloodied. Resist with
violence and you'd be shot. Even the docile paid a price. As the
soldiers hurriedly searched each building, they left behind a
wake of damaged merchandise and ruined personal property.
Mixed among the soldiers, a handful of embedded journalists
in military fatigues filmed the proceedings for a U.S. public
where many were eager to see those in the zones being

punished. What the public did not realize was the searches were leaving fewer troops to defend the perimeter of the zones and making it easier for the rebels to move supplies and messages in and out.

At the fringes of the slow-moving troops, knots of angry civilians watched, grudgingly giving way. The hatred in their eyes pleased Angel. They'd stop acting like sheep now.

Although the soldiers were drawing closer, Angel felt no fear about their hostage. The Baldies always fixated on searching above the ground. The gabacha was safely concealed below it. Still, he'd keep a careful eye on the soldiers' progress. If they began looking in the sewer system, he'd have time to send Pedro and move their prisoner.

At the rate the sweeps were going, it wasn't likely the Baldies would cover half of Zone B before the deadline. But that would be more than enough for their purposes. By then, word of the inevitable violence of troops searching house-to-house would spread to every corner of the zone. The people inside the wall would be enraged again. And if the gabachos didn't release the El Paso Eight...well, he'd mourn his comrades, knowing they'd given their lives to breathe fire back into their struggle.

Yes, Angel assured himself, everything was going according to El Frente's plan.

———

Bill Perkins got into the Buick and shook his head. "Sorry, Hank," he said dejectedly. "Nothing in Garcia's inbox today except spam. I checked every message for attachments and even looked for hidden text in the headers. Nothing."

Evans's face tightened into a scowl. "Sonuvabitch," he muttered, starting the engine. For the last two days, Hank had insisted he and Perkins meet clandestinely after work to evaluate the progress of Hollywood Squares.

"I'm doing my best, Hank," Perkins said, hanging his head.

"It's okay, Bill," Hank said, his grimace fading. "I know it's not your fault."

Evans pulled away from the curb, easing the sedan into the evening traffic, unable to shed his despair. After two days of fruitless effort, Hollywood Squares was beginning to look like a dry well. Still, there had to be some way to penetrate the Latino Liberation Front. "What have we overlooked, Bill?" he said, turning onto one of Arlington's main drags.

Perkins scratched his head. "Damned if I know, Hank."

On the road ahead, Evans noticed the videoboard on a megachurch flashing an animated Bible passage: *Faithful are the wounds of a friend, but the kisses of an enemy are excessive.* Looking at the glowing words, Evans was struck by an idea.

"Bill, can we send a message over the Hollywood Squares connection?"

"Actually, yeah," Perkins said, looking puzzled. "But why would we want to do that?"

"I might have an idea," Hank said, squinting in concentration. "Can you access Garcia's e-mail remotely?"

"No, it's on a secure server at the office."

Evans hit the gas pedal and the Buick lurched forward, throwing Perkins back in his seat. "Hey, what are you doing, Hank?"

"We're going back to Langley," he said, hunched over the wheel, his chin jutting forward.

"Now?"

"Yeah, we can't waste any time. I've got a message to Garcia that has to go out tonight."

---

Sipping a glass of orange juice at his chalet's dining table, Ramon Garcia was clearing the spam from his laptop when he ran across an e-mail he could not ignore. There, amid the claims for longer erections and can't-miss stocks, was a message from someone named Honda Garganta—Spanish for "Deep Throat." The subject line was equally intriguing: *A friend in the U.S. government.*

After double-clicking on the e-mail, Ramon read the message, his mouth agape.

Mr. Garcia,

I know you have nothing to do with the kidnappings. Help me find the abductors and someone in U.S. government will publicly absolve the HRNA.

Honda Garganta

Ramon glanced at his Rolex. Mano's daily call was due in less than ten minutes. Too anxious to wait, he retrieved the satellite phone from its charger and called his comrade. After his confrontation with Octavio, he'd racked his brain for a way to stop Perez. If this message was legit, it might be the break he needed.

The phone in Mano's pocket vibrated silently as he neared the rotunda at the center of the cemetery. Shunned by the superstitious and invariably deserted, the burial grounds on Verona Street had recently become one of his regular spots to call Ramon. Settling into one of the concrete benches, he answered the phone.

"I just got an e-mail we should talk about," Ramon's familiar voice said from the receiver. After reading the message to Mano, he asked, "What do you make of it, mi hermano?"

"It's probably a hoax," Mano said, suddenly restless but not sure why.

"That's possible. But let's assume for a moment it's not,"

Ramon answered. "This could be a chance to help the hostages—and clear our name in the media."

Mano rose to his feet. "Look," he said, his voice tightening. "I don't think we have time to speculate about this message unless we're sure it's real."

"The message *looks* suspicious, I agree," Ramon conceded. "The e-mail address is from a generic domain and it was sent six hours ago—around nine p.m. in Washington. That's not exactly business hours. But, you know, these things actually make me think it's authentic. Anyone staging a hoax could have easily made the message appear more official. To me, this looks like someone in the government trying to open a back-door channel."

"Or it might be a trick by the CIA trying to crack your e-mail security."

"You're not thinking very clearly about this, amigo. If the CIA can reach me with an e-mail message, then they're already inside. No, this isn't a trick. I suspect it's a lone wolf— an intelligence operative who's freelancing. Even the name suggests that—Honda Garganta."

"I don't get the name."

"Honda Garganta—Deep Throat—was the code name of the CIA official who set up a secret pipeline to the press during the first Nixon's Watergate scandal." Ramon paused. "Mano, if this is someone in Washington who's trying to do the same with us—"

"What are you saying, Ramon?" he interrupted angrily. "That we turn in our own people?"

"Just because they're our own people doesn't mean we should tolerate atrocities," Ramon said, his voice growing tense. "What El Frente has done is—" He stopped, his breathing audible over the line. "Look, Mano, we don't have much time, so I'm going to be blunt," he said, his voice calm again. "We both know your son will be in danger if we expose

El Frente. All I want to do is take down Perez, not kids like Pedro who are just following orders. This is a distasteful situation, but it's also an opportunity we can't pass up, mi hermano. Until this e-mail came along, the needle law kept us from alerting the feds to El Frente without putting our own people at risk. Just tell me where they can find Angel. I'll take care of the rest. You'll have a chance to warn your son," Ramon added. "We need to stop El Frente, Mano, and I can't do it without you."

Mano lowered his head as a wave of shame washed over him. He knew Ramon was right. They needed to stop El Frente. But the tug of blood was too strong. He'd tried to pretend Pedro no longer existed, that his son didn't matter anymore. He'd been lying to himself. "I'm sorry, Ramon," he said hoarsely. "I can't do this."

"I can understand why this is hard for you, Mano. But you'll have time to warn Pedro."

"I know my son, Ramon. He won't listen." *He's too much like his father—and that will cost him his life*, Mano kept to himself.

The line was silent for a moment. "I don't have any children, Mano," Ramon said somberly. "But I can understand how you feel. I won't ask a man to endanger his own child. I'll try some of our contacts in the other zones. At least we have that option now."

Mano ended the call and began walking home among the tombstones.

# THE EL PASO EIGHT HOSTAGES:
## *DAY 5*

**S**imon Potts switched channels on the hotel room's plasma screen to Seoul's CBS affiliate as he hurriedly tucked the last of his toiletries into a well-worn travel bag. The CBS coverage was not much different from the news bulletins on the other U.S. networks.

Staring into the camera, the somber-faced anchor said, "For those of you just tuning in, I will repeat the news released through a Reuters embedded journalist less than an hour ago...An attempt to save one of the El Paso Eight hostages by a military rescue team in the San Antonio Quarantine Zone has ended in tragedy. Details remain unclear but it appears the team was led into an ambush. We cannot yet release the identities or unit of the fallen soldiers but we can report that seven are dead and four others are gravely wounded. This turn of events five days from the abductors' deadline—"

Potts turned off the TV and zipped closed his travel bag. His flight to Portland, the southernmost international airport still operating on the West Coast, would be wheels-up in less than two hours. From there, he'd rent a car and travel south to Santa Clarita, his base for covering the Los Angeles Quarantine Zones.

While in the cab on the way to the airport, Simon sent an encrypted text message to Ramon Garcia:

Want 2 meet Suarez. Can u arrange?

Contacts were more important than cameras in this business, Simon reminded himself as he pocketed the vu-phone.

Garcia's reply arrived as he was about to board the plane to the United States:

Sorry. Too hot right now.

Frustrated, Potts flipped the phone closed. *I'm going back anyway.* There was a story here the mainstream press was missing. Ordinary kidnappers did not lure the government into ambushes. Whoever was behind the abductions was ruthlessly trying to provoke a harsh response. He knew it was not Ramon Garcia and the Hispanic Republic of North America. Nevertheless, his instincts told him the situation in the U.S. was about to explode—and he wanted to be there to cover it.

---

Angel and Pedro stepped through an ankle-deep stream left by the morning's rain along the bottom of the storm sewer. Passing through the concealed entrance to the tunnels, the footing grew drier as their hidden passages rose to higher ground.

With Pedro following closely, Angel moved in silence, worried about a growing problem. With the hostage deadline only five days away, he needed to be sure Pedro could be trusted. The boy's constant requests for their prisoner bothered him. Blankets, salves, special food...this could only mean he was growing attached to her. That was not good. Not good at all.

Turning into the corridor that held their prisoner, Angel hoped what he'd planned next would test Pedro's loyalty.

Pedro was puzzled by Angel's behavior as they entered Sarah's holding chamber. The mero had been unusually silent, his movements tense and edgy. Pedro knew goading the Baldies into house-to-house sweeps was the goal of El Frente's plan; Angel's ugly mood made no sense.

Without any explanation, Angel unlocked Sarah from the wall and forced her to kneel on the floor. The girl began to tremble as Angel pushed her head downward until her chin rested on her chest. "No move," he said to her harshly. He then pulled a Colt Python from his pocket, held it out to Pedro. "You shoot," he commanded.

Pedro's eyes widened in alarm. "The deadline is not for another five days, Angel," he protested.

"I say she die now."

Sarah began to tremble violently. "Please don't kill me. Please," she said, her head bowed toward the floor.

"Why don't we wait?" Pedro asked, meeting Angel's eyes.

Angel glared back at Pedro, still holding out the weapon. "Vato do what mero say. Are you vato?"

Pedro took the gun, his knees growing weak. He looked at Sarah and imagined her head exploding, her body twitching on the floor. A wave of nausea rippled through his stomach. He could not let her die. There had to be some way to stop this.

If he handed the gun back to Angel, the mero would shoot her himself. Could he turn the gun on Angel? If he did, he would have to kill him—Angel would not be bluffed. Then again, Angel was no fool. He would never put himself in danger like this. He trusted no one.

Pedro hefted the gun in his hand. The Colt he'd held many

times before now felt light. He grasped the revolver with both hands, deftly running his fingers over the ends of the bullet chambers as he raised the weapon. The gun was empty.

This was a test. It had to be. Angel wanted to see if he would kill their hostage. Going through with it was his only chance to save Sarah now.

*Please, Lord, please let this gun be empty,* Pedro prayed as he brought the revolver to the base of Sarah's neck and pulled the trigger.

*Click.*

The sound of the empty chamber echoed in the tunnel.

Pedro stood frozen, still holding the gun.

"Muy bien," Angel said, taking the Colt from his hand. "You are vato."

# THE EL PASO EIGHT HOSTAGES: *DAY 6*

The president rose from the couch and extended his hand as Henry Evans was ushered into the Oval Office. "Good morning, Hank. Sit down," he said, gesturing to an antique armchair flanking the plush sofa.

"Thank you, sir," Evans replied nervously, squeezing his heavy frame into one of the delicate seats. This was the first time he'd been summoned to the White House alone. His previous meetings in the Oval Office had been business-like affairs with Evans standing alongside Byrne while Nixon addressed them from his desk. With the LLF deadline only four days away, this private audience made Evans uneasy.

"I can only imagine what you're going through right now. If that was one of my girls ... ," Nixon said, unable to finish the thought.

"Keeping busy helps, sir."

"Yes, I've kept up with your reports. It doesn't seem like we've made much progress. And this ambush in San Antonio complicates our position. The public's calling for action, Hank."

"It's only a matter of time, Mr. President. They can't keep

eight hostages hidden in the zones forever," Evans replied, still clinging to the hope that Hollywood Squares might produce the break they needed.

"Unfortunately, time is one resource we don't have to throw at this."

"We could buy ourselves more time with a stay of execution, sir."

The president sighed, rubbing his temples. "We've explored a stay and our lawyers aren't sure if it's even legal under the needle law."

"Frankly, sir, what does that matter? If you order a stay, it'll be carried out. Arguing whether it's legal or not could give us the time we need."

"Look, Hank," Nixon said, knitting his hands tightly. "I've relied on your counsel to shape a lot of the policy of this administration toward the insurgency. Your work for me has been outstanding and I hope it continues." Nixon paused, met Evans's gaze, then shifted his eyes to the carpet. "But I don't think you're the right person to lead the hostage investigation any longer. I'm sorry."

Evans rose suddenly from the chair. "Mr. President, you're making a—"

Before Hank could finish, the doors on both sides of the room burst open and four Secret Service agents brusquely stepped inside.

Nixon stood and addressed the agents, his palms raised reassuringly. "Everything's okay," he said. "Mr. Evans was just getting up to leave." He then faced Evans. "Please forgive this, Hank," he said nodding toward the agents. "They're trained to respond like that when anyone makes a sudden move."

...*and they're expecting a hostile guest*, Hank added silently.

Gently touching Evans's sleeve, Nixon said, "We'll catch these men and punish them, Hank. I know it's not much of a consolation, but you and the other parents can rest assured these people will be brought to justice. We'll turn those goddamn Quarantine Zones inside out if we have to."

Staring at the presidential seal under his feet, Hank realized Nixon had issued his daughter's death sentence.

---

Miguel Cardona brought the VW Passat to the curb in front of the U.N. complex along Avenue de la Paix. Pulling a plastic vial from his coat, he unscrewed the cap, shook out two red pills, and swallowed them. After getting a voice mail from Octavio asking to meet right away, Cardona knew he'd be up late again and would need the dexies.

As the head of operations for the Latino Liberation Front, Miguel was responsible for relaying Octavio's orders to their dozens of cells back in the States. That usually meant late hours on the satellite phone—the price they paid for their decentralized structure.

The passenger door opened. "I haven't got much time," Octavio said, stuffing his large frame into the cramped front seat. "Just take the loop around the campus. What I need to say won't take long."

"Seems like our ambush hasn't provoked much from Nixon," Miguel said irritably, merging the car into the light traffic around the U.N. facility.

"Hijole, he's more gutless than I thought," Perez said puckering his lips. "That's why we need to talk, Miguel. I'm going to force that puto to get tougher," he said, then took a deep breath. "We're going to execute one of the hostages."

Cardona stared straight ahead, surprised at his indifference to Octavio's order. At one time, he'd been idealistic. The idea of killing a teenage girl would have appalled him. But after a while, it was like a butcher slaughtering cattle. You turned off your mind to the suffering. The exhaustion actually made it easier—although his temper had grown short. "When?" he asked finally.

"The sooner the better—and I want it to be the CIA guy's daughter," Octavio said, stabbing the air with his finger. "Nixon will have to hit back harder after that."

"She's being held in L.A. Zone B. That's Garcia's home turf," Cardona said, glancing at his boss. "He won't be too happy about that."

"Yeah, I know," Octavio said smiling. "That's the bonus."

———

The frayed nylon rope feeding through Pedro's hands scratched his palms as he lowered the long-handled wire cutter down the manhole. With the heavy tool safely at the bottom of the storm sewer, he dropped the rope into the hole and climbed down the steel ladder after it.

Reaching the bottom, he took off his backpack and placed it in a recess near the ladder. Hoisting the cutter on his shoulder, he hurried through the sewer, convinced he'd made the right decision. Angel's order to shoot Sarah last night had ended his loyalty to El Frente. For a long time he'd doubted the LLF's way of fighting. Realizing they were prepared to kill a helpless hostage had ended any doubts.

Entering the earthen tunnel that led to Sarah's cell, he thought of his father. He hated to admit it, but the old man had been right about one thing. Protecting people took more courage than hurting them.

The sound of footsteps approaching in the dark made Sarah's heart start pounding in fear. After the Panchos' fake execution, being alone no longer seemed so frightening.

"Sarah...It's Barry," she heard from the darkness. Directing the weak beam of her plastic flashlight toward the entrance, she saw the masked Pancho carrying something with two long handles on his shoulder.

"What is that?" she asked, her voice cracking with fear.

"It's okay," he said, soothingly. "This cutter was easier to get than the key to your handcuffs. I'm not going to let anyone hurt you, Sarah. I'm going to get you out of here."

*Is this another mind game?* The Panchos seemed to be tormenting her, trying to break down her will. Maybe if she played along, she might find a chance to escape. "What if your boss catches us?"

Ignoring her question, Barry said, "Look, what happened before...it was a test to see if I'd really do it—but I figured out the gun was empty." He helped her to her feet. "I realize it must have scared you, but it was the only way I could keep helping you."

"Yeah, I believe you," she said, hoping it sounded convincing.

Barry lowered the long-handled tool from his shoulder. "We haven't got much time. Stretch out the links on your handcuffs," he said, bringing the jaws of the tool toward the chain tethering her to the pipe. "Now shine your flashlight here so I can see what I'm doing."

Pulling the chain taut made the handcuff dig into her chafed left wrist and she trembled in pain, making the flashlight in her right hand jerk erratically.

"I know it hurts, but try to hold the light steady, okay?" Barry said, struggling to get a solid grip on the chain.

"Sorry," she said, trying to ignore the searing pain.

Barry grunted with exertion as he pressed the handles together. "There!" he said triumphantly as the chain snapped free with a clink.

Sarah lurched back, suddenly free.

Barry laid down the cutters. "Let's take your food and water with us," he said bending down. "We're going to need all the supplies we can get."

With the Pancho crouching at her feet, Sarah saw the

chance she'd been waiting for. Raising the flashlight high with both hands, she brought it down on his head with all her strength.

Before he'd hit the ground, she was on the run.

The beam of her flashlight bounced wildly off the dirt walls of the tunnel as Sarah ran furiously, trying to gain as much distance as possible from Barry. The Pancho might recover in only a few seconds. She hoped it would be enough.

The tunnel snaked erratically, making it dangerous to run at full speed. She charged ahead anyway, more afraid of being caught than falling. As she rounded a bend, a wall appeared suddenly out of the darkness. She tried to stop but stumbled forward on the slick footing. *Dammit! I'm going to hit it*, she thought, extending an arm defensively as her body hurtled forward.

To her surprise, the wall gave way with a crash.

Shining the light around her, she saw the "wall" was some kind of plywood cover over the entrance to a concrete sewer line that led away in two directions. To the left was pitch dark. To the right, she could make out a glimmer of light. There was little time to decide—she ran toward the light.

Her strides were growing longer now as her leg muscles loosened, giving her a sense of hope. Drawing closer to the light source, she saw it was coming from an opening in the ceiling of the sewer line. After a few more steps, she saw the bottom of a metal ladder attached to the wall and a metal grate beyond it. A wave of exhilaration shot through her. She'd found a way out of this horrible black hole.

Reaching the ladder, she looked up and her heart stopped.

Coming down the ladder about ten feet above was a stocky, short-limbed man. He looked down, locking his eyes on her, a vicious scowl on his tattooed face. Although she'd never seen him without a mask, Sarah was sure this was the leader.

With the metal grate blocking her way, she bolted back the way she came, turning off her flashlight to stay out of sight. After several paces, she looked behind her and saw the leader's stocky frame drop onto the floor. It was a footrace now—with her life as the prize. Running blindly in the dark, she dragged a hand against the wall, using it to guide her.

She looked back again. The leader's flashlight beam was probing for her, not yet close enough to reach her. It looked like she'd managed to widen her lead thanks to her speed.

Without any warning, someone very strong grabbed her torso in the dark. She tried to scream but a hand covered her mouth. "If you want to stay alive, be quiet," Barry whispered calmly before carrying her several paces into the earthen tunnel leading back to her cell. "Stay here," he said softly. "If you move or talk, you'll get us both killed." Barry released her. The sounds of his footsteps shuffling away merged with the sound of the leader's, drawing closer.

A moment later, she saw the beam of the leader's flashing cover Barry. With his back to her, she could not see Barry's face, but he seemed to be limping. "Sarah must have broken out of the handcuffs somehow," Barry said as the leader reached him. "How bad did she hit me?" he asked, turning his head to show the leader a bleeding cut above his neck.

"No es nada," the Pancho said dismissively. "You go for her," he ordered, pointing down the corridor.

"I twisted my ankle chasing her," Barry said wincing. "You need to go after her. I'll get more vatos to help."

The leader nodded, then rushed away.

Once the leader's footsteps had faded, Barry pointed his flashlight toward her and said, "C'mon, Sarah. We need to get out of here."

She hesitated, uncertain if she should trust him—then realized he would not have lied to his boss unless he meant to help her. This might be her only chance to escape. "Okay," she said, running toward his beam.

As they ran together in the dark toward the ladder with Barry's flashlight guiding them, she noticed he was no longer limping. A few paces from the pool of light below the ladder, he stopped her.

"Sarah, I'm going to have to blindfold you, okay? I want to get you out of here alive but I can't let you see who I am or anything up there. It could hurt people I know."

"Please don't do that," she pleaded. "I won't tell anybody."

"I'm sorry. We don't have time to argue," he said, then directed the flashlight beam to a backpack tucked into a recess in the sewer wall. "There's a hoodie in there. Put it on."

Opening the pack, she found the hooded sweatshirt amid a collection of bottles and plastic bags and slipped into the garment.

"Good," he said before hurriedly tying a black cloth around her head, covering her eyes. He then pulled the hood over her. "The blindfold won't be as noticeable this way."

Back in the darkness again, she said, "I don't like this at all."

"It's just for a while, I promise. I need to get you some-where safe and you can take it off."

Blindly climbing the ladder, Sarah wondered if she would ever feel safe again.

―――――――

Hank poured the last of the gin into a tumbler then stared at the empty bottle. *One more thing that came up empty today*, he thought bitterly and hurled the bottle against the kitchen wall.

Oblivious to the broken glass, he carried his drink into the living room, rubbing his aching belly. Since leaving the

White House six hours ago, his stomach had churned with a succession of emotions...anger...humiliation... fear...despair.

Cradling the tumbler in both hands, he began to pace again—his gait unsteady from a near fifth of gin. After five nights without sleep, Hank knew he was verging on exhaustion—a bulb about to give off its final flash before burning out. Yet his mind kept working frantically, unwilling to give up the fight despite today's body blow. Would Garcia respond to his e-mail? What would the rebel leader say? What else could he do?

When the doorbell rang, Hank wondered if the sound was in his head. No one had visited his apartment before. After the second ring, he peered into the security viewer by the door. Michael Fuller, still in uniform, stood at the entrance to his apartment building.

Evans buzzed the captain through the exterior door, and a few moments later Fuller entered the apartment.

"I heard the news, Hank," Fuller said, taking off his hat. "It was a bad decision."

"Thanks," Evans muttered cheerlessly. "You want a drink?"

"No, I don't want to intrude. I came to ask a favor."

Evans nodded. "Whatever you need, Mike," he said, knowing Fuller's help was one of the few assets he had left.

Fuller stiffened, almost coming to attention. "I want you to arrange a leave of absence for me," Fuller said, eyes focused in the distance. "I'm not sure yet how long, but at least a week."

"What?" Hank said, his jaw suddenly slack. "I was counting on you, Mike. I just lost the best chance I had to save my daughter and you're bailing out on me four days before the deadline? I can't believe you're doing this."

"I've got my reasons, Hank."

"Yeah, sure," Evans said cynically. "Need some time to polish up your CV? Or are you just trying to get away from a sinking ship before you get caught in the undertow?"

"I'm not looking for another assignment, Hank. This is personal."

Hank drained the last of his gin. "Personal, huh?" he said, arching his eyebrows. "I suppose there's someone you've been meaning to look up for a while and this seemed like the perfect time."

"Something like that."

"Well, I'll do better than give you a leave, Fuller," Hank said, his face flushing with anger. "When you get back, your transfer papers will be ready. I'm through with you."

"That wasn't my intention, Hank."

"Please don't insult my intelligence," Evans said, tottering toward the door. "I've seen chickenshits abandon a wounded boss plenty of times in my career." Throwing open the door, he said, "You got what you wanted. Now get out."

His face impassive, Fuller put on his hat and left.

Alone again, Evans looked into his empty glass and felt tears on his cheeks for the first time that day.

# THE EL PASO EIGHT HOSTAGES: *DAY 7*

Since leaving El Frente's underground complex, Pedro had guided Sarah through alleys and empty buildings, keeping a distance from anyone on the streets. Now, with their destination in sight, Pedro felt a wave of relief. They'd been very fortunate to get this far undetected.

Walking through the narrow passage between two storefronts, they crossed the street onto the grounds of an abandoned elementary school. Entering the gym through the back door, they arrived at a fenced-in alcove once used to store outdoor sports equipment. Pedro led Sarah into the makeshift jail, donned his ski mask, and removed her blindfold.

"If you make a sound or try to escape, you'll get us both killed. Do you understand?" he whispered.

Sarah nodded mutely and he stepped outside, securing the chain-link gate with a combination lock from his backpack. Returning to the gym's rear entrance, he scanned the surroundings through the broken-out window. The area looked clear—no one had followed them.

He'd planned Sarah's rescue as best he could, scouting out

a site to secure her and taking along food and water. But the obstacles he faced were staggering. He was now a fugitive from El Frente *and* the U.S. government with a captive who would flee at the first opportunity. She was blond, fair, and green-eyed in an area where all three were conspicuous. A battalion of soldiers was conducting house-to-house searches to find her, and her left wrist carried a manacle. And yet, part of him was proud.

"Barry," she called out softly, her fingers laced in the chain-link fencing.

He raised his index finger over his mouth, then walked back to her. "I told you not to talk," he said sternly.

"Look," she whispered. "If I'm putting you in danger, why don't you just let me go?"

"I can't do that." He'd considered releasing Sarah, but with troops in the area, he'd quickly dismissed the idea. Under questioning, Sarah would alert the Baldies to the presence of El Frente's underground complex and catch them flat-footed. He would not risk betraying Angel, Isabel, and the vatos of El Frente—although he knew Angel would kill them both if he found them.

"Why not?"

Answering her question was dangerous. If Sarah knew there were Baldies looking for her, she might try something foolish. "Remember what I said about asking questions. It's better if you don't know."

"I'm not a child, Barry."

Pedro suddenly realized their exchange was unpleasantly familiar—only this time he was playing the role of his father. The comparison bothered him and he tried to change the subject. "How old are you anyway?"

"How old do you think I am?" she asked, sitting down on the floor beside the fence.

He shrugged. "I don't know...fifteen or sixteen?"

The corners of her mouth dropped. "I was hoping you thought I was older. I'm sixteen," she said. "What about you?"

"Sarah, I—"

"I know. I know...Don't ask questions."

"Are you hungry?" he asked, taking off his backpack and sitting on the floor beside her on the other side of the fence. "I brought food and water."

"You really thought this through, didn't you?" she said, tilting her head. "I know I'm not supposed to ask you anything but I can't help wondering why you're doing this."

"I couldn't let them hurt you. You're not the enemy."

Sarah looked away for a moment, then met his eyes again. "Barry, my parents taught me not to be prejudiced. Most people I know—most Americans—they're not your enemy. They just think Hispanics have turned against this country, that they won't do things our way and don't want to learn English."

Pedro laughed softly. "I can hardly speak Spanish. Same goes for my mom and dad. We wanted to be Americans, Sarah. But America didn't want *us*."

"You're different, Barry," she said, putting her hand against the fence. "You're not like the others—full of hate for Americans."

He studied her pale hand for a moment and said, "How many Latinos have you known?"

"Well...the Quarantine Zones have been around since I was little. I think there may have been some Hispanics in my preschool."

"So other than me, you haven't really gotten to know any Latinos. What I'm trying to say is that each of us is as different as your people are."

"How do you know what we're like?"

"I may have lived in a different neighborhood but I grew up watching the same shows you did—those shows were about people like you, Sarah, not me."

Sarah sighed. "Not easy being different, is it?"

The personal talk made Pedro uncomfortable. "I better go take another look around," he said, starting to rise to his feet.

She touched his hand through the fence. "I haven't said thanks for what you did. I should have."

When Pedro returned from his patrol, they had their first meal together: burritos and water bottles passed through the fence.

Night fell, and Pedro's fear of being found lessened as the hours passed. His talks with Sarah grew more relaxed and intimate as he unpacked the blankets he'd brought and they stretched out beside each other on the floor, cocooned by the darkness, the chain-link fence between them.

Sarah's tales of school, computer games, and sports fascinated Pedro. What she viewed as mundane, he saw as foreign and exotic. Listening to Sarah, Pedro was shocked to learn she was not happy with her life. Despite being smart and pretty, she still considered herself an outcast in her world, someone too different to be fully accepted. Pedro understood her feelings. For the first time, he saw his own bravado in a different light—as a need to belong.

As Pedro talked about his own life, he found himself revealing more than he wanted to—especially about his father. He'd disparaged Mano's lack of courage. Yet in telling Sarah about his father's decisions not to fight, they sounded better than Pedro thought they should.

Despite coming from different worlds, Pedro realized he and Sarah were alike in a way that really mattered. They were both loners. He'd never had a conversation like this with anyone before. Listening to Sarah, it seemed she never had, either.

Sometime near dawn, their conversation spent, the pair succumbed to sleep.

Now, with daylight streaming into the gym from the bank of windows near the ceiling and Sarah still asleep,

Pedro mulled his next move. Their supplies were nearly gone and he could not risk leaving Sarah alone to get more. His hastily planned rescue had saved Sarah's life, but as things stood now he'd only put off the inevitable. They'd be caught if they stayed here much longer. He'd need help to save Sarah but resisted the answer that kept coming back to him.

As Sarah awoke and drank the last of the water, Pedro realized he had no other choice.

If he was going to save Sarah, he would have to go home.

———

Trying not to wake the baby in the next room, Rosa climbed out of bed, put on her robe, and walked quietly toward the kitchen to start a fire. Mano usually returned at dawn and she took pride in having a meal ready for her husband. Hearing the back door open, she entered the kitchen expecting to see Mano. What she found instead left her speechless.

Dirty and disheveled, Pedro stood by the door, accompanied by someone in a hooded sweatshirt. As Rosa looked closer, she noticed the person under the hood was a girl wearing a blindfold. "What is this, Ped—"

Before she could finish, Pedro placed his index finger over his lips. "No names, okay?" he said, nodding toward the girl. "This is Sarah Evans. You've probably heard of her. Someone with wings is looking for us."

Rosa understood Pedro's reference to Angel and quickly grasped the situation. "The man of the house will be home soon," she said calmly. "Are you being followed?"

Pedro shook his head. "No one knows where we are."

Rosa embraced her son, tears of joy forming in her eyes. "Sit down," she said, leading them both to the table. "I imagine you're hungry."

Soon the smell of fresh eggs frying in the skillet filled the kitchen. Pedro picked at his food, but the girl ate ravenously despite the cumbersome blindfold. "This is good, ma'am," she mumbled.

"Eat slowly, dear," Rosa cautioned, patting the girl's shoulder. "I don't think your stomach's seen much food for a while."

"Sorry. I've been eating okay. Barry's made sure of that. It's just that I'm pretty sick of tortillas," Sarah explained.

Rosa smiled. The girl did not appear to have been mistreated. She was proud her son had protected this girl from the worst. Clearing away the dishes, Rosa heard Mano enter the living room and rushed to intercept him.

Mano closed the door and saw Rosa hurry into the living room. "Pedro is here and he needs our help," she said without preface.

The news did not cheer him. "What does he want?"

"He's got one of the girls El Frente kidnapped with him. He took her away somehow and Angel is looking for them."

Mano's eyes widened in alarm. He locked the front door, then moved to the windows and looked around outside. "They could have followed him."

"Pedro didn't think so."

"Angel's no fool. He knows where we live and that Pedro might come here. His vatos have probably been watching our house. Where are Pedro and the girl?"

Rosa pointed toward the end of the hallway that ran the length of the house. "In the kitchen."

"Close all the curtains," Mano said and headed for the kitchen.

Pedro rose to his feet when Mano entered the room. "Papi," he blurted, forgetting Sarah was present. "I just want to tell you—"

Mano raised his palm, cutting him off "We don't have much time. Take the girl into your old bedroom and get down on the floor. Rosa, get Carlos and join them. All of you need to stay in that room, no matter what happens. Do you understand?"

They all nodded in agreement. Pedro looked awestruck by his father's resolve.

Moving to his bedroom, Mano retrieved the Glock he kept under the mattress and grabbed two ammo clips from the nightstand. Back in the kitchen, he placed the automatic pistol out of sight atop a high cupboard and hid the extra ammunition under the sink. Mano was betting the lives of his family that Angel would enter through the kitchen door at the rear of the house, the approach that would give the mero and his vatos the most cover.

He pulled a chair near the hidden weapon, poured himself a cup of chicory, and sat down to wait.

———

Angel studied the white stucco cottage, contemplating his next step. A few months ago, he would have sent for more Verdugos. But rounding up his reluctant vatos would take hours now. Pedro and Sarah could slip away in the meantime. He could not risk losing them again.

There were two men inside, most likely armed, along with two women and a child. He had three armed men—and the element of surprise. The odds favored him, but this play would be complicated.

Angel did not want to hurt Mano or his wife and baby. The big man still commanded a great deal of respect in the barrios, and killing him would hurt El Frente with their people. No less important, Mano was a comrade who had saved Angel's life more than once.

Sparing Sarah and Pedro, however, was out of the question. Sarah had been condemned to death and he was honor-bound to carry out the order. As for Pedro, his insolence could not be forgiven. He had to be punished as an example.

Sending one vato to cover the front entrance, Angel and another Verdugo circled the house and found all the curtains closed. They would have to enter the house blind. Moving to the back door, Angel tried the handle and discovered it was unlocked.

Their guns drawn, Angel and his vato stepped quickly into the kitchen and found Mano seated in a corner, drinking coffee. Startled, Mano rose to his feet. "No move," Angel growled, his Python trained on the big man.

Angel smiled, pleased at his good fortune. In less than a minute, he'd neutralized his most dangerous obstacle.

Mano raised his hands over his head. "I'm not armed."

Angel nodded to his vato, and the husky Verdugo expertly frisked Mano. "Nada," he reported to his mero.

"I no want hurt you, Mano," Angel said coolly. "Pedro... girl... Dónde están?"

"They left through the front door a while ago," Mano said, his arms still above his head.

"You lie. I have vato in front. No one go there."

"Then search the house."

"Ve y mira," Angel said to his vato, and the Verdugo disappeared down the hallway.

With the odds now evened, Mano knew he had only seconds to act. When Angel's attention drifted toward the vato in the hallway, Mano grabbed the Glock atop the cupboard with his upraised hand and leveled the weapon at Angel. "Put down your gun," he whispered, staring over the sights of the Glock.

Caught with his own weapon pointed down, the mero did as Mano ordered.

Mano stepped behind Angel, using the mero as a shield, and pushed the tall kitchen cupboard to the ground. The crash of the cabinet was followed by the hurried footsteps of the Verdugo approaching through the hallway.

When the vato charged into the kitchen, Mano shouted, "Drop your weapon!"

The young man froze for an instant, seeing his mero's predicament, then tried to aim his gun.

Mano fired three shots, striking the Verdugo in the chest. Before he crumpled to the ground, the vato got off two wild shots. One of them struck Angel in the throat. Gushing blood from his carotid artery, Angel slumped to the floor.

Mano grabbed their guns and moved into the hallway, positioning himself so he could watch both entrances to the house while lying on the floor. When the door into the living room burst open, Mano took aim and waited to see how many Verdugos would enter. A lone vato cautiously crossed the threshold, crouching with his gun leveled, seeking a target. Before he could find it, Mano squeezed off four quick shots. The man collapsed against the doorway.

After searching outside the house for more of Angel's men, Mano returned to check on the vatos inside. Angel was still alive, sprawled in a widening crimson puddle, his breathing labored. Mano knelt beside him, gently lifting his head. "You were always very brave, hermano," he said softly to the fallen mero.

After a moment, Angel's eyes glazed and his chest stopped heaving. Mano checked the mero's pulse as his own eyes welled with tears. Angel was dead.

Mano rose and entered the room where his family had taken shelter. "We need to leave this place right away. The Baldies will be coming to investigate the shots."

"I'm sorry, Papá. Bringing her here was stupid," Pedro said, gesturing toward Sarah. "I put all of you in danger."

"No, m'hijo," Mano replied, putting his large hand on Pedro's shoulder. "You did the right thing."

Pedro's eyes grew moist. After a moment, he said, "I'll help Mamá pack up her things."

"Good," Mano said, walking out of the room. "Bring everything she needs to take into the kitchen. We'll be leaving through the back door."

Stepping into the hallway, Mano reached high on the wall and removed the section of crown molding that hid the satellite phone. Grasping the silver device, Mano heard Rosa call out in alarm from the bedroom.

"Mano! The baby!" she shouted as fifteen-month-old Carlos burst out of the bedroom, tottering toward the kitchen.

Instinctively, Mano bent down and scooped up the toddler. An instant later, he heard a crash behind him and turned to look.

The satellite phone, shattered in several pieces, was on the floor.

Mano closed his eyes, trying to remain calm. Until the next courier arrived, they'd lost their lifeline to Ramon.

# THE EL PASO EIGHT HOSTAGES:
## *DAY 8*

**R**ubbing the sleep from his eyes, Mano entered the living room of their new house. On a stack of cinder blocks in the corner, Rosa was assembling her shrine to the Virgin of Guadalupe like an Army commander christening a new HQ with the regimental flag. Although Mano was not a believer, seeing Rosa's shrine made the house feel like home. The place certainly needed a welcoming touch.

The troops had already searched the three-bedroom Mission-style house, which a widowed DDP official, Hilda Ortiz, had gladly given up for them. While that made it relatively safe from the Baldies, the house and its furnishings had suffered considerable damage. Still, it served their purposes. Mano and Rosa had taken one corner bedroom with Pedro and the baby in the other corner and Sarah locked in the windowless room between them.

"You're up early," Mano called out, crossing the room wearing only a pair of jeans.

"Shhhh! You're going to wake up the others," Rosa whispered over her shoulder. "Go back to bed, mi amor. You were up most of the night."

"None of us got much sleep last night," he said yawning. "Why are *you* awake?"

She tightened the collar of her robe and made the sign of the cross. "We need Our Lady's protection, Mano. Pedro told me why you can't just release the girl with all the Baldies around. I need Our Lady to find a way for Sarah to get home safely—for her sake and ours."

Mano knew Rosa's prayers had already been answered—it was only a matter of time. Once their courier arrived and he got word to Ramon, they could contact Honda Garganta and arrange a site somewhere outside the zone to pick up the girl. But the longer they held her, the greater the risk. At least the most immediate danger they faced was gone—Angel and El Frente. But from long habit, he decided to tell Rosa none of this. "I think we'll find a way to get her home," he said truthfully.

Rosa walked to him and took his hand. "I know it's dangerous having Sarah here, but I'm proud of our son, Mano."

Remembering Pedro's part in the attack on the mall, Mano was not so ready to forgive. Still, he did not want to hurt Rosa. "We don't know what else he may have done, but saving the girl showed he knows what's right."

"Ever since Pedro left us, I've prayed for you to forgive him. God shows his mercy in strange ways. I'm very happy, mi amor." Rosa put her arms around Mano's waist, resting her cheek against his bare chest. "I'm very proud of his father, too. You saved all of us, Mano. In all our years together, I'd never seen that part of you with my own eyes," she said, nuzzling his skin.

Relishing Rosa's warmth, Mano stroked her hair, continuing the caress to the small of her back. He wanted to savor the embrace—and see where it might lead them. But there was still unfinished business. "We need to do something about Isabel," he said, lifting Rosa's face. "She may not know her brother's dead, querida. I need to go to their house and tell her what happened."

Rosa sighed, clearly disappointed their romantic moment had evaporated. "Of course—you're right," she said, breaking their embrace. "But are you sure it's a good idea for you to tell her? The news is going to hit Isabel hard, Mano. She may blame you."

"I don't want to lie to Isabel—and besides, she's too young to be left alone. We need to take her in."

Sitting on the arm of a sofa with missing cushions, Rosa took her husband's hand. "I know you feel a debt to Angel for what happened, and I agree Isabel needs a home, mi amor. But where are we going to put her? We've already got a captive in the house."

"We can't leave her alone, Rosa. I'll ask Teresa to take her."

"Your sister already has three children, Mano. You can't ask her to do that."

"Isabel will only need to stay with Teresa until we can release the girl."

"I've got a better idea," Rosa said with a knowing smile. "Celia could use some help in her shop and around the house. I could ask her to take Isabel in."

Mano nodded. "Yes, that makes sense for both of them, You think Celia will agree?"

"Celia's getting pretty weak. I think she'd jump at the chance for some help," Rosa said, then pressed his hand to her chest. "One other thing, mi amor. Why don't you let me break the news to Isabel? I'll stop by Celia's first and make sure she'll do it. Then I'll ask her to come with me to see Isabel. It might be easier for Isabel to grieve with women around her."

Mano was relieved but didn't want to admit it. "Are you sure you want to do this?"

"Who would want to tell an orphan her only brother is dead? I'll do it because it's the right thing to do—like our son did," she said, then gently pushed her husband toward the bedroom. "Now go get some sleep."

With Mano back in their bedroom, Rosa went to the kitchen and quietly started a fire. Hilda Ortiz had been generous, leaving them a fully stocked kitchen and a supply of wood. Rosa filled the largest pot she could find with water and placed it over the fire.

Pedro had made sure Sarah was well fed and unhurt, but the poor girl was filthy. Once she had Sarah cleaned up, she'd visit Celia's and take care of the grim chore with Isabel. A short while later, with the pot nearly boiling, she woke Pedro and brought him into the kitchen.

"Sorry to get you up but I'm going to get Sarah cleaned up and I want her to know you're around," she told her son. Although Sarah seemed to be cooperating, she was still a captive and Pedro's presence would keep her from getting any crazy ideas.

"You'll need to put on a mask if you're going to take off her blindfold, Mamá."

"What?" she said, putting her hands on her hips. "And look like some kind of cholo holding up a liquor store? No, Pedro. I won't do it."

"You have to, Mamá. She might identify you after we release her."

"Pedro, the Baldies already know your father and me. They haven't caught us yet. There's no way I'll do this."

"Hijole," Pedro said, shaking his head. "There's just no arguing with you about some things, Mamá. Am I supposed to stop wearing a mask, too?"

"We're not criminals, m'hijo," she said, touching her son's face. "We shouldn't act like it."

Rosa carried the hot water to the bathroom and poured it into the tub, adding cold water from the tap. After laying out towels and soap, she unlocked the bolt on Sarah's door and tapped on it softly.

The knocking awoke Sarah. She looked around the dimly lit room, trying to get her bearings. The sliver of light below the door reminded her she was no longer underground, and she sighed with relief. "Is that you, Barry?"

"No, it's his mother," the voice behind the door said. "May I come in?"

"Sure," she said, gathering the sheet around her although she was still dressed.

When the door opened, Sarah gasped. For the first time since her ordeal had begun, she was looking at a smiling human face. The woman was younger than her own mom and beautiful, with dark eyes and black hair. The sight warmed her, like seeing the sun after a rainstorm.

"I see you're a little shocked," the woman said gently.

Recognizing the voice, Sarah struggled to match it with the person standing before her. "I pictured you a lot older," she said, then realized she'd been rude. "Oh, I'm sorry, ma'am."

"Being told she looks young never hurt a woman's feelings," she said with a soft laugh. "But calling me 'ma'am' makes me feel ancient. Why don't you call me Mamá? It'll make things a lot less confusing."

Awkwardly, Sarah raised her palm. "Hi, uh, Mamá."

"There's someone else here you might want to see." Mamá waved her hand and a very tall boy stepped into the doorway. "This is my son—the one you call Barry."

Sarah covered her mouth, staring in astonishment. "You're, like...just a kid," she said, looking at Barry's youthful face.

Barry looked down, a small smile betraying his embarrassment.

Sarah studied Barry, mesmerized. He wasn't handsome in a *GQ* kind of way, but his sensitive brown eyes and firm-set jaw made him attractive all the same.

"Sarah, would you like to wash up?" Mamá said, breaking Sarah's trance.

"Sure," she said, still stunned.

Mamá led her into the bathroom and closed the door. "Take off those clothes and wrap this towel around you," she said, turning away to give her privacy. "When you're done, give me your clothes."

After handing Barry's mother her dirt-stained clothing, Sarah said, "I can't believe I've been wearing these all this time."

"You can take a bath now. I'll bring you something to wear when you're done." Mamá closed the door behind her.

Staring at the cardboard-patched window, Sarah suddenly wondered if she could open it. Then she realized all she had to wear was a towel. Barry's mother was no fool. In any case, would she really escape right now if she could?

These people weren't terrorists. They were a family. From what she could tell by the sounds of gunfire at Barry's house yesterday, his father had fought with the leader. They'd left that house in a hurry after all the shooting, which meant Barry's family had lost their home trying to save her. Barry had even cut the handcuff from her hand in what sounded like another family's house while they waited for Barry's father to find this new place.

She now believed Barry was telling the truth when he said they'd release her when they could do it safely. His family would be arrested if they took her to the troops, she understood that. She only wished they'd trust her enough to let her go. She wouldn't rat on them—not now. *How can I convince Barry to trust me?* she wondered, stepping into the tub. The sensation of the water on her skin made the question melt away.

Sarah lowered herself into the warm water and closed her eyes, enveloped in bliss. She'd never imagined a simple bath could feel so good. She laid in the tub for a long time, letting the water soothe her, before finally starting to scrub with some strange-smelling soap. As she was rinsing off, she heard a knock on the door.

"Sarah, you need to come out now," Mamá said through the door.

"Okay, just a minute," Sarah answered before getting out of the tub and drying off.

The door opened slightly and a hand came through holding a white garment. "Here, put this on."

Slipping into the white sundress, Sarah looked at herself in the discolored cabinet mirror. Judging by how loosely it fit in the bust and hips, she was certain it belonged to Barry's mother. All the same, she felt exotic in the borrowed dress.

"Are you dressed?" Mamá called out from the hallway.

Sarah opened the door. "Thank you—for the bath and the dress."

"I'll try to get you something that fits better later." Mamá smiled. "I've got to go out for a while right now. Barry will be here if you need anything," she went on, guiding Sarah back to her room.

Sarah sat on the bed, combing out her hair, reveling in the joy of feeling clean. After days of being bound and blindfolded, roaming free in a furnished room felt like a birthday gift. She lay back on the bed and stretched out, feeling the smoothness of the sheets caress the bare skin of her arms and legs.

A knock on the door made her sit up, suddenly embarrassed.

"I have something for you," Barry said behind the door.

"Just a minute," she answered, smoothing out her dress and fluffing her hair with her fingers. "Come in."

Barry entered the room carrying a stack of magazines. "My mother said that . . . Wow! You sure look different."

"Do you like it?" she asked, fanning out her dress. "I'm pretty sure it's your mother's."

"You look nice," he said, smiling.

"Thanks," she answered, feeling herself blush.

"I think you're going to like these," Barry said excitedly. "The lady who lived here has a huge collection of old magazines. They're like super valuable in the zones because paper is so scarce."

"Tight," Sarah said and patted a spot next to her on the bed. "Sit down. Let's look at them."

With Sarah turning the pages on her lap, they fell into an easy conversation about the odd styles in the decades-old issues of *People* and *Soap Opera Digest*. "Oh, my God, look at that hair!" Sarah said laughing, leaning close to him, feeling his warmth. She looked up, meeting Barry's eyes. "Do you like my hair? It's the first time you've ever seen it washed."

"Yes, it's very pretty."

"Does it smell clean?" she asked, slowly placing her head against his chest.

Sarah could feel his warm breath on her scalp. "Yes," he said softly.

In a day of firsts, Sarah felt something she'd heard about but never really known—passion. It was like a fever, or hunger, or an ache. She wasn't sure which. All she knew was she wanted to hold Barry, to feel his body against hers.

She reached for his hand and wove her fingers into his. "Barry...," she whispered, brushing her lips against his, enticing him into a kiss. Closing her eyes, her old self seemed like a stranger now, someone who'd been deaf to music that had been playing all along. She'd seen how fleeting life could be—this chance to know love might be her last.

Barry embraced her and she lay back on the bed, drawing him down to her, longing to be touched, giving in to the desire she knew they'd both held back.

It was the first time for both of them. She was patient and Barry was gentle.

# THE EL PASO EIGHT HOSTAGES: DAY 9

In the gathering dusk, the rear door of the prison bus opened, throwing a weak yellow light onto the broken pavement. The detainees filed out slowly between a gauntlet of soldiers leading to the North Gate of Los Angeles Quarantine Zone B.

"Hurry up," a soldier said, shoving one of the prisoners. When the man complained, the trooper knocked him to the ground. "That's for the hostages, Pancho," the soldier said angrily. After the last of the captives was inside the high concrete wall, the soldiers locked the rusting door.

From a crude hut inside the wall, a DDP volunteer wearing a blue armband approached the nearly two dozen men. "Where are you from, hermanos?"

"San Diego," several of them answered.

"Bienvenidos a Los Angeles. Please follow me," he said and led them several blocks to a storefront with a hand-painted sign that read DEFENSA DEL PUEBLO. Entering the large main room, the man with the blue armband said, "Please wait here. A DDP officer will interview each of you."

Among the last escorted to a private office was a man in his early thirties of average height and build wearing jeans and a plaid work shirt. As he entered the room, a hefty woman behind a metal desk gestured toward a battered plastic chair with the air of a schoolteacher. "My name is Hilda Ortiz. Your name?"

"David Ayala," he answered. His flat vowels and hard consonants made the DDP officer look up from her papers, suddenly apprehensive.

"Hablas Español?"

"I don't speak much Spanish. My father's Cuban, but my mother is from Iowa."

She nodded knowingly. "The language always comes from the mother," she said, making a note on her form. "Do you have any family in Los Angeles?"

"No. I'm single. My parents are in the Newark zone. I came to work in San Diego just before the Quarantines."

"What kind of work did you do?"

"I was a pharmaceutical rep."

"Do you have any knowledge of civil engineering?"

"No. I was a business major in college."

"Have any experience with plumbing, masonry, carpentry, or electrical work?"

"I'm afraid not."

"I presume you know which end of a shovel to hold?"

"Yes."

"Good. La Defensa Del Pueblo can use your help in cleaning up after the Army searches and in our community development projects. The pay's not much, but it'll help keep you fed. If you're interested, come back here tomorrow morning at six. We'll be handing out assignments. You can find temporary housing in the high-rises on Sixth Street. You'll see the apartment towers in the south from the street outside. The Army has already swept that area so you won't be harassed. One final question," Ortiz said, leaning forward in her chair. "Señor Ayala, you were transferred here because the Baldies in San Diego detained you as a suspected insurgent but could not prove it." She paused, letting her meaning sink in. "Did they have any cause for their suspicion?"

"Not when they arrested me, but I feel differently now. I want to fight the gringos."

"I see," she said, studying his brown eyes. "How do you feel about the hostages?"

"They're gringos. They got what they deserved."

The woman nodded slowly and waved her hand toward the door. "Thank you, Señor Ayala. I hope we'll see you here at six tomorrow."

After Ayala left her office, Ortiz signaled her comrade in the blue armband to step inside. "Have someone keep an eye on that one," she said. "He seemed a little too eager."

Michael Fuller walked out of the DDP office feeling good about his first attempt at undercover work. It had been easier than he'd expected. In the distance, Fuller saw the high-rise Ortiz had mentioned and began walking toward his new home.

Half an hour later, with the last of the daylight gone, Fuller gazed through the missing balcony door at the ragged outline of Quarantine Zone B from eleven stories up. Under a rising crescent moon, East Los Angeles was a dark mass of low buildings ringed by the lights of the perimeter guard posts. Here and there, the faint glow of a fire broke the gloom. Like a white gash piercing the dark were the headlights of the Army vehicles conducting the sweeps, a twenty-four-hour exercise in futility.

Built less than a decade ago, the public housing high-rise where he now stood had been a vertical ghetto even before the QZ walls went up. Without electricity to run the elevators, the upper floors of the fifteen-story building had become a refuge for the most desperate. Anything of value above the sixth floor had been scavenged; doors, cabinets, windows, flooring, plumbing fixtures, pipes, even the electrical wiring had been ripped out.

Settling down for the night in the barren two-room apartment, Fuller piled scraps of drywall in front of the hall doorway to warn him of any intruders and stretched out on the concrete floor. He was exhausted but could not sleep, his mind racing with the events of the last three days.

Asking Hank to arrange his leave of absence had been painful. But if he'd told Evans the truth, Hank would have been forced to scrub this infiltration. The second in command at the CIA could not authorize an attempt to save his daughter without a similar plan to rescue the other hostages. It would have been a political disaster.

Still, Fuller knew there was more driving him than saving Sarah Evans. Quarantine Zone B was the logical place to look for her—and the last known whereabouts of Manolo Suarez. This mission might give him a chance to settle some accounts with the rebel leader.

Fuller shook his head, trying to clear away the thoughts of revenge. With only one day left until the hostage deadline, his focus had to be on Sarah. He knew the house-to-house sweeps were political theater. If there was any chance of saving Sarah, he'd need to find it through stealth.

Getting himself inserted into a busload of detainees being transferred from San Diego had not been difficult for an officer with colleagues in the area. Arranging for his exit with Sarah had not been as simple. Eggbeater Eddie had balked at setting up a chopper extraction, but after Fuller mentioned it was for Evans's daughter, Eddie relented. The colonel had agreed to send a bird for them when he activated the transponder on the underside of his belt.

Most astonishing was how well his cover had worked inside the zone. People saw what they expected. Outside the walls, they saw a brunet with dark eyes. Inside the walls, they saw another Latino. His hardest task, however, was still ahead. Tomorrow, he would need to ask questions about Sarah—and that would raise suspicions.

# THE EL PASO EIGHT HOSTAGES: DAY 10

When Mano heard that the DDP had captured an infiltrator, he rushed to the onetime pawnshop where the spy was being held. A vato standing guard at the store said, "We've got him in the basement," and pointed toward the door at the back of the shop. The wooden steps creaked under Mano's weight as he hurried downstairs.

Against the wall of the musty cellar was a barely conscious man bound by his wrists to the pipes along the ceiling. Angry welts covered his face, and blood oozed from his mouth. Beside the prisoner, Eladio Cortez, a minor DDP official, held a short length of garden hose.

"This pinche cabron still won't tell us who he is," Cortez said, coiling to strike the prisoner again.

Mano grabbed Cortez's arm. "That's enough, Eladio."

"Enough?" Cortez said angrily. "When the chingado Baldies detained my brother, they handcuffed him to a wall and made him stand for forty hours without sleep. After that, they waterboarded him. This hijo de puta is only getting what he deserves."

"What makes you so sure he's a Baldie?"

"He told Señora Ortiz he had no family in our zone when the Army brought him here yesterday. Today we caught him showing people this picture and asking if anybody had seen his niece." Cortez handed Mano a wallet-size photo. It was a school portrait of Sarah Evans.

"He might be a reporter," Mano said, tucking the photo in his breast pocket.

"Would a reporter be carrying this?" Cortez said, handing Mano a small square of green plastic with a slot in the center. "I found it on the inside of this chingado's belt. It looks suspicious."

Mano recognized the Army-issue rescue transponder, a device that sent out a homing signal when the small antenna bar inside was extended. Thankfully, the transponder was not activated. "I'll take this," he said, pocketing the transponder.

Mano lifted the prisoner's face and saw the man's eyes widen involuntarily. *He recognizes me... but from where?* Then he remembered. This was the man who'd tried to detain him outside Jo's house. "I know this man. His name is Fuller," he said, recalling the name the soldier from the helicopter had called out. He was a captain.

"You see! I knew he was a gabacho! Let me gut him," Cortez said, drawing a switchblade from his pocket.

"Put away your knife, hermano," Mano said firmly. "Look, I know your brother was tortured by the Baldies. But that's not a reason to take it out on this man. Leave him to me."

Cortez glared at the prisoner. "I hope I have the pleasure of wasting your sorry ass," he said to Fuller before leaving.

Mano sent the vato guarding the shop for clean water and bandages then cut Fuller down. Keeping him covered with his Glock, Mano helped the battered officer to the floor. "This is the second time you've tried to infiltrate this zone, Fuller. You're either a brave man or a fool."

Fuller tried to answer but was racked by coughs instead.

"You mean there's a difference?" he finally said.

A faint smiled crossed Mano's lips. "No, not really," he said. "Whatever the reason, I admire your guts."

Fuller slowly propped himself against the wall and looked up at his captor. "I used to feel the same way about you, Suarez—until you started butchering civilians and kidnapping teenage girls."

"The Latino Liberation Front took the hostages, not the Hispanic Republic."

"Spare me the company line, Suarez. I've heard Garcia spout the same crap from Geneva."

"Somebody in your government believes it."

"Bullshit."

"No. I can prove it," Mano said, dropping to one knee near the officer. "You were sent to take me down two years ago because someone on your side homed in on our LAN. Correct?"

"I'm not going to divulge..."

"Save your breath, Fuller. I *know* that's how you located me. A couple of days ago, we learned your spooks cracked our network encryption, too. Want to know how we found out? Someone from your government sent a message over our secured network saying they knew we were not behind the kidnappings and asked for our help."

"Who?"

"Whoever it was, wanted it kept secret. The message came from someone who called himself *Honda Garganta*—Spanish for 'Deep Throat.' Unfortunately, we knew nothing at the time that could help you with the kidnappings."

Fuller laughed. "You expect me to believe that?"

"I wish it was funny. Because we rescued Sarah Evans from the LLF yesterday. But we can't release her with all your troops around."

"Why don't you ask this Honda whatever guy to set up a

remote rescue?" Fuller asked, eyes narrowing suspiciously.

"Our communications are down."

"How convenient," Fuller answered smirking.

"We both want the same thing, Captain," he said, dropping Sarah's photo into Fuller's lap. "To see Sarah Evans gets home safe."

Fuller laughed drily. "Sure, and I want to see California become part of your Hispanic Republic."

"Fuller, you can get Sarah out of here—with this," Mano said, holding out the transponder.

Fuller studied Mano's face for a moment. "All right. You turn the girl over to me and release us. I'll get her out of here."

"It's not that simple, Captain. First, you'll need to tell me about your extraction method. I can't let you walk outside and bring a company of your troops down on us when you activate your homing signal."

"Of course," Fuller said sarcastically. "I tell you my extraction plans so you can have an ambush ready. Nice try, Suarez."

Mano sighed. "This is getting us nowhere and we don't have a lot of time," he said, rising to his feet. "I'm going to send for someone who'll be more convincing."

Fuller swallowed hard, his voice strained when he spoke. "So Cortez wasn't your A-team on torture, eh?"

Mano shook his head. "You're a difficult man to persuade, Fuller."

———

"Why are we going outside?" Sarah asked as Barry unwrapped the blindfold.

"I don't know yet," he answered, wrapping the black cloth around her head. "My father sent for you."

"Your father?" she said, suddenly intrigued. She'd only

seen Barry's father once since they'd dispensed with her blindfold. He seemed serious but kind, like a gentle bull—someone you felt safe around. Looking at Barry's father, she could imagine the man Barry would be one day.

"Yes, my father—and the messenger said we should hurry," Barry said, fastening the blindfold and pulling the hood of the sweat suit over her head.

She touched the cloth over her eyes. "Do I have to wear this again? You know I won't ever tell on you."

"I know that," he said, touching her cheek tenderly. "But you're going to be questioned someday, Sarah. With the blindfold, you can tell them you don't know where to find us and it will be the truth. You could get in trouble for lying."

She realized what Barry said made sense. He was trying to protect her—and his family. "All right," she said nodding.

"C'mon," he said, guiding her toward the door. "You'll have to be quiet while we're outside."

They walked hurriedly in silence for several blocks. The warmth of Barry's hand on her arm brought back a memory she'd relived many times during the last two days.

She was still not really sure why she'd made love with Barry. Was she trying to win his trust? Was she relieved to be alive and afraid to die a virgin? Had she really fallen in love with him? Maybe all these things were true. Whatever the reason, she had no regrets. The child she'd been before was gone, replaced by someone who now saw how fortunate—and how empty—her life had been.

After she'd followed Barry for a long distance, he took off her blindfold inside a gutted pawnshop.

"This way," Barry said, leading her to the back of the building and down a stairway. In the far corner of the dimly lit basement were Barry's father and a man with a bandaged face.

Mano watched the teenagers enter the room. "Sarah," he

called out, waving for them to come closer. "There's some-one here you should talk to."

Walking toward them, Sarah's eyebrows rose in surprise. "Captain Fuller?"

"Yes, it's me, Sarah. Are you okay?" Fuller said anxiously.

"Yeah," she said. "I'm fine."

"Ask her anything you want, Fuller. We'll leave you two alone," Mano said and then retreated to the stairway with Pedro behind him.

As Fuller and Sarah talked in the corner, Pedro leaned close to Mano. "What's going on, Papá?"

"Fuller is an Army captain. He infiltrated the zone to res-cue Sarah—and he can get her out of here safely with this," Mano said, holding out the transponder. "But he has to trust me enough to tell us his extraction plan. I hope he will after he talks to Sarah."

Pedro looked down. In the dim light, Mano thought he could see tears forming in his son's eyes.

"M'hijo, you did a brave thing rescuing Sarah. You proba-bly saved her life," Mano said softly. "I leave it up to God to keep score. But I think this makes up for what you did at the mall in Santa Clarita."

Pedro slumped against the wall, covering his face. "I never did it, Papi. I never did it," he said, crying softly. "I gave my word to Angel—my word as a man. But I put the bomb in an empty office. Then I lied to him about it. All that time, I pre-tended I was a vato. But I was lying. And now, I help Sarah and..." He shook his head. "Each time I do something I think is right, it hurts."

Mano put his hand on his son's shoulder, tears welling in his own eyes. "Honor doesn't come cheap, m'hijo. I've never been prouder of you."

"Suarez," Fuller called out from the corner. "I think we have a deal."

The four of them stood at what had once been the ninth hole of a long-abandoned golf course.

"You can take off the blindfolds now," Mano said to Sarah and Fuller.

Sarah hurriedly lowered her hood and unbound her eyes, squinting at the glare. "I almost forgot what the sky looked like."

Pedro took the black cloth from her hand. "I'll burn this when I get home."

"No, I'd like to keep it," Sarah said, taking the blindfold back.

Fuller dropped his hood and removed his blindfold, handing it to Mano. "My part of the deal is done."

"Here you are, Captain," Mano said, giving Fuller the transponder.

Fuller pulled out the transponder's tab, extending its antenna. "We have about five minutes, Suarez. Care to tell me why a man like you would turn against his country and his comrades in uniform?"

Mano stared into the distance, then looked back at Fuller. "For the same reason the American colonists turned against the British," he said, then glanced toward Pedro. "And for the same reason a son rebels against his parents. Sometimes they forgive each other when it's all over. We'll see."

"I hope you're right," Fuller said.

Sarah stepped closer to Pedro. "So your last name is Suarez," she said shyly. "What's your first name?"

Pedro looked at his father, who shrugged. "Fuller knows all our names. Go ahead and tell her."

"My name is Pedro."

She touched his cheek, looking into his eyes. "Pedro...I wish we could have met some other way."

Pedro looked away. The four of them stood in silence then,

knowing their lives had intersected for a brief time but there was little chance they'd ever meet again. After a while, the throbbing of a helicopter rose in the distance. As the craft drew closer, the wind from its rotors made them stagger, whipping their hair and clothing.

With the chopper nearly on the ground, Fuller faced Mano. "I met a man of honor today," he said saluting.

Mano returned the salute. "Likewise, Captain."

Sarah held Pedro's face in her hands, looking into his eyes. "I won't forget you," she said, then turned and ran toward the craft.

After watching the helicopter rise into the sky and disappear into the distance, Mano put his arm around his son, and they began their walk home.

# THE EL PASO EIGHT HOSTAGES: *DAY 11*

**G**ood morning, señora," Pedro said to Celia, entering the curandera's shop. "My mother told me you'd stopped by last night and wanted me to come see you."

"Ah, and you're here so early. What a fine young man you are, Pedro," Celia said smiling. "Thank you for coming." She took his arm and shuffled slowly toward her apartment at the back of the store. "Isabel insisted she needed to speak with you privately." Pedro followed the curandera silently through a door that opened into a living room almost as cluttered with religious effects as the old woman's shop.

From the living room, they passed into an arched alcove. "She's been very anxious to see you," Celia said, knocking on the door. "Isabel...Pedro is here," the curandera called out before shuffling away.

Isabel opened the door. "Please, come in," she said with a sad smile, her eyes glowing intensely. "Sit down." She gestured to a metal folding chair beside the bed.

"I should have come to see you sooner," Pedro said, still standing. "My family's been in danger...I—I really can't say more."

"Angel never told me anything about his business. You don't need to explain."

Her answer brought Pedro a measure of relief. It meant she didn't know the details of her brother's death. He'd explain them to her someday, but this was not the time.

"I'm sorry about your brother," he said softly. Then, wanting to show his sympathy, he walked to her and stiffly put his arms around her, patting her back. Isabel pressed her forehead against his chest and began to cry, holding him tightly against her. He waited patiently as she vented her grief. When she finally released him, he said, "Angel was very brave, Isabel."

"Yes, he was," she nodded, wiping her cheeks. "He felt the same about you."

A pang of guilt seized Pedro. Angel would have considered him a coward if he'd known the truth about the Santa Clarita mall. "I'm not so sure he was right."

"No, you've never talked big. But Angel knew he could count on you. That's why I needed to see you," Isabel said solemnly. She retrieved a small bundle from under the bed and handed it to him. "It's the phone to El Frente. I made sure to bring it with me."

––––––––

The News Alert icon in the lower right of his editing program blinked into life as Simon was adding a new caption to the footage from his Quarantine Zone flyover. *Nineteen bulletins*, Simon noted. This must be it.

As the eleventh day of the crisis had arrived, most people around the world were waiting anxiously for news of the hostages. Clicking on the icon, Simon scanned the list of headlines—all of them about the hostages. The news was not good.

Grabbing the remote control, he turned on the hotel room's wall plasma. A news anchor, staring soberly into the camera, was reading from the teleprompter. "...all the female hostages seized by the Latino Liberation Front ten days ago are believed dead. We cannot confirm the identities of the victims but the one-page statement from the Latino Liberation Front released at noon Eastern Time was accompanied by the photographs of seven bodies. Due to the disturbing nature of these images, we have chosen not to air them." The newsman then gave the network's Web address for viewers who wanted to see the photos. *Somebody there scored a coup with this Internet idea*, Potts noted as he muted the TV and logged onto the URL.

The station's servers had crashed under the volume of traffic.

For the next half hour, Potts surfed the news channels, waiting for the next shoe to drop. On CNN he caught a fade cut to the presidential seal. *Here we go*, he said to himself and parked on the station. Moments later, the image of George Whitehead Nixon appeared on the screen. After the usual platitudes about a time of crisis for the nation, Nixon got to the meat of his message. "I will order the immediate execution of the eight convicted terrorists held in El Paso. In addition, I will ask the Pentagon to return three Army divisions from overseas deployment to increase the security around the Quarantine Zones. We cannot let this kind of tragedy happen again."

When the president was finished, Potts scanned the stations again. He stopped to watch a street interview with a middle-aged man in a suit. "...this is outrageous. We can't let them get away with this. I think Nixon should take someone out of each Quarantine Zone and have them shot." Several interviews that followed echoed similar sentiments.

Simon turned off the set. As he had expected, the public anger was intense—and being directed against all those in the zones. He went back to work, hoping the project he had under way would focus the anger where it belonged.

After hurriedly kissing Rosa good-bye, Mano stopped at the front door and turned around. "One more thing...If Hilda Ortiz stops by, tell her the DDP leadership is meeting at our usual place at one this afternoon."

"I will, mi amor," she said. "Be careful—the Baldies are going to be looking for revenge," she added as he rushed outside.

Alone for the first time since she'd heard the news, Rosa thought of the families of those poor girls and covered her mouth. To see pictures of your daughter, mutilated. The idea horrified her. She'd lost a daughter, seen her buried in the frozen ground covered only with a burlap sack. But that was a death of neglect by the Baldies. This was wanton killing. Deaths made to hurt.

A knock at the door made Rosa jump. She approached the entrance warily, looking through the window. Celia was waiting outside, two plastic bags in her hands.

After Rosa had ushered her in, Celia said: "Is Don Manolo home?"

"No, Celia. He had to go—some kind of meeting with the DDP to discuss how they can prepare for the Baldies. They're expecting trouble." Rosa took the bags from the curandera. "What's in here? They're heavy."

"Candles—that's why I want to talk to Don Manolo. He has the influence to help the entire barrio hold a novenario."

"I heard of a novenario from my mother, Celia, but I'm not sure what that is."

"We need to light candles or small fires in every home and pray for nine days to honor the souls of the dead. Those poor girls El Frente killed deserve our prayers," Celia said firmly.

"I'm not sure everyone is as selfless as you, Celia. Candles and firewood are scarce."

"Yes, we'll suffer—but that's why we have to do it. The Baldies know how precious candles and firewood are to us," she said. "I believe most people are decent, Rosa. They'll behave that way if they're given a chance. But when people are angry and want revenge, they'll do very cruel things— even if they regret them later. If we show the Baldies our sacrifice, that will speak louder than words."

"I think this gesture comes from a good heart, Celia," Rosa said, touching her friend's arm. "But I think we might be wiser to spend our time protecting our supplies and finding shelter for our leaders. These senseless killings are going to create more misery for all of us."

"Rosa, if the Baldies believe we support these killings, nothing will spare us from their attacks, no matter what we do. Except for those few in El Frente, our people are disgusted by this horrible crime, but if we act like criminals, then we convict ourselves. If everyone in our barrio takes part in the novenario, the Baldies will understand we share their grief."

Rosa remembered her own words to Pedro when she'd refused to wear a mask. This was the same gesture on a larger scale. "All right, I'll tell Mano about this and explain why it's important," Rosa said. "In the meantime, let's light a candle and pray."

---

"Welcome back to Outpost Bravo, Hank," Major Greg Johnson said, extending his hand as Evans stepped off the helicopter.

"Hello, Greg," Hank said, with a perfunctory handshake. Johnson had been one of the many who'd shunned Hank during his last days here. Now the camp's number two Army intel officer wanted to be his friend again.

"Your daughter and Fuller are still being debriefed," Johnson said as they walked toward the hangar. "They'll be done in an hour or so. You can wait for them in the VIP boarding area."

"I'd like to see them now."

The major stopped. "My CO wouldn't like me breaking with protocol, Hank."

"Let me put it this way, Greg," Evans said icily. "My boss reports directly to the commander in chief of the United States. Now, do you want to get into a pissing contest with me, or are you going to bring my daughter and Fuller to me now?"

After staring at Hank for a moment, Johnson said, "I'll see what I can do."

"Thank you," Evans said drily and walked into the VIP boarding area.

A few minutes later, the door opened and Sarah Evans burst into the room.

"Daddy!" she called out smiling, her arms spread wide. Wearing oversize fatigues, she looked surprisingly healthy as she bounded across the room and locked him in a hug.

Hank fought back tears as he held his daughter, unable to put into words the agony he'd suffered and the joy he now felt. "I never gave up hope, Sarah. Never," he said, holding her a very long time.

A knock on the door made them gently step apart. "Come in," Evans said hoarsely.

"Hi, Hank," Fuller said, entering the room, a tight smile on his face.

"I'm sorry I doubted you, Mike," Evans said, looking down. "There's no way I can ever repay what you've done—but I'm sure as hell going to try."

Fuller nodded in acknowledgment and said, "Look, Hank. I know you and Sarah have a lot of catching up to do, but there's something we need to talk about in private."

"Can it wait, Mike?"

"I wouldn't ask if it wasn't important."

Hank patted Sarah's back. "Hon, you stay here. Mike and I will go for a walk and be right back, okay?"

Sarah smiled. "Sure, Dad. I'll be fine."

Walking along the tarmac outside the waiting room, Fuller said, "G2's covering up what happened, Hank—with Sarah and me. The story they're going to release to the press is that this was a successful rescue from the HRNA. But that's not what happened," Fuller said, his jaw growing tight. "I was captured. The only reason Sarah and I are alive is because Manolo Suarez let us go. His son was one of the kidnappers for the LLF, but the kid couldn't go through with it and took Sarah to his dad. What the Hispanic Republic has been saying all along is true. These terror attacks have been coming from a fringe group."

"Are you sure?"

"Trust me, I was skeptical, too. But Sarah's the one who finally convinced me."

"I see why you needed to tell me about this. I heard the news about the other hostages on my flight coming in. The public thinks all the hostages are dead. With three divisions coming home, all hell's going to come down on the zones."

"Yeah, we're playing right into the hands of the LLF. I don't want to see all the work we've done to end this war get scrapped by another politician."

"I agree, Mike. I'll call Helen and get this straightened out—or I'll go public if I have to."

"There's one other thing," Fuller said, coming to a stop. "We may have an ally in the spook community. Somebody calling himself Honda Garganta sent a message to the HRNA telling them they'd be cleared publicly if they helped us save the hostages. You know anything about that?" he asked, looking Hank in the eye with a hint of a smile.

Evans answered slowly, measuring his words. "I don't think mentioning this Honda Garganta would help our cause right now."

"Good," Fuller said, smiling broadly now, "because I didn't say anything about it in my debriefing."

---

"Papá!" Pedro called out as his father emerged from a defunct movie theater on Whittier.

Mano turned and smiled when he saw his son.

"I've been looking for you all day," Pedro said, catching up to him. "I know you're busy but I've got something that could be very important."

"What is it, m'hijo?"

Pedro looked up and down the street. "We should go somewhere private."

"Okay, let's go back inside," Mano said, nodding toward the theater. "Our meeting's over."

Walking into the battered lobby, Mano said, "Please forgive me if I seem impatient, Pedro. We've got a lot to do right away."

Pulling the satellite phone from his pocket, Pedro handed it to Mano and explained about his visit to Isabel.

"Have you used this phone before?" Mano asked, studying the black device.

"No. All I know is the number and my code name."

Mano turned on the power and heard a dial tone. "It's got a charge," he said, nodding with encouragement. The black device looked very similar to the silver phone he'd used for years—until he'd broken his four days ago. Their regular courier was scheduled to arrive tonight, but it would be days before the new phone arrived.

"Can you call Ramon with it?" Pedro asked, leaning toward him.

"Let's find out," Mano answered, then scratched his head, trying to remember the number he'd always speed-dialed. "Ah, yeah," he said, tapping on the dial pad.

The sound of ringing on the line raised a smile on Mano's face—until he got a recorded message. "*Leider hat sich ihre Zahl ist nicht Teil Ihrer Service Plan,*" a woman's voice said.

"I can't connect," Mano said, exhaling slowly. "Seems the only people we can reach with this phone are our enemies." As he said those words, an idea bubbled into his consciousness. *This phone could be a weapon*, he realized suddenly. With the rough sketch of a plan already forming in his mind, he asked Pedro: "Do you know who Angel spoke to at El Frente?"

"No, he never told me—he never even used the phone when I was around."

Mano nodded, understanding the dead gang leader's caution. "Do you know a way to record a conversation on this phone?"

"It's easy if you have a computer. You can connect the earpiece to the headphone jack and record an MP3."

"I know where I can get a laptop," Mano said, recalling the equipment he'd cached from Jo's house. "Can we both listen to the conversation as you're recording?"

"Sure."

"Then I think we can use this phone against El Frente," Mano said, and began explaining his plan to Pedro. An hour later in Ramon's library, with their equipment ready to record, Pedro dialed one-eight-seven on the phone.

"Bueno," a male voice answered curtly.

"This is Flaco."

"Flaco?" the voice on the line said warily. "En que zona estas?"

"Sorry, ese. Don't speak Spanish."

"What zone are you in?" the man said in perfect English.

"L.A. . . . Zone B."

"Hold on a minute," he said. The line was silent for a moment.

Pedro covered the mouthpiece. "I think he knows something's wrong," he whispered to his father.

Mano shook his head. "He's just checking his records. Don't worry," he answered softly.

"What the hell's been going on there, Flaco?" the man said angrily. "We had to issue a press release about the hostages without a confirmation from your zone—and your zone was given the execution order before any of the others."

"Angel is dead, man," Pedro said. "The girl...our hostage...she escaped for a while. But we caught her again. That's how Angel got axed."

"You have the hostage now?"

"Yeah."

"She's to be executed immediately."

"You want me to kill her?"

"What else do you think 'executed' means, marero?"

"Can't do that."

The line was silent for a second. "What? Why not?"

"I don't know who you are or what authority you have to order that, homes."

"You can't be serious. Put another member of your gang on the line."

They had not expected this. Pedro looked at Mano, his eyebrows arching in distress.

"No," Mano mouthed silently, shaking his head.

"No," Pedro said into the phone.

"Listen to me, cholo," the man said, his voice tight with rage. "I'm Miguel Cardona, the aide to Octavio Perez. Perhaps you've heard of him in your little Eslo barrio?"

"Yeah, I've heard of him."

"Well, that's who wants this done—and he wants it done *now.*"

"All right, chill, ese," Pedro improvised.

"And we want pictures, you understand? Send them by the usual channel."

"Tight," Pedro said and ended the call.

"You imitate a vato way too well, m'hijo," Mano said smiling. "Now we need to get the recording to Ramon—along with an idea your mother and Celia had."

# THE EL PASO EIGHT HOSTAGES: *DAY 12*

**T**he elevator door opened on the seventh floor at Langley and Hank Evans stepped out unshaven, tired, and angry after two cross-country flights in as many days.

Striding past Helen Byrne's stunned assistant, he opened the door to her office and walked inside.

"Did you think you'd put me off by not answering my calls?" he said, standing before her sleek mahogany desk, his arms crossed defiantly.

For several seconds Byrne stared back, slack-jawed. "What's gotten into you, Hank. Have you been drinking?" she finally managed to say.

"Worse than that—I've been reading. And what I've read has made me very pissed," he said, his jowls trembling. "You've given a story to the press about my daughter's so-called rescue when you know full well Sarah and Michael Fuller both gave the same account—that they were released by a leader of the Hispanic Republic. Now, I realize this fiction you've created helps put some positive spin on the way the rest of this hostage crisis has gone for—"

"Now, hold it right there, goddammit," Byrne interrupted,

rising to her feet. "Are you suggesting we give comfort and aid to our enemies? Because that won't just cost you your job, my friend, you'll be looking at jail time, too."

"Take me to court, Helen. I'd like nothing better. Because I've got two witnesses that will prove you lied."

"All right, let's calm down here," she said, sitting down again. "Close the door, Alan," she called out to her assistant, who promptly complied. "What do you want from me, Hank?" Byrne said calmly.

"A full retraction of the story."

"Why is that important to you? Your daughter's back safe. Hell, you even stand to bask in a little glory yourself."

"You just don't get it, do you? Look, Helen, I'm as worried about my career as the next guy. But what you're doing is going to bring a bloodbath on people who don't deserve it. And the worst part is, it's going to make it harder for us to end this insurgency. We damn near had them beaten. But you're going to let the extremists win."

"Well that's all a matter of opinion, Hank. And it's an opinion very few Americans share," Byrne said, leaning forward in her chair. "We've got people rioting at the gates of the White House calling for air strikes and executions. Turn on a TV, open a paper, or go online. People want blood for blood. And it's not just here. All over the world, people are denouncing the deaths of those girls. We can't back down now, no matter what you do, Hank. You think it's easy to convince a nation you're right when the polls show two-thirds of the people think you're wrong?"

Evans leaned forward, placing his hands on her desk. "No it's not easy. It's called leadership," he said before leaving Byrne's office.

Taking the elevator to the third floor, he walked to Bill Perkins's cube. "We need to talk," Evans said, motioning with his head for Perkins to follow.

The pair walked silently until Hank led them outside into the courtyard. "I want you to send a message to Ramon Garcia, just two words: *thank you*. And make sure you sign it from me—not Honda Garganta. After that, I want you to destroy the Hollywood Squares link. Erase it totally."

"You sure about that, Hank," Perkins said, his eyes widening.

"Yeah. My career here is over, Bill, and I don't want you to go down with me."

Perkins swallowed hard. "What are you going to do, Hank?"

"You'll be better off reading about it in the papers."

# THE EL PASO EIGHT HOSTAGES: *DAY 15*

**S**itting at his laptop, Ramon smiled serenely and clicked the Play Again button on a video already seen more than eighty-seven million times in the last two days on VuTube. Since being uploaded, the three-minute video had been featured in countless media sources and discussed incessantly by pundits and bloggers.

Though millions had seen the work of filmmaker Simon Potts, few had ever seen the man himself. Breaking tradition with his previous productions, Potts was in front of the camera in the video titled *Flames of Hope*.

The video opened with Simon on the roof of a skyscraper in downtown Los Angeles, microphone in hand, his ebony skin reflecting the yellow glow of the ground behind him.

"I'm standing in front of Los Angeles Quarantine Zone B, an area that's had no electrical power for nearly three years. This is normally a dark place at night, but as you can see, the people inside the wall have lit signal fires—thousands of them. They tell me these fires will burn for nine days in a memorial tradition called a novenario."

In quick succession, other overhead night views of

the illuminated Quarantine Zones appeared as Simon continued his narration in voice-over.

"Similar novenario fires are burning in El Paso, Phoenix, Santa Fe, San Antonio—in fact, all of the people in North America's Quarantine Zones have joined together to send the world a collective message."

Simon appeared before the Quarantine Zone once again.

"What you see behind me is a symbol...a symbol of hope...a people sending a message with the only tools they have. These fires are precious. They use fuel that's scarce inside the walls of the Quarantine Zones. But the people inside this wall are sacrificing a scarce resource to show their grief...to show their compassion...to show their loss for the senseless deaths of seven young lives. Like the rest of the world, the people inside this wall are appalled by that brutality—even if those who perpetrated that horrible deed did it in the name of their cause."

Potts's image was replaced by a succession of shots from his Quarantine Zone flyover...hungry children...a hopeless old man...a desperate mother.

"For over five years, the people inside this wall have endured violence, starvation, and despair. Amid a nation that leads the world in its standard of living, the people inside this wall live at a subsistence level. And yet today, there are many who call for more violence against these people. They want to punish them all for the crimes of a few."

The Quarantine Zone scenes faded to a long shot of the White House.

"That misguided anger is being used by some in the highest places of power. They hope to curry favor by appealing to our baser instincts, to boost their political fortunes by fueling hate."

The screen switched to a CNN interview captioned: HENRY EVANS III—FORMER ASSISTANT DIRECTOR, CIA. In a tight close-up that featured his eyes, Evans said: "My daughter was one of the hostages taken by the Latino Liberation Front. She was rescued and released by a leader of the Hispanic Republic of North America. The reports of her rescue issued by the current administration distort the truth and make the people who saved my daughter look like the culprits. I've resigned my position with the CIA in protest."

Returning to the night view of the Quarantine Zone, Potts concluded his coverage.

"The world will judge our reaction to the slaughter of these seven innocent young women as much as they'll judge those who took their lives. One act of cruelty will not atone for another. The fires you see here tonight are the flames of hope for peace and compassion."

The screen faded to black as Barber's *Adagio for Strings* played during the credits.

Ramon was certain this video had saved lives. Since its release, the protests calling for retribution had dropped dramatically. Although there were many who still blamed all Latinos for the deaths, the voices of reason were now being heard amid the shouts for vengeance. Talk of air strikes, shelling, and executions was now limited to the GlobeNetDaily and other fringe media sources. What had made the video so powerful was the sense of unity it presented, something their new communications link with all the zones had made possible.

Glancing at the time, Ramon powered down his laptop and retrieved the satellite phone from his desk drawer. Mano would be calling soon—for the first time since his phone had gone down.

The new phone felt strangely familiar as Mano entered Ramon's number. After two rings, Ramon answered, sounding excited. "Hola, hermano," he said brightly. "Seems you managed quite well without me the last few days."

"It's not an experience I want to repeat."

"Well, then. I'm glad you missed me," Ramon said laughing.

"Don't grow a new hat size, viejo."

"I gathered from your courier messages that Pedro has returned," Ramon said, his voice becoming serious. "That's good to hear."

"Rosa and I are happy to have him home."

"If there was any part of you in that boy, I knew he wouldn't stay with El Frente."

"Thanks, Ramon. He's still very young but he's been forced to grow up fast."

"Well, Pedro certainly has a knack for intrigue. Thanks to your caper, Señor Octavio Perez has resigned as our U.N. delegate. Let me tell you, Mano, it was a pleasure playing the recording for him. I told him he'd better hope longevity runs in my family because if I die—even if it's from pneumonia—a copy of the recording will be released to the media and the local constabulary wherever he might be."

"That's it, Ramon?" Mano asked, his eyebrows furrowed. "He ordered eight girls killed, along with hundreds of others before that—and he just gets fired?"

"Things aren't always black and white, Mano. Suppose we'd turned that recording over to the authorities. Octavio's prosecution would have still tarnished the HRNA—he was, after all, an official delegate. Besides, that recording would never hold up in a court of law."

"So you're happy with what Octavio got?"

"Hardly. But I'm happy he no longer represents our people."

"I'm glad you're the diplomat."

"Speaking of diplomacy, our stock went way up on that front thanks to Simon Potts. I'm being invited to committees again. For a while there, we were complete pariahs. Potts's video has turned our image around—except in the States. That's the downside right now."

Mano's teeth clenched. "I don't like the sound of that."

"You shouldn't. The three divisions Nixon's bringing home should be fully deployed on U.S. soil in a few weeks. These are hardened troops and they're well equipped, Mano. They're used to fighting an enemy that uses human beings as artillery. We'll be getting more supplies and weapons for the fighters. But I'm afraid our people are going to suffer, mi hermano."

The realization sobered both of them and with little more to say, Ramon ended the call.

Mano looked down at his shiny new phone. Holding it gave him the sense of a new beginning, a combination of anticipation and dread. The last few days had changed his world. He was sure of that. How it would all play out, he was not so certain. He'd regained his son, but lost a comrade. The novenarios had averted a bloodbath, but a hardened army now waited in the wings. There seemed to be no gain without some kind of loss. But then again, when had his life ever been different?

Putting the phone in his pocket, Mano walked into the night.

# READING GROUP GUIDE

## Characters

- How do the central characters change during the course of *House Divided*? Who changes the most? Who changes the least?
- Which character did you find most interesting? Which did you identify with most?
- What surprised you most about a character?
- Did you find any of the characters disturbing?
- Was Mano and Pedro's relationship typical of father and son? What role, if any, do you think ethnicity played in Mano and Pedro's relationship? Given their very different upbringings, how would you compare Pedro's and Sarah's relationships with their parents?
- When Sarah is abducted and held in captivity, what effect did the "Stockholm syndrome" have in her attitude toward Pedro and his family?

## Issues

- Do you think an ethnic conflict like that portrayed in *House Divided* could ever take place in the U.S.? If so, what trends present today could lead to such a conflict? And what could we do to avoid the nightmare scenario presented in the novel?

- How did demagogues and factionalism on each side escalate the conflict?
- What did you learn about Hispanic culture from *House Divided*?
- How do we respect the cultural heritage of the U.S.A.'s diverse people while retaining a unified national identity?
- In the interest of national unity, should we ignore past injustices like the internment of Japanese-Americans during World War II, slavery and Jim Crow segregation, the annexation of lands from Hispanic landowners following the Mexican-American War, and the displacement of Native Americans during the colonization and westward expansion of the United States?
- Under the same circumstances, how would you have acted differently than the Latino characters in *House Divided*?

*¿Prefiere usted discutir el libro en español? Visite www.hachettebookgroup.com.*

# ABOUT THE AUTHOR

Cuban-born Raul Ramos y Sanchez grew up in Miami's cultural kaleidoscope before becoming a longtime resident of the U.S. Midwest. Following a successful twenty-five-year advertising career that included founding an ad agency with offices in Ohio and California, Raul turned to more personally meaningful work. *House Divided* is the second book of the *America Libre* trilogy, which Ramos began in 2004 with the input of scholars from the U.S.A., Latin America, and Spain. Besides developing a documentary for public television, *Two Americas: The Legacy of Our Hemisphere*, Raul writes for a variety of publications and hosts MyImmigrationStory.com—an online forum for the U.S. immigrant community. To find out more, visit www.raulramos.com.

# MISSED RAUL RAMOS Y SANCHEZ'S FIRST NOVEL?

Provocative and chillingly credible, *America Libre* reveals what could happen to America when smoldering ethnic tensions ignite a Hispanic liberation movement and a second civil war.

"A sweeping, intense novel of extremism, fear, and consequences."
—*Publishers Weekly*

"Provocative!"—*USA Today*

"A must-read for all, no matter where you draw your line in the sand."
—James Rollins, *New York Times* best-selling author

If you enjoyed *House Divided,* then you're sure to love these emotional family dramas as well—now available from Grand Central Publishing.

### *Sisters, Strangers, and Starting Over*
Belinda Acosta

A woman must come to terms with the death of her estranged sister while learning to become a mother to her orphaned niece, in this second novel of the Quinceañera Club series.

Look for the first novel in this series,
*Damas, Dramas, and Ana Ruíz*

### *Try to Remember*
Iris Gomez

"Lyrical, poignant, and smart, as compassionate and hopeful as it is heartbreaking...a novel you will never forget."—*New York Times* best-selling author Jenna Blum

### *Tell Me Something True*
Leila Cobo

"A bittersweet journey about coming to understand and forgive the indiscretions of one's parents through the simple act of living one's life."—*Miami Herald*

Look for future books from Leila Cobo